God in His Infinite Wisdom
DEATH, DEFIANCE AND BILLY PENN'S HAT

Mary DiMauro

Paperback ISBN: 978-1-54399-759-0

eBook ISBN: 978-1-54399-790-3

Table of Contents

God in his infinite wisdom made men
and women different.

—*Philadelphia Police Commissioner Joseph O'Neill, the United*
States District Court for the Eastern District of Pennsylvania, 1975

PROLOGUE

Philadelphia, Pennsylvania 1975
Federal Courthouse

————————————•••————————————

AFTER TESTIFYING IN FEDERAL COURT IN THE CASE OF THE
United States versus the City of Philadelphia, Commissioner Joseph
O'Neill walked out of the federal courthouse at Sixth and Arch Streets
in Philadelphia, accompanied by an entourage of police department
commanders. As he reached the top step of the courthouse, he was
approached by a local journalist.

"Commissioner, Kit Gibbons from the *Bulletin*. Do you have a
minute to answer questions?"

O'Neill looked down at Gibbons through his black-rimmed
glasses, and when he spoke, his tone was dismissive. "Only a minute."

"I was present for your testimony in court today. Do you
expect that the City of Philadelphia will settle on the court suit and
eventually welcome female patrol officers to the rank and file of the
police department?"

"Women are welcome in the Juvenile Aid Division of the police
department. It's suited to their abilities. Women have no place in the

patrol or detective divisions of the police department. There will be no settlement in this case. We will fight this court suit to the end."

"Will you confirm the reason you cite is, and I quote, 'God in his infinite wisdom made men and women different'?"

"Yes, that's right."

"Could you be more specific, Commissioner?"

"As I said, that sums it. Now, if you will excuse me, I have a police department to run."

"Commissioner, one more question. What will you do if Judge Weiner rules against the City?"

O'Neill walked away without responding.

"Did you really expect him to answer you?" asked Tom Weitsen, a reporter from the *Philadelphia Inquirer* who overheard the exchange between Gibbons and the commissioner.

"I don't understand why he doesn't just concede. I thought the world was way past treating women like this. Philadelphia is the birthplace of the Declaration of Independence and the Bill of Rights. He even has Title VII of the Civil Rights Act going against him."

Weitsen grinned as he ran a hand over his bald head. "It's nice to see you haven't become jaded yet. I'm not a betting man, but I predict that if O'Neill and Rizzo have their way, they'll build buildings higher than City Hall and the Billy Penn hat before they welcome women to patrol work in the Philadelphia Police Department."

PART I

Philadelphia, 1985

I expect to pass through life but once. If, therefore, there be any kindness I can show, or any good thing I can do to any fellow being, let me do it now, and not defer or neglect it, as I shall not pass this way again.

—William Penn

ONE

A. J. HARRIS (POPULARLY CALLED "AJ") WAS EXHAUSTED. THE Philadelphia police officer sat in her green '79 Dodge Dart, parked in the lot of her apartment complex in Chestnut Hill, and she stared into the blackness of the night. The rain pounded against the roof of her car, and her body trembled. She was in no state to think clearly or process the implications of the day's events.

Taking a deep breath, she spoke to her reflection in the rearview mirror.

"Pull yourself together, Officer Harris," she said, forcing her voice to sound strong, sure, confident.

And then, in quick sudden movements afforded by her long legs and her years in the army, she ducked out of the car and made a run for her apartment building. Head pounding, heart racing, and thoughts rushing through her head like wind through a tunnel, she reached the stairwell and made her way to the second floor. Her emotions sapping her energy with each step, she wiped a wet hand across her face in a hopeless attempt to see through the rain and tears. She shook the water from her short, curly hair.

Philadelphia weather in late November could be bone-chilling—but the weather was not the reason AJ couldn't stop shaking. She couldn't vanquish the vision of Jack's face when she asked about all of the women. Or the tone of Detective Wexler's voice earlier that day, when he'd threatened to destroy her career alongside that of her best friend, Sam Kelly.

As AJ opened her apartment door, she heard her telephone ring. She looked down at her wrist to note the time on her watch.

"It's 2:00 a.m. It's not the time for me to listen to any more of your lies, Jack Nathan," she said out loud. AJ collapsed into her leather armchair, resting her head against the well-worn back and closing her eyes. A moment later, she dropped her head into her hands and leaned into her knees. Images flicked through her mind—Jack with the other women, the way he'd looked when all three of them showed up at his door. Looking sorry he'd gotten caught, but not sorry he'd done it. Images of the retirement home, the case she was so close to cracking, if only she could just nail down what exactly had happened there. And then Wexler's face, threatening her career if she didn't back off.

"This is as screwed up as it gets," she said, still speaking aloud to the storm-darkened room. "How can you go from a happy life and bright future to as low as you can go in the span of twelve hours?"

One thing was for sure, AJ wouldn't go through all of this pain again. She was sure of that. She exhaled, her eyes still closed.

She didn't know how much time had passed—a minute? an hour?—when she felt the cold steel of her own service revolver against her temple. In her last moment, the faces of her best friends flashed across her mind, and one final tear fell from her eye.

"I'm sorry, Sam," AJ whispered. The report of the gunshot dissipated into the night.

TWO

———————————————•●————————————————

OFFICER JOHN MORRIS WAS A PATROLMAN WHO CHERISHED nothing more than rules and order. Whenever he was confronted with a possible crime scene, he ticked through the points of his training like he had a checklist in front of him. The first thing Morris noticed was the door of Apartment 203 was ajar, and then he heard the sobbing inside the apartment. The police radio had dispatched the call as a hospital case. So who was making that noise?

His hand resting on the handle of his gun, Morris announced himself as a police officer and slowly pushed the door open. He quickly realized he was not responding to a hospital case.

On the floor of the apartment lay a slender, blond-haired, six-foot-tall, white male crying hysterically, a handgun lying next to him. His hands were covered in blood, and he was holding the unmoving body of a fair-skinned black woman with an apparently fatal head wound. Morris immediately recognized the man as a narcotics officer with the Philadelphia police. Jack Nathan. Morris knew him, all right, but never thought very highly of him.

Recognizing the possibility that more than one weapon might be present, Morris pulled his service revolver from its holster.

"Slowly move away from the body with arms raised and let me see your hands," Morris said, keeping his voice level and just the right amount of loudness. He didn't want to startle a man who might be armed, but he also wanted Nathan to comply with the command.

Nathan looked up, seeing Morris in the doorway for the first time, but he didn't look surprised. Instead, his face was contorted in emotions Morris didn't know how to categorize—grief, sorrow, regret?

"It's not what you think," Nathan said through sobs. But he followed the directions anyway and raised his hands.

Morris motioned Nathan to the far wall of the apartment, away from the body and the gun. Frisking Nathan, Morris recovered a .357 Smith & Wesson handgun. With his own weapon still pointed at Nathan, Morris stooped down to press two fingers against the woman's neck. No pulse.

Morris moved to handcuff Nathan and then removed the bullet from the gun he recovered from Nathan. Morris then took custody of the .38 caliber Smith and Wesson 4" revolver on the floor next to the body. Using the hand radio that he had secured to his belt, Officer Morris notified police radio that he was at the scene and that it was a "5292"—the code for a dead body, not a hospital case.

"This is an officer-involved shooting. Please send a supervisor to the scene," he said.

The dispatcher's voice crackled back at him. Fire Rescue squad and a police patrol wagon were on the way to the location. Morris then looked over the scene and noticed that there was only one access to the apartment. It was the front door, and the door did not appear to show any signs of being forced open.

Officer Nathan leaned his head against the wall, his body still wracked by sobs. "Morris, I didn't do this. I called nine-one-one. She shot herself. It's her service revolver."

Morris paused his inspection of the scene for evidence of what had happened and considered Nathan. "Save your story for the detectives," Morris said. "In the meantime, you have the right to remain silent. You might want to exercise it."

Within minutes, Fire Rescue and a patrol wagon arrived. Rescue pronounced the victim dead, and Morris called for a second patrol wagon. Upon hearing the Rescue Squad's pronouncement, Nathan slid down the wall to the floor, his shoulders shaking with soundless sobs. Morris directed the crew of the patrol wagon to transport Officer Nathan to the Homicide Division at the police administration building at Eighth and Race Streets. It was referred to as the "Roundhouse" by most of Philadelphia, but within the rank and file of the police department the building was referred by the acronym PAB.

After Nathan was taken away, Morris could concentrate fully on the potential crime scene. It was only then, with a jolt, that Morris recognized the woman splayed on the floor, Angela "AJ" Harris. The streetwise, self-confident, almost cocky friend of Kate Rossi, the same two-squad sergeant in the Fourteenth District who would be relieving his squad at 7:00 a.m. Morris took a moment to contemplate his next steps.

Morris usually found it easy to emotionally detach from a crime scene, but knowing the victim was A. J. Harris would make detachment difficult today. *Christ*, Morris thought. It was hard to imagine her dead, even with her lifeless body before him. He'd thought she was on top of the world. He had just seen her perform at a police fundraiser last month. She was drop-dead gorgeous, with mesmerizing, translucent green eyes; she looked like Halle Berry with a holster. But even more than that, Harris had a warm presence that drew all the energy in the room toward her—and the talent to back it up, with a voice like Whitney Houston's. She had seemed more like a Miss America contestant than a street cop. On the surface, at least, she had everything going for her. But after fifteen years on the job, Morris had learned never to be surprised. Especially if she was involved with Jack Nathan. Nathan was good-looking and carelessly confident, the kind of man you didn't want to spend too much time alone with your sister, wife, or daughter. *Having Jack Nathan in your life wasn't a smart move for any woman*, Morris thought.

Morris had seen police work ruin the lives of good people who let the bad seep into their dreams. No, not their dreams—their nightmares. Morris hoped he'd know to walk away when wrestling in this garbage made him forget the smell of roses. But today, the garbage stank, bad. It was difficult to see a beautiful young life end this way.

Morris shook his head as if he could shake these thoughts away. What had happened was for the detectives to figure out. It was his job to protect the scene and make the notifications. After radioing dispatch and headquarters and then notifying the operations team at the district, Morris dialed the Fourteenth District to contact Sergeant Rossi.

Standing in the operations room of the Fourteenth District, Kate Dominic Rossi wore her sergeant stripes proudly. As one of the first women promoted to the rank, a recipient of the commendation for valor when she was shot on duty responding to a bank robbery, and the wife of Lieutenant Ray Rossi, Kate had mastered command presence—from her tailored uniform to her military posture.

Kate had just dismissed roll call and was completing the tactical plan for the day when the corporal called her name across the operations room to take a phone call. Kate picked up the phone. "Sergeant Rossi."

"Sarge, this is Officer Morris from last-out shift," Morris said, referencing the 12:00 a.m.-to-8:00 a.m. shift. He spoke bluntly. "I'm calling to inform you of an officer-involved shooting. Fire Rescue squad pronounced Officer A. J. Harris DOA at the scene. The cause of death appears to be a single gunshot wound to the head. My condolences, Sarge. I wanted you to know as a professional courtesy before police radio notified you."

Kate could hear the sincere regret through the crispness in his voice. Kate felt like she had been punched in the gut.

"What do you know, Morris?" she managed to ask.

"It appears that the cause of death was a single gunshot wound to the head," Morris said again, but Kate still couldn't believe it. "I'm not sure, but I'm guessing it was a shot from a police service revolver—probably hers. Officer Jack Nathan, from narcotics, was on the scene when I arrived. He said he had found her, she was already dead, and he called nine-one-one." Morris paused before voicing what was niggling at the back of his mind. "What doesn't make sense is that the call came in as a hospital case. I'd like to hear the tapes from police radio. I guess something got lost in translation. Anyway, Homicide and mobile crime are on the way, and Officer Nathan was transported to Homicide." Morris paused as he looked at the 75-48 form that he had filled out. "Oh, and no forced entry."

"Thanks, Morris. I'll notify the captain's office and come out to the scene."

As she hung up the phone, the on-duty lieutenant said, "Police radio is requesting a supervisor at Chestnut Hill Arms Apartments. The sector cop reported a DOA who is an active-duty police officer."

"I know," Kate said. Her voice cracked as she said, "It's A. J. Harris."

The lieutenant turned to the corporal. "Tell radio that I will take the scene," he said. "I'll be out of service for a while." He glanced back at Kate. "Sergeant Rossi will stay in service and respond to radio calls until I return."

Time is what we want most,
but what we use worst.

—William Penn

THREE

———————————•———————————

DETECTIVE JAMES WEXLER ARRIVED AT THE POLICE HEAD-
quarters, referred to as the "Roundhouse" by the police and public
alike, at 6:00 a.m. on the dot for the Homicide day shift. He was
unusually early. He filled up his coffee cup, propped his feet on his
desk, and read files until the call came in.

When Wexler overheard Detective Bill Reynolds, the night-
shift deskman, inform the duty lieutenant that A. J. Harris had been
found shot in her apartment, Wexler swiveled in his chair so quickly,
he spilled the coffee he was gulping all over his yellow shirt and
brown plaid sports coat.

Wexler nearly leaped out of his chair and rushed over to
Reynolds and the lieutenant.

"I'm the early man for day shift. I've got the case."

Detective Reynolds, responsible for assigning cases to the
on-duty detectives, objected. "No telling how busy day shift will be,
and we're running light on manpower since several detectives are in
court," he said. "I'm assigning this to the overnight shift."

Ignoring Reynolds, Wexler turned to the lieutenant. "Lieu,
I'm the only one here, and someone should get out to the scene

immediately. Reynolds is trying to give his buddies overtime, and I thought HQ is trying to limit OT."

"You're here almost two hours early. Too early even for an early man," Reynolds said. Glaring back at Wexler, he repeated, "I'm assigning this case to the overnight shift."

After a moment of silence, the lieutenant nodded to Detective Reynolds.

"If we can avoid paying overtime, we should. Assign Wexler."

Reynolds nodded, his mouth pursed in resentment, and all but threw the police report at Wexler.

Thirty minutes later, Detective Wexler arrived at Chestnut Hill Arms to process the crime scene. He even beat the mobile crime unit. Wexler listened without comment as Morris provided a brief description of what had transpired after he arrived at the apartment. Wexler then began going through the apartment like he was serving a search warrant.

The way Wexler was rummaging through drawers made Morris cringe. Wexler wasn't being thorough; he was being disrespectful.

"The crime scene is in the living room," Morris said aloud before he realized he had spoken.

Wexler stopped and glared at Morris, trying to use every bit of his six-foot-one-inch broad frame to intimidate him.

"That's why you never made detective, Morris. You don't know how to process a crime scene."

Before Morris could respond, the mobile crime unit arrived and both men refocused the conversation.

An hour later, Wexler was back at the Roundhouse. He walked into the Homicide interview room and looked at Officer Jack

Nathan, who was sitting at a gray metal desk with his face in his hands. Looking up as he heard Wexler enter, Nathan exhaled.

"God, I'm glad it's you, Wexler."

Wexler raised a questioning eyebrow and said, "Nathan, you know the drill. I need to read you your Miranda warnings. Don't say anything until you sign off that you understand your rights."

"Yeah, I know, but I didn't hurt her," Nathan said. "I could never hurt her."

Wexler rolled his eyes. "Nathan, shut up. We are going to do this by the book."

After Wexler advised Nathan of his Miranda warnings, Nathan insisted on relating his story. Wexler listened, taking an occasional note and rubbing absently at the coffee stain on his shirt. Nathan began by describing the women in his life. There was, of course, his wife, Betty.

"I'm not living with her anymore, but we aren't officially divorced yet, you know. And sometimes, yeah, we're still, uh, close. When she gets a little needy, we hook up sometimes. For old times' sake and all that." Nathan shrugged. Then there was his relationship with Harris, which had been on and off for about a year. And the final point in the love triangle was a woman named Lisa Venter.

"It's complicated," Nathan admitted. "But AJ was my soul mate. She was the reason I bought the bracelets."

"Whoa," said Wexler. "How did we get to soul mates and bracelets? What do bracelets have to do with anything?"

"I am trying to tell you. You need to understand the bracelets to understand what happened. I met AJ at a police fundraiser, and we noticed each other right away. She sang with Ray Rossi's band, Anti-Corruption. While the DJ was spinning records, I asked her to dance. The DJ played the song 'Always and Forever'—corny, I know, but we felt an immediate connection between us." Nathan's face softened at the memory. "She was the love of my life. The bracelet was meant for AJ. But, as I said, things got complicated. My ex-wife was lonely, and it was hard for me to make a clean break from her. We've known each other since high school." Nathan paused and lowered his head into his hands. "This is all Lisa's fault."

"How's that?" asked Wexler.

"I was at the FOP lounge one night after the four-to-twelve shift, and I got drunk because I had a fight with AJ. Lisa was someone I could always talk to about my problems. She was my go-to person when I was at odds with AJ. It was before Valentine's Day, and I made a joke about what I was going to give all my loves for Valentine's Day. She said she would go shopping with me—a lady's touch, you know. We went down to Jewelers' Row, and Lisa picked out the bracelets. Three of them—one for AJ, one for my wife, and one for Lisa for helping. I decided to engrave them with 'Forever.' I thought Lisa understood it meant that I would always be her friend—just friends. Now, though, I think she was setting me up—even back then."

Things happened, as things happened with Nathan and women, and the situation soon got complicated.

"After a while, I realized that I couldn't handle the stress of three women in my life, and I had to decide. It was easy to choose, really. I had to break it off with Lisa. I thought that I was letting her down easy. I told her I was going to tell my wife the same thing—that I was going to file for divorce and stop seeing her, too." Here, Nathan paused. "But I miscalculated with Lisa. She went to both my wife and AJ. The three of them all showed up at my apartment together, wearing the bracelets.

"I'll never forget the look on AJ's face. The other two yelled at me, but she just stared at me. I wasn't sure it was hurt or hate in her eyes. Maybe both. She broke the bracelet in front of me and left my apartment. She was the first to leave. After the other two got tired of screaming at me and left, I tried to call AJ's apartment, but she didn't answer.

"I knew that I couldn't lose her. I wanted to be with AJ for the rest of my life. I couldn't sleep, and I kept calling her. At about 2:30 a.m., I drove to her apartment, but she didn't answer. I drove home and couldn't sleep. Then, I remembered I had a key. I drove back to her apartment and used the key about 5:30 a.m. That's when I found her, dead." Nathan shuddered. "She shot herself with her own service revolver."

"You had a key and didn't bring it with you the first time. Do you think that story is believable, Nathan?"

"It's the truth. I was so fucked up I didn't remember."

"Now that is the first thing you said that I believe. You are fucked up."

Nathan put his hands in his face and then ran his fingers through his brown curly hair. He started to cry again.

"Knock off the waterworks, Nathan. Let's get back to it. Why do you think she shot herself?" Wexler asked.

"Because she loved me and she was afraid she had lost me."

Wexler gave Nathan an exasperated look. "You are an arrogant motherfucker if you think I'm gonna believe that," he said. "How about this for a story: she threatened to out you to Internal Affairs for moral turpitude, and you got so angry, you shot her."

"She loved me," Nathan protested. "That whole thing at my apartment, it must have just destroyed her. She had been asking for a commitment from me since Lieutenant Rossi married her friend, Kate." Nathan shook his head violently. "I loved her, I could never hurt her. This is all that bitch Lisa's fault."

Wexler stared at Nathan, frowning for a minute before finally saying, "I guess it shouldn't surprise me that you think you are the victim here. You make me sick. OK, Mr. innocent victim, how about agreeing to take a polygraph and paraffin tests?"

"Yeah, I'll agree, but I have to tell you I shot a weapon. The paraffin test won't mean anything. I was at the pistol range yesterday, and so was AJ. You saw us there. Didn't you?"

Wexler scowled at Nathan. "I'd like it on the record that you are willing to take both tests."

"Sure. I know the drill."

Wexler left the interview room to make arrangements for both tests. When he returned, he was carrying a typewriter and a pile of 75-49 investigation report forms.

"We're gonna get formal now," Wexler said briskly. "Let's focus on the confrontation at your apartment."

As Wexler typed, Nathan described again, this time in more detail, the visit from AJ, Betty, and Lisa the night before, and then he explained how he had found himself in the victim's apartment early that morning. When he finished interviewing him, Wexler had Nathan read and sign the statement, and another detective escorted Nathan to the polygraph and paraffin tests. In the meantime, Wexler wanted to make sure ballistics was lined up to check the handguns against the bullet fragments recovered by the medical examiner.

Wexler was reading his notes at his desk when the on-duty lieutenant, Ted Farrell, called Wexler into his office and asked him for a debrief on the investigation. Wexler walked into the office, shut the door, and eased onto the worn couch across from the lieutenant's desk.

"Turns out Pretty Boy Nathan lived up to his nickname," he began. "Nathan was working three women at the same time. He told me that the third woman, Lisa Venter, turned them all against him. She orchestrated this meeting of all three ladies to retaliate against Nathan for breaking off their relationship last week. When the women met to compare notes, Venter made sure they realized Nathan had bought them all the same Valentine's Day gift—a sterling silver bracelet with a heart charm and the word 'forever.'

"Nathan says Venter got A. J. Harris and Betty Nathan into a frenzy before the three women drove to confront him at his apartment—a residence off Cottman Avenue in Northeast Philadelphia. They were all wearing the bracelets. Nathan described the scene as ugly, but he claimed there were no threats of violence or suicide. Harris broke the bracelet in two and threw it at him before she left, about 11:20 p.m. She seemed more hurt than angry, he says, but who knows. He doesn't seem to have a good handle on women's feelings, if I may say so. His wife and his other girlfriend were still angry, so he concentrated on calming them down."

"So, what do you think?" Farrell asked. "Are those tears a sign of grief because he loved her or guilt because he killed her?"

"I think she killed herself," Wexler said. "But Nathan agreed to take paraffin and polygraph tests."

"You did Mirandize him, didn't you? No shortcuts on this one, Wexler. Internal Affairs will be brought in to oversee this investigation."

"Yeah, I Mirandized him. I actually had to tell him to shut up so I could get to it. I'm doing it all by the book. Bottom line, though, this is gonna be a quick and easy investigation—it's a suicide. I think Harris went off the deep end when she realized her boy was also still doing his ex-wife and an FOP groupie on top of that. In a funk, she took herself out. Using her service revolver was a classic cop move." Wexler smirked.

Farrell glowered back at him. "You think this is funny, Wexler?"

Wexler ignored Farrell and continued, "The story is like an episode of Peyton Place. I think it is an obvious suicide—I think we will find that she used her own service revolver—but don't worry, I'm gonna make sure all my ducks are in a row."

"I want facts and not your theories, Wexler," Farrell said. "You work the case until you have the facts. No conclusions or leaks to the press, and if asked, your statement is that circumstances are under investigation. Understand?" Wexler nodded, and Farrell continued, emphasizing his next words carefully. "Her father is an army chaplain. He is a captain at Scofield Barracks in Hawaii. He has served his country honorably, and his daughter was a respected member of this department, in spite of her poor choice in men. I don't want any cheap shots at these people because you get your jollies hating police women. Am I clear?"

"I'm clear," Wexler said. But under his breath, he muttered, "One less whore in the PD."

"Oh, and Wexler?" Farrell barked as the detective strode out of his office. "Find a new shirt. You've made a mess of that one."

Death is not the greatest loss. The greatest loss is what dies inside us while we live.

—Norman Cousins

FOUR

THE LADIES' ROOM OF THE FOURTEENTH DISTRICT POLICE station was an afterthought, originally intended for use by the public but turned into a ladies room because there were a limited number of bathrooms in the station. It was cramped and bare, with chipped yellow tiles, no window, and a smudged mirror over the single sink, where water dripped from the rusting faucet, no matter how tightly Kate Rossi turned the handles. Kate listened to the steady drip, drip now, willing the sound to fill her mind, to take over the racing thoughts and gruesome images. She leaned against the closed door, her arms wrapped tightly around her chest, her hands gripping her shoulders to keep from shaking as unstoppable tears seeped from her eyes.

Finally, Kate took several deep breaths and pushed forward to look in the mirror. She winced when she saw her mascara-smudged eyes. Kate pushed a strand of brown hair over her ears and brushed a hand across her bangs, fixed her face, took more deep breaths, and walked back into the operations room to make some calls.

First, Kate called her husband, Ray, at the Roundhouse, the main headquarters for Philadelphia. Unfortunately, his line was busy. Her next call was to the Central Detectives Division to speak with

Samantha Kelly, but Sam was out of the division, attending court at City Hall, and wasn't expected back. This wasn't going well. The next call, though, was more successful; after only one ring, Michelle Jones picked up.

"Detective Jones," Jonesy responded in a husky voice.

"Jonesy, this is Kate. I don't know how to tell you this except to just say it. AJ is dead."

After thirty seconds of silence, Jones asked, with shock evident in her voice, "What happened?"

"I'm not sure. Jack Nathan was on the scene."

"Don't tell me that idiot killed her?" Jonesy spat the words with hatred spewing from each syllable

"I don't know. Morris, who was on the scene, said there were unanswered questions."

"Does Sam know?"

"I called Central Detectives, and the deskman told me she is in court today. I'm going to ask Ray to find her."

"If Ray can't find her, let me know, and I'll drive to City Hall. I'll call Walt to help me find her."

There was a moment of silence, neither knowing what to say next. Finally, Kate said, "Keep in touch," and Jonesy said she would.

Next, Kate dialed the Philadelphia Police Research and Planning unit for the third time and was relieved to hear her husband's warm voice answer the phone. "Lieutenant Rossi."

"Ray, it's Kate."

"Good morning, cutie. Miss me already?"

"Ray, it's AJ. She's dead."

After a moment of stunned silence, Ray said, "I'll be there in half an hour."

"No, Ray, I'm OK. I was able to catch up with Jonesy but not Sam. I think Sam is in court at City Hall, and I can't leave the district. Would you drive there and find her and tell her before she hears it in the hallway at City Hall?"

"Of course," he replied. "Call me in about an hour."

Acceptance of what has happened is the first step to
overcoming the consequences of any misfortune.

—William James

FIVE

• •

GREG LOCKE WAS WALKING SWIFTLY TOWARD THE SECURITY
door at the PAB, on his way to find Sam Kelly at City Hall, when
the Homicide detective made eye contact with Ray Rossi. Rossi was
walking toward the exit like he was also on a mission, and Locke
instantly knew the reason: he, too, had just learned of AJ's death.

Locke had known Rossi for most of his eight-year tenure in
the Philadelphia Police Department; he was a happy-go-lucky guy
who never seemed to lose his cool. In addition to being the commanding officer of research and planning, Rossi was a moonlight-
ing musician—he played the saxophone and was the lead singer for
a group of cop musicians who called themselves Anti-Corruption.
They performed, for the most part, at police benefits and the weddings of police officers and their relatives. Ray's smooth style, baritone singing voice, and Dean Martin stature made him one of the
most likeable bosses in the department. As their gazes met, they
both realized the other knew about A. J. Harris.

Locke offered his hand for a brief shake and said, "I'm guessing
you heard about AJ."

"Yeah, Kate asked me to find Sam in City Hall. It'll be a
tough conversation."

Locke nodded and waved his hand. "Ray, I know where she is, and I'm on my way. I'll take this notification off your hands."

"Thanks. I wasn't looking forward to the task. In the meantime, I'm going to take a ride to the Fourteenth District to see my wife."

Walking toward their respective cars, the two men silently contemplated the impact of the tragedy on their personal lives.

The short drive to City Hall provided Detective Locke with time to organize his thoughts. Locke knew that Sam was going to be devastated when he told her about AJ. He guessed she might initially cry, but the deeper consequence of this heartbreak would reveal itself over time. He knew that if history was an indicator, Sam would try to detach from everyone around her and manage the heartbreak alone.

For the three years Locke had known Detective Samantha Kelly, she had avoided talking about herself or sharing her feelings unless he prodded. Locke found Sam to be an interesting dichotomy. Her five-foot-four slender build; brown eyes; brown, shoulder-length curly hair; and quiet demeanor gave the accurate impression of a reserved and hardworking detective. Though it was rarely evident, she had another side: a fiery temper that would make a grizzly bear take pause. Sam approached most situations with a quiet, approachable, collaborative enthusiasm. But, occasionally, when confronting a perceived injustice, she reacted with ferocious abandon.

Most of the other cops liked her because she was focused on being a good detective and never talked of burning bras and women's rights. She never spoke of the women's court suit against the department by the Justice Department, but because of public disclosure, it was widely known that she had refused the financial settlement portion of the settlement. That gesture didn't detract from her friendship with A. J. Harris, Kate Dominic, and Michelle Jones, who were very vocal about discrimination in the Philadelphia Police Department.

Locke's respect for Sam's unique style and ability to puzzle through an investigation grew during the time he had worked with her at Central Detectives. He initially regretted his transfer to the Homicide Division the year before because he limited his ability to work with her on cases, but he didn't regret the decision when he found her receptive to a personal relationship with him.

Sam had natural ability to create positive energy in the squad, sharing her investigations because she always seemed energized by identifying a crime pattern, identifying a doer, or serving a warrant for bad actors. Even old timers like Johnny Hogan were energized by her. After she worked with him on a couple of cases, he actually went to alcohol rehab. Partnering with Sam gave him a new sense of purpose. Hogan was a great detective in his day, but the job and alcohol had left him behind. As Hogan's decline was noticed by everyone, so was Sam's role in his rebound.

Sam was able to find a way to get along with most everyone, with one exception. Detective James Wexler and Detective Samantha Kelly were like oil and water from the moment they met. Wexler, an arrogant misogynist, annoyed lots of cops. He was widely known as "Detective Strapper," referring to a South Philly insult meaning a "dumb-ass loser." Unfortunately, Sam never just ignored Wexler but met his antagonism measure by measure. The hostilities between them started the day they met and rose to a new level in a fight over a typewriter.

Locke was pretty sure the feud would escalate to a war. The news that Wexler was the assigned investigator for AJ's shooting could be a flash point, and Locke cringed at the thought of Sam's reaction. He concluded that it would be best to hold that piece of information in his back pocket until Sam had time to process AJ's death.

Philadelphia City Hall was built between 1871 and 1901. Its exterior is made of granite, marble, and limestone. The most significant architecture is the freestanding staircase in each interior corner. Greg Locke took the winding staircase in the southeast corner, two stairs at a time. As he turned into the third-floor corridor, he scanned the crowd of police officers and civilians milling about outside the courtrooms. It only took a few seconds before he saw Detective Sam Kelly in the crowd.

Sam was staring out the huge window, looking down at the rush-hour crowd quickly moving through City Hall's courtyard. Noticing a familiar suit and walk out of the corner of her eye, she turned and saw Locke striding toward her. She smiled at him, admiring how well his broad shoulders, dark wavy hair, and five-foot-ten-inch frame fit his navy-blue pinstripes. As he closed the distance between them, she made eye contact, saw the concern in his deep brown eyes, and knew something was wrong.

"Hey," she said with a slight but confused grin. "What are you doing here?"

Locke steeled his voice against any emotion and said, "Can we take a walk?"

Sam's heart sank, then started racing as her mind flashed back to the day that AJ told her that her brother and parents were killed in an automobile accident.

As they walked to the end of the corridor and entered the secluded stairwell, Sam studied Locke's profile for any clue of what he was going to tell her. Locke knew she was searching his face for information and decided not to look at her until they had privacy.

Surveying the area to confirm they were alone, he reached for her hand. Making eye contact, he kissed her palm. Sam felt Locke tremble. Her mind raced, and her eyes widened as they stared at each other. "Come on, Locke, you are scaring me. What is it?"

"Sam, AJ was found dead in her apartment."

"No," Sam gasped. As she felt her legs give out, Locke put his arms around her waist and pulled her to his chest to steady her. His chin on her head, he stroked her arms and back, wondering if she would break down and cry.

He could feel and hear her take deep breaths.

After several long minutes, Sam asked, "Who is the assigned detective?"

Locke fought a grimace by swallowing. "Wexler. Wexler is the assigned."

"Damn," she said. Her head spinning, leaning against Locke's chest, she squeezed her eyes to fight back out-of-control emotions. When she thought she could talk, she said, "Thanks. I appreciate that you found me before I heard it in the hallway."

They didn't speak for another minute, but it felt like an hour to Locke, who was waiting for her to say something.

"Thanks, Locke, I appreciate that you reached out to me before I heard it in the hallway." She said, her voice sounding robotic.

"Sam, don't talk to me like I'm a sector cop making a notification. It's me. Are you OK?"

"I know who you are," she said more curtly than she wanted to sound. "Sorry. I just meant that I appreciate that you went out of your way to make sure I didn't hear someone talking about it. But I do need to get back to the courtroom now." Sam tried to push away from Locke, but he tightened his hold on her.

Whispering in her ear, he said, "I'm sorry, baby. I know this sucks. Why don't you come with me now? We can take some time to regroup. I'll call the DA and explain."

Sam hesitated but managed to gather her resolve once again. Without looking at him, she shook her head and again in a tone harsher than she intended, said, "No!" Immediately realizing how she sounded, she followed saying, "I mean, I am good. I can handle this. Unless there is some last-minute continuance, the DA needs me to testify today. How about I meet you at the PAB afterward? I want to swing by Homicide and catch up with Michelle. I guess Kate and Ray know, right? Did you have plans tonight? Could we spend some time together? Am I babbling?"

Locke kissed the top of her hair. "I'm just glad you're talking. I spoke to Ray Rossi, and yes, Kate and Jonesy know. Let me give you the key to my apartment. Why don't you just go directly to my apartment after court and get some rest? I'll bring you dinner."

"No, I need to go to the records unit, and I also need to pick up some photos at the crime lab. I'll meet you at Homicide. Jonesy should be there, and I'd like to see her."

"Whatever you think is best," he said. Inwardly, he recoiled at the possibility that Sam would run into Wexler. The last thing she needed today was a showdown with him.

Locke didn't want to leave, but he knew she wouldn't change her mind. He decided not to press her. He released his hold, kissed her cheek, said goodbye, and watched her walk down the corridor to the courtroom. At first she was tentative, unsure, but then her gait became more confident the farther she traveled down the hallway.

As Locke walked to his car and drove back to Eighth and Race, he wondered at Sam and her reaction. Something bothered him. She had been upset and deep in thought, but she didn't seem shocked. She asked one question, and she didn't cry.

"It's not like you, Sam. Why didn't you ask more questions?" he said to himself, not realizing he had spoken aloud until he noticed the curious glance of the driver next to him stopped at Twelfth and Market. He nodded lamely and sped up when the light flashed green.

You will not be punished for your anger;
you will be punished by your anger.

—Buddha

SIX

"WEXLER, A CALL ON LINE THREE," THE HOMICIDE UNIT DESK-man called out.

The detective, who had been reviewing an interview, looked up and said, "Got it." He picked up the phone and said, "Wexler."

"Wexler, this is Detective Michelle Jones. I was transferred to Homicide three-squad from South Detectives last week. I'm a friend of A. J. Harris's. I was told that you are the assigned. I was hoping you could provide some information—"

"Were a friend." Wexler interrupted.

"What?"

"You were a friend, you mean. She's dead."

"OK. She was my friend. Can you help me understand what happened?"

"No."

"Why not?" asked Jonesy in an incredulous tone.

"You don't need to know."

"Would you be saying that if I was one of your male buddies?"

"Here's some advice to you, Detective Jones: stay away from my investigation. If I find you poking around, I'll consider it interference, and I'll make a complaint to the brass. You got that?"

Although momentarily silenced, Jonesy soon responded in a flat, controlled voice. "Wow, I reserved judgment when I heard you're called 'Detective Strapper.' I guess I was wrong."

"What can I say? Oh, I know what I can say. How about this: kiss my ass. You got that?" Wexler said, and he slammed the phone down.

Sam spent the next several hours at City Hall in a daze. She was relieved when her court case was eventually rescheduled to a future date. As she walked into the attendance office to check out of court, she felt the stares of other cops. But no one said anything to her beyond brief hellos.

Sam usually took the bus whenever she could, but today she decided a walk from City Hall to Eighth and Race would clear her head; she'd felt a migraine building ever since Locke had told her the news. She pushed through the heavy doors of City Hall and left the court behind her. Walking by the John Wanamaker Store at Thirteenth and Market Streets, she was struck by a desire suddenly to see the Christmas light show. Before she could talk herself out of it, she was through the doors and gazing up at the lights.

The Wanamaker light show was a Philadelphia Christmas tradition. Sam tried to make a point of seeing it once every Christmas. The show had two features that Sam loved: a pipe organ playing Christmas carols, and the comfortingly familiar voice of John Facenda, a local TV icon and the voice of NFL films. Standing in Wanamaker's grand hall, Sam was lost in memories of Christmases past, with trips to the light show and the knee sock hung at the family fireplace on Christmas Eve. Her parents were gone, her brother was gone, AJ was gone, and life felt empty and cruel. But for a moment, standing there bathed in light and sound, Sam could reach into the past.

When the show was over, Sam walked at an easy pace down Market Street, amid the hordes of shoppers and businessmen and women. Her mind was overwhelmed by an avalanche of thoughts and memories. Seven years of friendship. AJ had been there when Sam's entire family died. She knew how hard it had been. Now she was gone—one last link to her past, and a friend who could never be replaced. Sorrow trembled through her.

Sam began taking deep breaths, pushing back against the memories and emotions. *Be strong. Be sharp. Above all, let no one see you like this.* By the time Sam entered the squad room of the Homicide Division, she thought she felt calm and clear-headed. But it didn't last long. She surveyed the squad room for Jonesy or Locke, and instead she saw Wexler sitting at his desk. He saw her at the same time. She quickly glanced away and walked toward the deskman.

Determined not to be ignored, Wexler rose and strolled over. "Is this a personal visit, Detective Kelly?" he said. "Should I be offering condolences for your loss? I actually wondered sometimes—you and Harris were *so* close. But it seems like she went for guys after all—unfortunately, the wrong guy. What does it say about the judgment of women who hook up with losers?"

"I don't know. Why don't you ask your wife?" Sam said coldly, making sure not to blink first.

Bull's-eye. Wexler's bloodshot gray eyes narrowed, and he took another step toward her.

"It's so sad she blew her brains out just because she didn't want to share her boy toy with his wife and other girlfriend. What an efficient guy, buying Valentine's gifts in triplicate."

So Wexler was already treating AJ's death as a suicide. Sam felt fury shoot throughout her entire body, but she kept her voice devoid of emotion and stepped closer to him. "Wexler, if I thought for a minute you could investigate your way out of a paper bag, I might be really pissed to hear you say that. Your lack of investigation skills doesn't surprise me. It just makes me fear for Philadelphia."

Wexler took another step toward Sam; now they were inches apart. "My skills are good enough to know that you didn't even flinch when I mentioned the Valentine's gifts. How did you know about them? Were you with Officer Harris last night? Could you be a witness, Detective? Should I escort you to an interview room?"

Sam didn't back down. She moved closer too, so close she could see the pores of his nose and the gray in his mustache. Staring straight into his eyes, she said, "You want to know what I know, Wexler? I know that the next time you get an investigation right, it will be the first time. I am surprised at how quickly you are moving to close this investigation. The question is, why?" Sam pressed her finger to her chin, still inches from Wexler's face. "Hmmm, let me think. Does a determination of suicide provide the misdirection you need to distract from what you know really happened? Should you be escorted to an interview room?"

Wexler's face flamed with anger. He balled up his right fist and grabbed her black trench coat with his left hand. "You fucking bitch."

Sam looked down at his fist and whispered, "Your move, Wexler. Lots of witnesses." Sam raised her voice. "So, is there any reason you need to recuse yourself from this investigation, Detective? What is your involvement in the circumstances of Officer Harris's death?"

"Are you making an accusation?" said Wexler through gritted teeth, gripping the lapels of her trench coat with white knuckles.

"Should I be?" Sam challenged.

At that moment, Locke and Farrell walked into the tense office and quickly moved forward to intervene.

"Take your hands off her, Wexler," Locke commanded in a steady voice.

"Always the hero, Locke?" Wexler shot back, glowering.

Farrell nudged the two detectives apart and ordered, "Wexler, my office."

Wexler and Sam continued to glare at each other. Neither moved. The lieutenant raised his voice. "Now, Wexler!"

Turning to Sam, Farrell asked, "Do you need something, Detective?"

"I was looking for Detective Jones and Detective Locke, sir."

Lieutenant Farrell motioned toward Locke. "Locke, your shift is over. Please escort Detective Kelly out of the building."

Locke nodded and grabbed his coat and briefcase before nudging Sam into motion. "Let's go. Jonesy isn't here," Locke said. They walked in silence to Locke's car.

Many people resented my impatience and
honesty, but I never cared about acceptance as
much as I cared about respect.

—Jackie Robinson

SEVEN

NEITHER SAM OR LOCKE SPOKE UNTIL LOCKE'S BROWN BUICK
Riviera made its way down Callowhill Street from Sixth Street. Sam
leaned back against the seat's headrest and massaged her temple
absently. Locke moved his right hand from the steering wheel and
brushed his knuckles down Sam's left cheek. She looked at him and
smiled, but it seemed forced.

"You have to be more careful with Wexler," Locke said. "For a
moment, I thought he was going to hit you. What's worse, it looked
like you wanted him to hit you."

"It would be a small price to pay if it got him removed from the
investigation," she said flippantly.

"Samantha, don't bait him. You won't like the consequences."

Attempting to ignore his comment, she said, "You know, you
only call me Samantha when you are very serious or very nervous.
It's your tell. So which is it this time: nervous or serious?"

"Both. Nervous that you are reckless around Wexler. Serious
because I know this sucks, and I want to help. Why don't you just let
go and have a good cry?"

Sam raised an eyebrow and gave him a disgusted glance. "I never thought I'd accuse you of chauvinism. Do I need a good cry because I'm a woman? Do you ever need a good cry?"

"When my father died, I cried on and off for three days. I felt terrible for my mother, my sister, and myself," he said softly.

Sam blew out a breath. "OK, you got me, Greg. That was a cheap shot. You are not that guy. I'm sorry."

Locke reached over and squeezed her hand. "Promise me that you won't be so reckless with Wexler," he said, quietly.

Not wanting to lie, Sam redirected the conversation. "Locke, Wexler said AJ committed suicide."

"Yes."

"Yes, what?"

"I understand Wexler thinks AJ's death is a suicide."

"You know that is crap. Wexler is an idiot in general, and I think he would blow the investigation regardless, but this time, I think he's up to something."

Locke glanced over at her thoughtfully but didn't agree or disagree. After another moment of silence, Sam whispered, "If anything ever happens to me, you have to promise that Wexler will not be the assigned investigator."

The unexpected request sent a chill down Locke's spine. He reached for her hand and said, "Samantha, nothing is going to happen to you. I have your back, but help me out here. Stop baiting Wexler."

Feeling nauseous and light-headed from a migraine that had started when Locke visited her at City Hall, Sam closed her eyes and leaned her head against the seat's headrest. Her pleading voice cracked as she whispered, "Really, Locke, you are calling me 'Samantha' again…"

Sam sighed and continued, "I have never asked a favor and normally wouldn't but——"

Noticing her complexion had turned as white as a sheet, Locke interrupted her. "I would do anything for you. I hope you know that, Samantha." He glanced at her as his right hand left the steering wheel and slipped behind her neck. He gently rubbed his thumb gently along her neck.

"You are calling me Samantha again, but I'm going to ignore it for now," Sam said. Fighting back the nausea and light-headedness, Sam continued, "You know, AJ would never commit suicide, no matter what happened. Wexler is way off, and I think purposely. I think I pressed his buttons today."

"You think!"

"Could you find a way to have the investigation reassigned? The chief likes you. I'm sure he could do it. I know they wouldn't let Jonesy handle it, but they would probably trust you to be objective."

Locke's stomach sank. He felt deflated and empty suddenly, like a popped balloon. "Samantha, there is no way the investigation would be reassigned to anyone. If I even suggested it, we'd both look foolish."

Sam never opened her eyes or acknowledged Locke's response. The migraine bloomed, and the events of the day caught up with her. She slumped into darkness and slept for the rest of the drive.

A woman is like a teabag—you can't tell how strong she is until you put her in hot water.

—Eleanor Roosevelt

EIGHT

LOCKE PULLED UP TO HIS HIGH-RISE APARTMENT BUILDING across from the Philadelphia Museum of Art. He tried patting Sam's hand and gently shaking her shoulder, but still she slept. She was so pale. *Should I take her to the emergency room?* No, he decided. She didn't need any more excitement. He lifted her over his shoulder and carried her to his apartment. Thankfully, he passed only one neighbor along the way. Joe looked startled at first but quickly joked, "They say cops are Neanderthals. I just didn't believe it. Need any help?"

Locke didn't slow his pace. "No, it's OK. She's very tired and had a rough day. She'll be fine once she's had something to eat."

After unlocking his apartment door, fumbling the keys in his left hand, he carried Sam to the bedroom and laid her on the bed. He propped her head up with pillows, dampened a washcloth with cool water, and put it on her forehead, coaxing her to consciousness by gently calling her name and patting her hand.

When Sam opened her brown eyes, she was dazed. Locke kissed her once on her forehead and then he rested his nose on hers, their eyes so close he could see the deep flecks of gold in her irises.

He whispered, "Please don't ever do that to me again. Samantha, you scared me to death."

She blinked and looked at him, confused. "What happened?"

He leaned back a little to give her some space. "I was driving. We were talking. You passed out. I was going to rush you to Hahnemann Hospital, but I knew you'd never forgive me if I took you to the emergency room after the day you've had. Plan B was to bring you here. I brought you here. I promise not to seduce you." He winked, hoping it would make her smile.

It worked. Sam chuckled a little. "Sorry," she said, massaging her temple. "If I didn't have a major headache right now, seduction might be appealing. But you could begin by feeding me. I haven't eaten all day. I guess the self-imposed starvation got the best of me."

"How about I order a pizza from Mr. Morgan's? And I have a couple of Moosehead beers in the fridge. The perfect prescription for a headache."

"Thank you, Dr. Locke. Pizza sounds yummy—that is, if you promise to stop calling me Samantha. No beer. I can't mix anger, despair, and alcohol." She cleared her throat. "Do you mind if I steal some aspirin and close my eyes for a couple minutes? Just a little while, though. I need to catch up with Kate and Jonesy, but I need some time. Do you know if AJ's parents were contacted? Damn, I'm rambling again."

Locke had noticed her rubbing her temples and had already started to search his medicine cabinet. He smiled gently, handing her a glass of water and aspirin. "Beginning at the top—here is your aspirin. Mr. and Mrs. Harris were notified. Kate and Ray Rossi made the call. I checked in with them while you were still at City Hall. Ray said the call was pretty tough on Kate, and AJ's father and mother were completely devastated. They're flying up from Scofield Barracks, in Hawaii, as soon as they can make the arrangements. Yes, you are rambling. Rambling is *your* tell. You do it when you are very upset or very happy."

Watching Sam swallow the aspirin, Locke continued tentatively, "Could we talk for a minute before you nap?"

"Yes," said Sam, straightening a little in the bed and setting her glass on the nightstand. "But let me start. I'm sorry. I put you on the spot. I get it, Locke. I had a moment of desperation, and I crossed the line when I asked you to somehow get the investigation from Wexler. That was lousy of me." Sam touched his hand and quietly asked, "Forgive me?"

Locke caught her hand and brought it to his lips, and then he climbed into the bed next to her, pulling her into his embrace. Sam rested her forehead on his chest, her head under his chin. "Sam, you've had a terrible day. There's nothing to forgive. But I don't want to talk about that right now. I want to talk about what Wexler said. Was he right? You know something more, don't you?"

Sam pulled back a little to look into his eyes. Her voice wouldn't work, so she only nodded, a small but deliberate movement.

"Talk to me, Sam."

She looked away, staring thoughtfully at the bedroom ceiling. When she began speaking, her voice was quiet but controlled. "AJ called me last night from Northeast Philly. She was at a pay phone. At first, she was upset. She told me that Jack's ex-wife and his other girlfriend had shown up at her apartment yesterday. They told her that Jack had been screwing all three of them." She shook her head a little and said, "Her words, not mine. Anyway, from what AJ concluded, Jack was trying to dump girlfriend number three, and girlfriend number three took revenge by exposing the truth to his ex-wife. The two of them decided to team up, and they turned up at AJ's door next. She was devastated and disgusted. The girlfriend told them about the Valentine's Day bracelets, and they thought it would be a nice touch to bring them along when all three of them went to Jack's apartment to confront him.

"I was at the division when AJ called me. She'd just left Jack's apartment. We talked for a while. The only time she cried was when she told me he bought the Valentine's gifts in triplicate. She called him every foul name she could conjure and described all the ways he deserved to be tortured. I told her I had never heard of some of her torture methods, and she said it was because she wasn't finished teaching me everything she knew. We both started laughing hysterically, and then we reminisced about how she taught me how to curse. I thought by the end of the conversation that she was in a better place. I asked if she wanted to meet me either at Baker Street or at her apartment, and she said that she wanted some time to herself, but she would see me in the morning.

"Before she said goodbye, though, she said something strange. She told me that she thought we may have trouble coming our way in the form of Detective James Wexler. Honestly, she almost sounded as upset about that as she did about Jack's trysts and gifting habits. I tried to press her for details, but she wouldn't say more. I should have pushed harder." Sam shook her head as if to clear her thoughts and continued, "I have no clue how or why she would have crossed paths with Wexler yesterday, and why she would bring it up then. Anyway, I hope I don't see Jack for a long time. I'm not sure I could hold back from killing him. He may have surpassed Wexler on my hit parade of men I'd like to put six feet under."

"Remind me to avoid your hit parade, and while I know you don't mean 'kill' literally, be careful where you say that. If either man shows up dead, you could be the prime suspect."

"Yeah, you are probably right. I'll watch what I say. But on the other hand, I would probably be a good suspect." She chuckled.

Locke raised an eyebrow. "Not one of your funniest lines, Gracie Allen."

"Where is your sense of humor? It's a little funny, George Burns." She laughed as she tapped his nose.

"OK, I admit that I can't deliver a comedic line like Gracie Allen, so I'll be serious," she continued. "I never liked Jack. I always thought Jack was a jerk, but buying gifts in triplicate was a level lower than I even imagined for him. AJ and I talked about his arrogance and stupidity until about 1:30 a.m. I thought she was OK—at least, temporarily. We agreed to meet at City Hall because she had court, too. I was waiting for her when you came walking down the hall."

"Sam, you should have told Wexler you spoke to AJ before…"

"I don't trust him, Greg. I'm not sure what he's up to. Did you notice his reaction to me?"

"Everyone in Homicide noticed his reaction to you."

"OK, you've made your point, Locke. I'll watch my step where he is concerned. Now, my head is killing me. I'd like to close my eyes for a few minutes."

Locke kissed her on the forehead, smoothed his hand over hers, and turned out the light. "Get some rest," he said. "I'm off to Mr. Morgan's to pick up the pizza."

Sam was still feeling woozy when she awoke to the telephone ringing a short time later. She was just making sense of her surroundings when she heard Locke's voice in the other room. "I agree, it is a good idea," he said, his deep voice muffled through the wall. "See you soon."

Several seconds later, Locke opened the bedroom door, walked in, and sat on the bed next to her. He took Sam's hand, kissed her palm, and asked, "How are you feeling?"

"A little foggy, but OK," she lied.

He cupped her face in his hands and brushed her lips with his. "Feel like a road trip?" he asked. "Are you up to driving to South Philly to see Kate and Ray? Jonesy and Walt will be there as well. We can take the pizza, but you should eat something before we leave. Being that I'm his best customer, Mr. Morgan himself gave us a steak sandwich that a customer ordered and never picked up."

"You would make a good nurse," Sam said, winking at him. "Yes, I would like to take the road trip, and yes, I'd love to share the sandwich."

Sam sat up, swung her feet over the edge of the bed, and stood up slowly. She straightened her suit as she looked at the full-length mirror on the outside of the bathroom door. Noticing that her navy-blue suit wasn't badly wrinkled, she said, "Thank God for polyester blend." As she smoothed her skirt, she added, "But the suit aside, I do look like I could haunt houses. Give me a minute to fix this." She circled her hand in the air in front of her face.

Locke smiled, relieved Sam seemed to be feeling better, and went into the kitchen to put the sandwich on a plate.

Friends help you move. Best friends help you move bodies.

—Unknown

NINE

———————————————• •———————————————

In Girard Estates, homes were passed down through generations of families. Ray Rossi had inherited one such home in this prestigious section of South Philadelphia from his grandparents. After Rossi married Kate, her mother, Carmella Dominic, wasted no time applying her flawless, classic Italian sense of design to create an impressive home for the newlyweds.

When Greg Locke and Sam Kelly arrived in the Rossi home, Carmella and her husband, Len, were leaving. Carmella embraced Sam. "Samantha, the pain you girls are feeling breaks my heart. Please don't be a stranger to us. We are here for you," she said. "Come over for Christmas dinner. Len will be making his meatballs, and I'll make your favorite pepper pasta."

Sam nodded. "I would love that, Carmella."

Locke quietly surveyed the group. He noticed that Kate and Jonesy were still flushed from crying, and even the faces of Carmella and Len were tired and worn by tears. Ray's concern for Kate was obvious in the way he looked at his wife.

Jonesy's tall, lanky boyfriend, Walt, who worked in South Detectives, sat in a navy-blue wingback chair and stared into a glass of scotch while swiping his hand over his graying mustache. It was a depressing scene, and Locke wondered if it would get worse. The three women exchanged lingering hugs, and more tears flowed—but none from Sam. Not yet.

Ray offered Greg something to drink, and he accepted a glass of scotch and took a quick gulp.

In an effort to lift everyone from their sorrow, if for a moment, Sam remarked on the dramatic changes to the house since she had seen it last. "Your mom and dad need to take up a new business," she said, taking in the remodeled slate fireplace and wooden mantle, dark hardwood floors in the foyer, and the marble countertops and artisan-tile backsplash in the remodeled kitchen.

"I'm jealous," Jonesy chimed in, picking up on the need to elevate the mood. "When your parents expand their tailoring business to interior design, they can practice on my house," she joked. "I won't even ask them to put a kitchen in the basement. I'm too lazy to go to the basement to cook." Everyone laughed.

"They are good to us, for sure." Kate agreed.

But the room still felt awkward, and silence ensued. Jonesy spoke up again, abruptly changing the direction of the conversation to what was on everyone's minds. "What is the protocol for this type of thing? Should we offer to help with the funeral, or is that too pushy?"

Kate said, "Ray and I spoke to AJ's father. He was very receptive to our help. They seem so nice. I wish we had taken the time to meet them when AJ was alive. AJ offered to take us to Hawaii for years. We kept saying we would save up for the trip, but we never got there. Lesson learned: life is short, and you shouldn't put off things that matter. Meeting her parents, while she was still here, mattered. God, it feels so strange and unreal to acknowledge she's gone.

"Anyway, they're flying in from Scofield Barracks in an army transport, and we will pick them up from Maguire Air Force Base. They are going to stay at the Bellevue Stratford on South Broad Street. We were going to drive them to the Chapel of the Four Chaplains on North Broad to meet with the undertaker and the minister to plan the funeral. You're all welcome to join us there."

"Yes, I'll join you. I made AJ a promise to sing her funeral song, and I want to keep the promise," Sam said to no one in particular.

Kate and Jonesy exchanged glances, as did Ray, Walt, and Greg.

"I think AJ was kidding when she said that. Anyway, do you think you'd be up to singing?" asked Kate. "None of us would want to send you in to an emotional tailspin—least of all AJ. I'm sure she was joking."

"I think she was very serious. And it doesn't matter if I'm up to it. I promised," Sam replied, her voice tapering off to a whisper. But then her voice grew stronger. "Is there any way to keep AJ's parents as far away from Wexler as possible? Based on my last conversation with him, he won't be kind. He's already going down the wrong path on this." Again in a low voice, she added, "I wish we could start on our own investigation right now."

Jonesy and Kate nodded in agreement. "We will do right by her, but after the funeral," said Kate.

The three men looked at each other, and Ray spoke. "Let's slow down and talk this through," he said, aiming for a reasonable tone of voice.

All three women turned to stare at the men.

"What is there to talk through?" asked Kate.

"This is a major blow to the three of you—I mean, to all of us. I think it is important that we—all of us—talk this through," Ray said. Greg and Walt nodded in agreement.

A minute of silence ensued, with each woman staring at her significant other with folded arms and a glare that could send the Amazon River into a deep freeze.

Ray broke the uncomfortable silence. "I spoke to Ted Farrell. He told me that Wexler is making a pretty compelling case for suicide."

"Really?" Jonesy said, unable or unwilling to disguise the anger in her voice. "That is very interesting. I work in the Homicide unit, and I was told I couldn't ask for details. I hate to disagree with you, Lieutenant, but Wexler's obvious hostility toward women doesn't inspire confidence in an objective conclusion."

Greg intervened quickly. "I think we can objectively say the hostility goes both ways. Because Sam mistrusts Wexler, she withheld information," he said. "Sam spoke to AJ last night. She may have been the last person to speak to her, but she didn't share that information with the assigned investigator. You can't expect him to run a solid investigation if his own colleagues withhold information."

Sam said nothing, but her icy stare communicated the dagger of disloyalty through her heart. Locke regretted his words immediately. Kate and Jonesy looked at Sam in disbelief.

Breaking the silence, Walt spoke. "Do you think you three might be too close to be objective?"

It was Jonesy's turn to send ice darts with her eyes across the room. "No," she replied sharply. "I think we are close enough to see things *clearly*. AJ would never commit suicide over her relationship with Jack, under any circumstances. Also, it is inconceivable that AJ would ever shoot herself in the head. We actually talked about suicide once, and she said she would never do that. She would take pills or jump off a bridge."

"Why would you ever talk about committing suicide?" Walt asked, his voice a mix of disbelief and concern.

"Oh, for Christ's sake, Walt, we're cops." Jonesy said impatiently. "We see terrible things, and we talk about it to try to figure out why people do the things they do. Haven't you ever put yourself in the position of the victim or the bad guy and wonder how you would do things?"

"Actually, no. I have never thought about suicide, and I don't sit around South Detectives and shoot the shit with the guys about committing crimes."

"You might want to try it before you knock it," said Kate. "Talking things through actually helps you understand people and situations. For instance, let's examine the facts about Jack Nathan. Why doesn't Wexler think it's strange that Nathan, who is at the scene when AJ is found shot in the head, conveniently talked AJ into going to the shooting range the day she died? Most cops would know that would make a paraffin test useless. And then he behaves like a freaking professional crier, grandstanding about how distraught he is, so the polygraph is inconclusive. I'm not buying it. And I could see a scenario where Wexler perceived AJ as a threat to his job. AJ could have said something in anger, and he responded in kind."

"Kate, I was hoping that information would help you not send you down a road—"

"What is this, an intervention?" Kate said. "I'm so sorry to have gotten this wrong. I thought we were all getting together because we needed to talk through how we are going to find justice for AJ. But the truth is, the three of you brought us together to lecture us on the limitations of our judgment or the lack thereof. I think we are having a Commissioner O'Neill moment—the next thing you're going to tell us is that God in his infinite wisdom made men and women different, and our feminine ways will hamper our objectivity and capabilities."

The men appeared to be stunned by Kate's accusations. Jonesy said nothing. Sam's pained stare never left Locke's brown eyes.

Ray was the first to speak, very slowly. "Kate, this has nothing to do with men versus women. I would be saying this to anyone in similar circumstances. We care about the three of you, and we thought our collective experiences would help the three of you process this tragedy. We are just trying to help. The three of you are very close to this case, and we don't want this to hurt you even more than it has. Doesn't it make sense to take a step back and review the facts objectively? The evidence points to suicide, and denial will cause you more pain."

"What about our collective experiences?" Kate said, spreading out her arm to encompass Jonesy and Sam.

"When I said collective, I meant—"

"Ray, don't say another word. We will both regret it," Kate said with fire in her eyes.

Walt reached out for Jonesy. Her eyes were glazed with anger and hurt. She put her hand up and took a step back. "Walt, don't touch me."

Sam finally spoke. "Well, thanks, guys. Appreciate the three of you saving us from ourselves."

"Sam," Greg said calmly. "AJ's death is a blow. Wexler leading the investigation compounds it for you. Would you consider that Wexler's involvement could affect your judgment?"

"OK, maybe you are right. Wexler is a lousy detective and an even worse human being, and I'm personally appalled by him. He has gotten it wrong more than once. But I guess we disagree about that, don't we?"

"All right, Sam. I agree the guy won't win any awards for his personality. Even if he is the world's biggest ass, this is America, Sam.

The last time I checked, it's a free country, and you are allowed to be an ass. Just because he isn't the kind of man you admire, it doesn't mean he is a bad detective. He is different from you, but I've seen him do good work. He isn't as a bad as you think."

"Said like a real man. I'm the intolerant one because I reject his misogyny, incompetence, and intimidation tactics." Sam's voice was riddled with bitterness and sorrow.

Locke maintained a poker face, but Sam's words cut him like a saber through his chest. He swallowed before responding in a very low voice. "That was harsh, Sam. I just don't want you to hurt yourself. I have always had your back." Her silence and angry glare told him that she didn't agree—not this time.

The minutes ticked by agonizingly. Walt paced while Greg and Ray repeatedly ran hands through their hair. Kate and Jonesy stood with their arms crossed, staring at the wall. Sam and Locke stared at each other.

Finally, Kate spoke. "I think we are *all* emotionally depleted. Why don't we call it a night? Good night, everyone." Kate walked up the stairs to the master bedroom and closed the door.

No one moved. They all contemplated the potential impact of an additional conversation and decided that leaving words unspoken and feelings unresolved would be best, at least for now.

Sam turned to Jonesy and said, "Can I hitch a ride with you to Manayunk? I took the train to court at City Hall today."

"Of course," Jonesy said, and then she looked at Walt. "I think you might be able to get a ride with Locke. Good night." The two women walked out of the house. Locke shivered, but not from the cold air that swept through the door.

After Jonesy and Sam left, Walt rubbed his face and chin with his hands and said, "Well, that was fucked up. Any thoughts about where we go from here?"

Ray shook his head but asked, "What are you thinking about, Locke?"

As if he were giving a briefing on an investigation, Locke recounted what he knew.

"Obviously, there is no official report yet, so I haven't seen any documents. I think you know most of it. The Fourteenth District sector cop, Morris, responded to a hospital case and found Jack Nathan holding her body in her apartment. Nathan was as dramatic as Kate said. He claimed to be the person who called 911. The radio room dispatched the call as a hospital case instead of a DOA. But by Nathan's account, she was dead when he arrived. I haven't heard the 911 tapes. I don't know if Nathan called it in as a hospital case, or if the radio room screwed the pooch. Nothing was gleaned from neighborhood interviews. There don't appear to be any witnesses who even heard a gunshot. There are no results from ballistics yet, but circumstantially it looks like her service revolver was the weapon used. One shot had been fired from her gun. It could be consistent with a suicide. A service revolver is usually the weapon of choice for a cop committing suicide. As Kate said, Nathan tested positive for gunshot residue, but he had been at the range with AJ. Nathan didn't stop crying long enough to take a legitimate polygraph.

"My gut tells me that she didn't commit suicide, and Ted Farrell thinks the same. We have plenty of suspects, including Nathan, his wife, and his girlfriend. I think Wexler intends to follow up with the girlfriend and ex-wife for sure. Girlfriend number three sounds like she could be pretty nasty, but something tells me that Nathan was her target and she did the damage she wanted. What Wexler doesn't know is that Sam spoke to AJ last night. Sam admits that AJ was distraught, but she didn't think she was distraught enough to take her own life.

"AJ made plans to meet with Sam today to talk about Wexler. Sam thinks Wexler knows something, and Wexler thinks Sam is holding back information. I think Wexler might be afraid of what Sam knows. The cat-and-mouse game that Wexler plays with Sam isn't going to help the investigation, and Sam is a walking volcano, just waiting to erupt. She was ready to bait Wexler into punching her today, hoping it would get him pulled from the investigation. Sam is usually a very levelheaded and reasonable person, but not when it comes to Wexler.

"I tried to convince her that Wexler isn't involved in anything underhanded and that she should let the process work. But you saw her thoughts on that."

Ray nodded thoughtfully. "If I was being completely objective, and not a man worried about his wife, I wouldn't be as dismissive about their instincts," he said. "I agree with them—the idea that AJ would shoot herself in the head is shocking. AJ cared about her looks. I'd never predict she would do something to damage herself, much less her face. But in that moment of desperation—who knows?"

Locke tipped his head in respectful disagreement. "I understand that, but Sam confided in me once that when AJ got divorced, back when she was in the army, she had considered just walking into the Pacific Ocean. And then Jonesy told us they'd talked about it, too, and a gun wouldn't have been the answer." Locke took in a deep breath and blew it out. "This sucks, no matter what happened. I don't want to lose Sam or see her suffer because she feels guilty that she didn't read the situation right and stop it."

Ray was staring up the steps toward his bedroom door. "I'm right with you, brother. Kate has never looked at me or talked to me that way. I was trying to close the book on this quickly for her sake, but I think I've let her down."

Walt nodded. "We need to fix this. I guess we should apologize, for starters. Even if they think we're wrong, they'll forgive us because they know we love them. That will count for something."

Locke gulped the last of his scotch and said, "I wish I shared your confidence. Sam is stubborn. Regardless, I can't let her put herself in harm's way with Wexler. Let's get going, Walt. We can be sure that we'll need all of our energy and our best game faces to get through the next week and beyond."

I have learned that people will forget what you said,
people will forget what you did, but people will never
forget how you made them feel.

—Maya Angelou

TEN

SAM STARED OUT THE PASSENGER WINDOW OF JONESY'S CAR, looking toward Boathouse Row on the Schuylkill River as they drove down Route 76 from South Philadelphia. "Isn't Philly beautiful at night?" she said softly. "I never get tired of looking at the boathouses lit up at night, and I love looking over the parkway from Locke's apartment. Lights at night can make everything look beautiful."

"OK, Sam. Stop avoiding it and talk to me. What the hell is going on?"

"You know most of what I know. She called me at the district last night, and she was upset. No, she was devastated. But we talked for so long, and I thought she was OK by the time we said goodbye. We planned to meet for lunch. I thought about meeting her at her apartment, but I was tired and had court today, and I wanted to get some sleep. Damn it, I'm making excuses. If I were a good friend, I would have driven to her apartment anyway."

"Sam, snap out of it and stop feeling sorry for yourself. We need to stay sharp and focused if we are going to figure this out. If you start questioning yourself, we will screw this up. Focus on facts, not emotions or what-ifs."

"You are right, for sure," Sam said, clearing her throat and adopting a more businesslike tone. "I think we should set four short-term objectives. Let's start by doing what AJ would want us to do for her. Let's support her parents in their grief and help them get through the funeral. Number two, I made AJ a promise to sing at her funeral, so I need to call Ray and Bobby O to help me out. No, don't look at me like that. Last Christmas after she sang 'Hallelujah' at Kate's parents' house, she asked me to sing it at her funeral. I agreed as a joke—but now it isn't funny." Sam whispered the last four words and shook her head to clear her thoughts. "Third, and in parallel, we need to find out how Wexler was assigned to the investigation. When he worked in Central, he found ways to cherry-pick his investigations because he only wanted cases he was sure would help him get his transfer to Homicide."

"Ah yes, I remember those days. The Wexler versus Kelly—battle of the sexes. If I recall correctly, you beat his numbers, but he got his transfer anyway." Jonesy chuckled. "Who would have guessed that between the four of us, mild-mannered Samantha Kelly would be Joan of Arc reincarnated!"

Sam laughed. "Wexler used to call me 'Joan of fucking Arc.' He would have enjoyed the accusation more if he really understood her story. He doesn't know shit about history, though. He was referencing the statue of Joan on the parkway. I hated the comparison, but I took great satisfaction from the fact that at least I never manipulated the deskman to cherry-pick cases. Half the time, I worked his rejects, and I still beat his numbers. I was glad when he was transferred to Homicide, thinking he was finally out of my life, but he is like a bad penny that keeps coming back. By my count, he has tried to jam me up with the PD four different times. Apparently, I am the only person who sees his manipulations and vindictiveness."

"No, you are not alone. I now have firsthand experience," Jonesy said, thinking of their encounter earlier that day. "Let's figure out how we keep the investigation open. I could talk to Lieutenant Farrell. Do you think Locke will work against us?"

"No, he will lecture me, and then he will quietly keep an eye on how it all plays out."

"You aren't mad at Locke, are you?"

"It's hard to stay mad at a guy who constantly has your back, literally. He backed me up twice when I was on the ground wrestling the bad guys. One guy was wanted for murder in Virginia and the other was a member of a drug posse. He doesn't think I realized it, but I know he was the one who distracted Wexler from hauling off and punching me when I wrestled the typewriter from him a few months ago."

"I didn't know you were so into wrestling," Jonesy said sarcastically. "I'm not really mad at Walt either, but I think Kate is furious at Ray. That said, I am sure that Mr. Suave-and-Debonair will work it out with Kate quicker than we will work it out with our guys. Let's touch base with Kate in the morning. She is always good for a plan."

"Just be careful of Wexler—he'll screw with you just to get to me." Sam paused a minute. "Maybe that's it! Maybe AJ was trying to tell me that Wexler was screwing with her to get to me."

"Possibly, but how does it all fit? Does it have anything to do with her death? Could he be afraid you would accuse him of something?"

"I don't know. I need to write down as much of the conversation as I can remember. After Jack, Wexler is the next best suspect. Even if it means playing another game of chicken with Wexler, I'm going to find out why he was threatening her."

"You mean 'we,' don't you? No more of this lone-wolf stuff, Sam."

"I don't want anyone else compromised. Anyway, I do well as a lone wolf."

"Wolves are more effective in packs." Jonesy countered. "Stay with the pack."

Courage is not a man with a gun in his hand.
It's knowing you're licked before you begin, but you begin
anyway and see it through no matter what. You rarely
win, but sometimes you do.

—Atticus Finch (To Kill a Mockingbird)

ELEVEN

TWO DAYS LATER, KATE AND RAY ROSSI PICKED UP AJ'S PARents, Chaplain Harris and Mrs. Harris, from the Bellevue Stratford Hotel on South Broad Street. They all drove north on Broad Street to the Chapel of the Four Chaplains to coordinate plans for AJ's funeral. Sam and Jonesy drove together from Manayunk to the chapel to meet with AJ's parents for the first time.

"You nervous, Sam?" Jonesy asked, behind the wheel once more.

"A little, but I think I'm still angry enough to keep from blubbering in front of AJ's parents. What's the news from Homicide, Jonesy?"

"I guess that question means that you're not interested in helping me through my bout of nerves. OK, then. The good news is that the case is still open. Per Lieutenant Farrell. Nothing much else has changed. The fact that Jack Nathan had gunshot residue on his hands and the fact that AJ had gunshot residue on her hands doesn't help the investigation, because they had both been at the pistol range that day. Jack is lawyered up and refuses to take another polygraph, now that he has stopped with the histrionics."

"Do you think Jack had the balls to kill her? Wexler, on the other hand—"

"Sam, I know you hate Wexler, but that is a leap. We don't know if he had a reason to kill her. If he was going to hurt someone, I think it would be you."

"AJ sounded as upset about Wexler as she was about Jack— maybe more, because she couldn't even talk about it. She only said she wanted to deal with one crisis at a time. The next day at Homicide, I bluffed him, and I know I saw something in his face. Locke admitted he saw it, too. Do you know how he became the assigned investigator? What are the odds it was a coincidence?"

"You are right about that. I found out he did snatch the investigation away from the twelve-to-eight shift. Bill Reynolds had words with Wexler because he wanted to give the investigation to the midnight shift. Wexler insisted on taking it as the early man for day shift. The on-duty lieutenant swung in favor of Wexler because he didn't want to approve OT."

"My Spidey senses are off the charts with him. I haven't connected the dots, but he is involved."

"Sam, he has nothing to recommend him as a good human being, but you can't accuse him of murder without evidence. Your typewriter battle with him is legendary, and now your face-off in Homicide is, too. Up until now, he was the one who looked foolish. Don't lose your objectivity and become the foolish one, or worse. I'll watch and listen. If Wexler did something wrong, we will sleuth it out."

"Sleuth it out? Jonesy, you sound like Agatha Christie. What has Homicide done to you?"

"You know what I mean, Sam. As long as there are unanswered questions and enough people who knew AJ are not satisfied, the investigation will remain open. At least until after she is buried. AJ had a loyal following of district cops, including her commanding officer. They will honor her final memory." Jonesy waited a beat. "Aren't you a little nervous meeting her parents?"

"No."

"I'm afraid I'll say something stupid. I'm not good at empathetic."

"You're not so bad in a crisis." Sam looked at her and smiled. "Don't borrow trouble, Jonesy. Just follow Kate's example and be assured that if anyone is going to screw up, it will be me."

The initial introduction between Sam and AJ's parents wasn't awkward. Kate and Ray managed the conversations and allowed Sam and Jonesy to nod quietly to questions until they relaxed. Sam felt like she already knew Mr. and Mrs. Harris from everything AJ had told her about them. As they worked through the logistics and the details of the funeral service, it was clear to Sam that AJ's parents were actually focused on comforting them.

Chaplain Harris kept making eye contact with Sam as the conversation progressed. Sam assumed it was because she was doing more listening than talking and he wanted to keep her included in the conversation. Finally, Chaplain Harris asked Sam if he could speak with her privately.

"Sam, I wanted to thank you for being my daughter's friend. AJ didn't make friends easily after her divorce, so I know how important the three of you were to her. Her love was obvious when she spoke of you. You were able to tap into the AJ we knew before she and David divorced. Before she married David she was confident and outgoing. She knew how to be the life of the party. When she took the microphone and sang, the crowd was putty in her hands." Sam swallowed but couldn't speak, so she just stared. Chaplain Harris gave her a compassionate smile and continued speaking but changed the direction of the conversation. "Your friends seem very sad. You seem very angry."

As Sam began to shake her head in protest, Chaplain Harris put his hand up in a stopping gesture. "Detective, I served as a chaplain in Vietnam. I know the grieving process. I'm guessing that you believe if you stay angry, you won't fall apart and cry. I also sense that something is troubling you in addition to grief. How can I help you?"

Sam shook her head in denial and struggled to find words to avoid continuing the discussion. "You are shaming me, Chaplain. I came to offer comfort. There is something wrong with this picture."

"I spoke to Detective Wexler," he said with a stare so focused, Sam couldn't look away but tried to hide her cringe as he continued.

"He told me that the investigation is in progress, and he couldn't provide me much information. Can you?"

Sam nodded. "There are a lot of unanswered questions." Her relief was obvious to Chaplain Harris, and he took note and decided to probe a bit.

Chaplain Harris's voice became almost lighthearted. "I spoke to AJ last week, and you know what she said about you?" Sam shrugged. "AJ told me, and I quote, 'Detective Samantha Kelly is the most instinctive person that I have ever met. She is probably the best detective Philadelphia has to offer.'" Chaplain Harris put his hands on her shoulders and made Sam face him. "Now that I've met you, I know she was right. I think you are up to any task you take on, and you are confident in that fact. You will tell me the truth about what happened?"

"Of course."

"Sam, we all hurt. You lost a friend. We lost our daughter and only child. We have always worried about AJ. A parent worries about their child, especially when a child isolates themselves.

AJ pushed everyone away for a time. After coming to Philadelphia, she seemed to blossom back into the happy person and extroverted person we knew when she was younger. She loved her job and her friends. To know that she knew the love of friends brings us a great deal of comfort. To meet you and her other friends, brings me even greater comfort."

"AJ and I were drawn together by many things, but she helped me navigate away from a bad marriage by sharing her own story and giving me the strength to preserve my confidence and self-esteem. She referenced you in every story. I felt like I knew you before we even met."

After a momentary pause, Chaplain Harris said, "I feel like I know you too. So much that I can see that you are struggling. Your friends are grieving. You are not—yet. Something has you angry. Don't let your anger consume you. It will destroy you. Use the skills you've been blessed with and seek the truth. Get your answers, find your justice, and move on and look to the future."

Sam looked at him with a sad smile. "That will be a challenge. I hope I can meet that challenge."

"Hope is good," said Chaplain Harris. Then in an abrupt change of the conversation, he said, "I understand you are going to sing at the service?"

"Yes, our friend Bobby O rewrote the lyrics to Leonard Cohen's 'Hallelujah,' which was a favorite song of your daughter."

"I met Bobby a few minutes ago. A friend, Reverend Leon Sullivan, is providing a choir and organist for the service. I think Bobby O is already meeting with them, and he is waiting for you to practice the music with them."

"The Reverend Leon Sullivan, the 'Lion of Zion'? Founder of the Opportunities Industrialization Center self-help movement?"

"Yes," replied the chaplain, "the very one."

"He is famous in Philly. AJ never told me she knew him."

"AJ didn't know him. I met him at a meeting in Washington and mentioned my daughter was a Philadelphia police officer. He reached out to me when he heard her name on the news. He referred to AJ as a pioneer for gender and racial equality. The four of you are pioneers. I know women were met with initial resistance, but I must admit I'm amazed. If the support we have received from the Police Department is any indication of the progress women have made to be accepted, it seems to be going in the right direction."

"The right direction—yes. I work with many talented and committed men and women. The department still needs to evolve. It's a job that few can really understand unless they work it. You see the best and the worst of people. I've been disappointed, shocked, and proud at times, but never expected to feel the bonds of friendship and loyalty I've developed."

"I think I know what you mean. Not exactly like the bonds developed by servicemen in combat, but something similar?"

"Yes, that's a good analogy. We relied on AJ's army training through the academy and then when we were assigned to the highest-crime areas in Philadelphia."

"Thank you. I can't tell you what it meant to us that she rediscovered confidence and, more importantly, happiness during her time in Philadelphia. A parent isn't always able to tune into their children long distance, but we knew the past several years were much better for her. I think they were the happiest years of her life." He paused. "I know it will take courage for you to sing at her funeral. It means a great deal to me and my wife. I know you will inspire us."

"I don't know about courage. I'm extremely nervous, but it means a great deal to me, too."

"The best cure for nerves is action. Why don't you join your friend Bobby O and the choir for your rehearsal?"

"Yes, sounds like my cue," Sam said, and she smiled at him.

"And Sam, if you need to talk, we will be here working through other details—we have a meeting with the captain and will be here until about 8:00 p.m. But I'm not just talking about tonight—we're here for you anytime."

When words fail, music speaks.

—Hans Christian Anderson

TWELVE

————————•●————————

THE FUNERAL SERVICE FOR OFFICER A. J. HARRIS WAS HELD on a cold, gray December morning with sleet driving against the slick streets and cars. The atmosphere surrounding the funeral was no more optimistic than the weather.

Ray and Kate Rossi, Michelle Jones, and Sam Kelly all emerged from their separate cars with their heads ducked down low against the icy rain and jackets pulled close to ward off the chill in the air. They met in the foyer of the chapel, where the splatter from shaken umbrellas already slicked the floors, and they quietly made their way to a pew marked "reserved."

The chapel was dedicated to four chaplains who sacrificed their lives in World War II. The chaplains came from different backgrounds—Methodist, Jewish, Roman Catholic, Dutch Reformed—but all four of them died on the same night, when the US naval vessel *Dorchester* was sunk by a German U-boat. In the face of certain death, the four chaplains spent the night ministering to the frightened, injured, and dying, and all four men ultimately gave away their life jackets so others might have a better chance to live. They stood arm-in-arm on the deck of the sinking ship, offering courage and prayer until the waves washed over them.

The chapel now was filled. Some attendees were dressed in civilian clothes, but most were Philadelphia police officers in uniform, with black armbands and black stripes across their badges. Police officers from the Sixth and Thirty-Fifth Districts represented the honor guard. Chaplain Harris and Mrs. Harris sat in the front pew.

Jonesy leaned over to murmur in Sam's ear, "Are you sure you're up to doing this, Sam?"

Taking a deep breath and swallowing hard, Sam pursed her lips into a forced smile and whispered, "I guess we'll soon find out."

Jonesy cast around for ways to distract Sam. "Who does Chaplain Harris remind you of?" she said, still keeping her voice respectfully low.

Sam cocked her head and considered. "He looks familiar, for sure. I can't place him. Maybe he just seems familiar because AJ spoke of him so often."

"How about an older version of Denzel Washington?"

"Who is Denzel Washington?" Sam asked.

"Dr. Philip Chandler from *St. Elsewhere*?"

Sam's eyes widened in recognition. "Absolutely, you're right! Now we know why AJ liked that show. But I think Chaplain Harris is the real deal. I bet he's even more of a badass than the character." Sam waited a beat to change the subject. "Are you talking to Walt yet? Is he going to be here?"

"Yes, we made up appropriately, and we're talking again. Why don't you try it? It might be good for your mental health," said Jonesy. "Walt said he was going to meet me here. He can give us a ride back to Center City if Locke doesn't come. Have you talked to Locke yet?"

Sam shook her head. "No, not since the other night. He left me a message at Central Detectives, but I haven't connected with him.

I guess part of me is avoiding him because I owe him an apology. I'm afraid that if I talk to him, I'll say something hurtful, or, worse, I might start blubbering. I'm guessing he will be here. Of course, the fact that he is so nice and I'm so rotten rightfully contributes to my self-loathing." Sam swallowed. Rambling again. "Anyway, thanks for the offer, but I'm lousy company right now. If my knight in shining armor doesn't show, I'll hop a ride in a squad car back to Central. I can go into work early. It should be a slow night. Maybe the sergeant will let me split early."

The air in the chapel had begun to shift; the seats were full now, and a hush descended over all assembled. Jonesy squeezed Sam's hand and said, "Good luck! I know this means a lot to you. You will do great. Mostly because you need to do this."

Sam winked. "Thanks, Jonesy." She stood up to find a seat with the Harris's and the Sixth District Commander, Captain Edwards.

The choir stood to sing "Our Father," and uniformed officers carried the flag-draped casket down the aisle to the front of the chapel. At practice with them the day before, Sam didn't think she could be even more impressed with their sound, but she was. Their voices echoed through the chapel and sent a chill through her. Chaplain Harris rose from his seat and walked past his daughter's casket to the pulpit, and Sam shivered again. Sam had just met Chaplain Harris, but she felt like she knew him already. She understood why AJ adored her parents. Watching Chaplain Harris preside over his daughter's funeral service was awe-inspiring, even despite the deep weight in Sam's chest that settled there the moment she heard the news about AJ.

Harris thanked those in attendance and spoke about his daughter, offering encouragement through his words. Sam knew that Chaplain Harris was devastated, but he presided over the service as if he were giving comfort to a family that had lost a loved one. Sam guessed Chaplain Harris managed his pain by comforting others. There was no mention of the circumstances of AJ's death; instead, the focus was on her life and his appreciation of the Philadelphia Police Department. Sam could hear an occasional sniffle; she didn't look behind her, but she guessed some of the sniffles came from Kate and Jonesy.

The captain of Sixth District followed Chaplain Harris with a eulogy. Captain Edwards remained professional, but he also seemed genuine. As an army veteran, he seemed to connect with Chaplain Harris. His eulogy complimented AJ for being a capable and resourceful officer with exceptional skills at adapting to situations and managing the relationship between the police and the public; he presented her with a posthumous award from the local business association for her work with them. Looking around the many faces assembled in the chapel, the captain also spoke about the pain of losing police brethren under any circumstances.

Sam was inspired by Captain Edwards's ability to stand up behind the podium and talk about AJ's strengths and the pain of losing her. But she felt nerves tangle in her stomach as her confidence dipped. Would she be able to fill her role in the service as well? When Chaplain Harris invited her to the pulpit, Sam took a deep breath and walked up, cringing at the noise her heels made as she walked across the marble floor. By the time she reached the pulpit, she could feel her legs shaking. At the altar, a choir member walked over to Sam and helped her into a choir robe.

Sam looked out onto the congregation of police officers, and her nervousness dissipated when she saw Kate, Ray, and Jonesy smiling at her. Her eyes moved up, past them, and she saw Greg Locke standing in the back of the chapel, his eyes on her. He nodded at Sam, and a calm fell over her. She was here to honor her friend and colleague; she would give it her all.

Before she spoke, though, Sam shifted her gaze to the chaplain and his wife. She surprised even herself—once she started speaking, her legs stopped shaking, and her voice rang out confidently.

"I am struggling with words, so I hope to eulogize A. J. Harris with her favorite song. But first, I want to give you all a little context.

"AJ, Michelle Jones, Kate Rossi, and I met in May of 1976 as recruits at the Philadelphia police academy. As the first group of female patrol officer recruits to attend the academy, we were venturing into uncharted waters for both our city and ourselves. The challenge of succeeding formed the basis of our friendship, but the mortar that held us together was AJ's confidence. When I think of AJ, I think of the Albert Einstein quote, 'In the middle of difficulty lies opportunity.' AJ inspired us to meet difficulty head-on.

"AJ called herself an army brat, and she laughed at us for exaggerating the challenges of physical training. We had little experience in running obstacle courses or competing at track meets. AJ took us under her wing and became our personal drill instructor. Before we ran a single yard, AJ decided we needed a theme song to motivate us. She chose the song of a Philadelphia musical group. At our first practice, she brought a tape recording of 'Wake Up Everybody' by Harold Melvin and the Blue Notes." Sam began singing a few of the lyrics the women had most related to.

The world won't get no better

If you just let be, no no

The world won't get no better

You gotta change the world, you and me.

Her own voice was clear and calm, and it powered her forward. "We exercised to the beat of the music, and we sang the words.

We practiced the obstacle course and the run for three months, and by the end of that time, 'Wake Up Everybody' had become our victory song. We did change the world when we successfully graduated—the first class of women to graduate from the Philadelphia police academy. But something happened in our own lives when we made a choice to change the world. We changed ourselves, for the better, as we've reached for that goal. AJ was our advocate through change, and she was my personal hero. I will miss her greatly, but I will always be inspired by her uncompromising commitment to our friendship and success.

"AJ had a beautiful singing voice, and, as you probably know, she would occasionally perform with a band you might be familiar with, Anti-Corruption. Last year, she performed a Leonard Cohen song called 'Hallelujah,' and afterward she asked me to promise that I would sing it at her funeral. I didn't like we were talking about this, but I agreed as long as she would promise to sing my funeral song, 'My Way' by Frank Sinatra."

Sam took a deep breath and continued, "I didn't realize that less than a year later, I would need to make good on my pledge. But with the help of my friends," she said, gesturing to the choir behind her, "and Bobby O, who rewrote the words, we will honor my promise."

She nodded to the organist and the choir and began to sing:

I've heard there was a secret chord

That David played, and it pleased the Lord;

I know how much you loved music, didn't ya?

Your faith was strong, but we needed proof;

You saw our struggle to seek the truth;

Your beauty and your spirit never threw ya.

You pushed us to compete with flair;
We ran until we had no air,
And from our lips, you drew the hallelujah.
Hallelujah, Hallelujah, Hallelujah, Hallelujah.
Yeah, I've seen your flag on the marble arch,
That will be our victory march,
But it's a cold, and it's a lonely hallelujah.
Hallelujah, Hallelujah, Hallelujah, Hallelujah.

By the last hallelujah, Chaplain Harris had walked to the pulpit and put his arm around Sam. Sam left the altar and drew Mrs. Harris, who was quietly crying, into a long hug. Sam walked over to the casket draped in the American flag and leaned down to kiss it. She raised her head and looked beyond the sea of blue uniforms with black-taped badges and made eye contact with Kate and Jonesy, who both nodded to her with tears in their eyes. The tears of many colleagues were flowing freely.

The congregation emptied onto Broad Street, and Sam found herself standing on the sidewalk on the north side of the chapel. Chief Inspector Stagliano, who commanded Central Division, walked up to Ray Rossi and shook his hand, then turned to Sam. The chief inspector tipped his uniform hat and said, "Detective Kelly, that was a beautiful tribute. That song is a favorite of mine. I've never heard it sound better."

"Thank you, Chief," she said, bowing her head. As the chief inspector walked away, Ray Rossi put his arm around Sam and walked her away from the others to have a conversation out of earshot.

"Sam, that was a beautiful rendition of 'Hallelujah.' With the choir and the chapel acoustics, there was an ethereal quality to it," Ray said.

Sam asked, with a half-laugh, "Is that good?"

"Excellent."

She softened her voice. "I'm glad you approve. It took every ounce of energy I could muster. I feel like Jell-O right now."

Ray squeezed her shoulder and said, "You've been suppressing grief. The music provided some relief. You touched everyone in that chapel. You need to sing more."

Sam smiled a little and said, "See how looks can be deceiving? I feel empty, inadequate, and pretty miserable right now."

Ray gave her a look that was equal parts stern and brotherly. "Look, I get it, Sam. We all feel the loss, but we have to rely on each other in times like these. We all regret what we said the other night. No one was challenging your instincts, especially Greg. Greg is a good guy who wants to help. Meet him halfway." He smiled at her gently and continued, "I know the last thing you need today is a lecture, so I'll stop. Kate and I are taking the Harris's to AJ's apartment, so I need to leave, but I want to ask a favor. Are you working tomorrow? Can you meet me at the PAB for a cup of coffee?"

Sam rolled her eyes but relented. "OK, my brother, as long as I don't have to listen to another lecture."

"Lieutenant Rossi, are you harassing my friend?" Kate said, walking over to interrupt with an attempt at levity.

Sam winked at Kate. "The lieutenant was giving me the kind of lecture that I would only accept from a senior officer or a big brother."

Kate laughed and then mentioned what Ray had said; they were leaving to take the chaplain and his wife to AJ's apartment.

"Sam, you said that you had a key to AJ's apartment. Did you bring it with you?" Kate asked.

"Yes, it's on my key ring," she said. She realized her hands were shaking as she dug through her purse to retrieve the key ring. But as she clumsily flipped through the keys dangling on the ring, she mumbled to herself, "I know it was here. Why can't I find it?"

Kate saw Sam's shaking hands and put a calming hand of her own on Sam's arm. "Maybe it's on another key ring. It's been a grueling week," she said. "I can talk to the apartment manager and have him open the apartment."

Grateful that Kate didn't press her to use her foggy brain to think, Sam nodded and hugged her goodbye.

After Kate left, Sam turned to Jonesy and Walt. Jonesy was staring through the sea of blue uniforms across Broad Street. "Sam, is that Beth over there?"

"What?" Sam turned and looked in the direction that Jonesy was staring.

"Why would your sister show up here? She didn't even like AJ, and you two have your complicated history. Is she that nosy?"

"Yes, she is that nosy," Sam said, scanning the crowd half-heartedly. The last thing she wanted right now was to talk to Beth. She was the only person who could make a terrible day like this so much worse.

"Sam, does Beth know Wexler?" Jonesy asked, still looking across the street.

Sam didn't see Beth or Wexler, and she had no interest in figuring out whether or why they were talking to each other. "If she's here, it's because she likes to keeps up the illusion with the rest of the family—all my sisters and brothers and their wives—that she is all-knowing. Being here establishes credibility for any false narrative she wants to craft. You gotta give her credit, because they usually believe her. Sometimes I think she should have gone into politics. She can spin a tale so successfully."

Jonesy rolled her eyes and responded with her usual sarcasm. "I think you just insulted politicians. But for sure, she has a weird interest in your life. Why don't you just confront her about this sort of thing?"

"I'm sure my reasons are rooted in despair," Sam said. She was feeling unusually honest and vulnerable after the service. "At first, I convinced myself I was saving my parents and family from conflict. We were raised to keep the peace at all costs. But I think the real reason is that it would never resolve anything. She lies so much, she starts to believe her own lies. I thought once she'd successfully screwed me over with the family, she would declare victory and leave me alone. Apparently, I was wrong. She keeps coming back like a bad penny. God only knows what she is up to now."

Sam quickly found out. Beth moved through the crowd and wrapped Sam in a brief hug. "I'm sorry to hear about AJ. I know that you two were close," Beth said. "Do you know what happened?"

Sam didn't speak, but she shook her head no.

"We're here for you, Sam. You've had so much loss in the past year. I mean, we all have, but you seem to be really shaken. Your family wants to help. Don't be such a stranger."

Sam just nodded mutely, and Beth mercifully walked away to greet others on the force.

Jonesy leaned over and whispered, "I can see why the rest of the family believes her. She reeks of sincerity."

"Maybe things have changed with her," said Sam uncertainly.

"And maybe pigs can fly," Jonesy said. Walt finished speaking with some of the patrolmen standing nearby and made his way back to them. "OK, I think Walt and I are headed home, but we will catch up when you finish your shift," Jonesy said. "You also need to make up with that hunk of a man over there. He looks lost," she said, winking at Sam.

"Not as lost as me," Sam said as she hugged Jonesy and Walt goodbye and scanned the sidewalk for Locke. He was talking to several officers from the Sixth District, but he kept glancing over at Sam. She walked over to him as the group was dispersing. She wasn't expecting rejection, but still she felt a momentary uncertainty. When their eyes locked, she was reassured by his smile.

"Hey, Locke, any chance you are going my way? Can I hop a ride to Central Detectives?"

Locke nodded. "I'm at your service, ma'am."

Warmed by his deep, familiar voice, Sam smiled and said, "Thanks. Do you mind if I say goodbye to Mr. and Mrs. Harris? They are flying back to Hawaii, and I won't see them before they leave."

"Sure. Do you think you could introduce me to them?" Locke asked.

After an introduction and a series of hugs, goodbyes, and promises to stay in touch, Sam and Locke walked to his brown '83 Buick Riviera.

"You are looking a little pale. Have you eaten today?" Locke asked.

"You missed your calling, Dr. Locke. No, I haven't eaten, and I am beginning to get hungry. Can I buy you lunch in exchange for the ride?"

Locke turned his head and looked at her directly. "Let me do better than that. How about we pick up two corned-beef specials from Mr. Morgan's and go back at my apartment? It'll give you a chance to relax before your shift."

In an exaggeratedly flirtatious voice, she said, "Why, Detective Locke, you know I can't resist your corned-beef sandwiches. Are you offering a bribe and expecting special favors from me?"

"I don't know. Will it work?" Locke asked, raising an eyebrow.

Sam tipped her head to the side. "Absolutely."

"Then yes," he said as he winked at her. Relieved at her light mood, he reached for her hand, but then he paused. "Your hands are clammy, Sam. Are you feeling well?"

Sam nodded without saying anything. She was trying to hide herself in the light banter, but she couldn't keep from wondering which day was worse—today, or the day she'd buried her parents and brother.

The art of acceptance is the art of making
someone who has just done you a small favor wish that
he might have done you a greater one.

—Martin Luther King

THIRTEEN

Sam stood at the wall of windows in Locke's apartment. Her eyes wandered from the Philadelphia Museum of Art to the late-morning traffic along the Benjamin Franklin Parkway and finally rested on the statue of Joan of Arc. The view from Locke's apartment was therapeutic for Sam. She loved looking out over the hustle and bustle of the city. But the real therapy was when Locke would inevitably walk up behind her, wrap his arms around her, and pull her back into his chest.

Locke did not disappoint. He pulled her into an embrace with one arm, nestled his face into the crook of her neck, and offered her a beer with his free hand. "How about a Moosehead?"

"Moosehead! I'm not sure. I need to go to work at four, and you know Moosehead goes right to my head."

"You have enough time, and you need to take the edge off. I'll keep you safe." He kissed her ear and whispered, "Drink up while I make the sandwiches."

By the time Locke walked back to the living room and announced that the sandwiches were ready, he was surprised to find that Sam had finished her bottle of Moosehead. He placed the sandwiches on the coffee table. When he sat next to her on the couch, he made sure that his leg brushed hers.

"AJ's parents showed amazing strength today," he said. "Her father must have dug deep to maintain his composure as well as he did. Captain Edwards was also impressive and touching. But your singing was transformational. AJ would have approved," he added, a half-smile revealing a slight dimple on his left cheek.

"Thank you. I'll probably ask you what you mean by 'transformational' another time. I can't process it now."

"I meant it as a compliment."

Sam put her plate down with a clatter and covered her face with her hands as her tears streamed quietly down her cheeks. Locke wrapped her in his arms and pulled her onto his lap. "Damn it, Locke, stop being so nice," she said, choking out a laugh. "I'm drained, and I can't combine alcohol and your sympathy. Look at me, I'm a mess now."

Pulling her tighter into his embrace, he said, "I think you need to cry. Let it go, baby."

Sam continued to cry, and ten minutes later, she had fallen asleep in Locke's arms. Locke laid Sam on his brown leather couch and covered her with the crocheted green blanket his mother had given him the previous Christmas. He stared at her, sleeping so peacefully, and he wondered if she had slept at all since AJ's death. He wished he could let her sleep until tomorrow, but he knew he'd have to wake her for her shift. He decided to let her sleep until half an hour before her shift started.

Sam awoke to the smell of coffee and the feel of Locke's light kisses on her neck. The sensations made her want to snuggle. "Hmm," she said, with her eyes still closed, "the perfect combination. Kisses and coffee."

Kneeling next to the couch, Locke murmured against her ear, "There is more where that came from—just say the word."

Sam opened her eyes, took the cup of coffee from him, and propped herself up on her elbows to sip it. She kissed him quickly on the cheek but ignored his flirtatious offer. "You are too good to me. I'm guessing it's time for work?"

Locke's brow arched. "I see Detective Kelly is back." He stood up and walked to the sliding glass door to study the city skyline aimlessly. "Yes, it's about time to get ready for your shift. Unless, of course, you would consider playing hooky tonight? We could have dinner and—"

Sam stood up, walked behind him, encircled his waist with her arms, and flattened herself against his back. "I hope you know how much I appreciate you. You have been so kind and patient with me. You nurture and feed me, and I've done nothing to reciprocate. I owe you, Locke. I'm sorry for the way I've behaved the past week."

"Does that mean you'll play hooky tonight?"

"Tempting as that sounds, I need a rain check. My promise is good, but I'm meeting with a complainant. Anyway, you need to get some sleep if you are going into work at midnight."

Locke turned toward her, wrapped his arms around her, and rested his chin on her head. "Maybe it is best for you to keep busy. I'm glad all of this is behind you, Sam."

Sam jumped from his embrace like his words had bitten her. "Behind me? What does that mean?"

Locke cringed, squeezing his eyes shut. Christ, why did he have to say that? But maybe he needed to have this conversation. With as much control as he could muster in his voice, he said, "Sam, let AJ rest in peace."

Sam stared out the window, her arms wrapped around her, and she replied, "Peace? What peace do Mr. and Mrs. Harris have? AJ isn't resting in peace. I'll not have peace, Jonesy will not have peace, and Kate will not have peace until we figure out why she is dead." Raising her voice louder than she intended, she said, "We sure as hell won't be able to depend on Wexler to figure it out."

Locke gently took her chin in his hand so she would look at him.

"Sam, I heard Wexler telling Lieutenant Farrell that the medical examiner said that AJ was pregnant."

Sam looked away from him and stared at the floor. She already knew, he realized.

"Damn, Sam, don't ever play poker with me." Locke shook his head as he exhaled. "I can see I'm not telling you something you didn't already know. How can you criticize Wexler for not getting it right when you are withholding information from him?"

Sam tried to look away, but Locke wouldn't let her.

"I don't think AJ knew for sure but suspected because she made a comment that being pregnant would be a final blow. I know what you are thinking." Sam looked at him with an arched brow. "A poor choice of words on her part, but I don't think she meant it that way. However, this is exactly why I didn't share it with you or Wexler. You think it's another reason she would commit suicide. AJ didn't think like that. She would have chosen to have the baby, but she knew she had a *choice*. A baby would be another reason to live, not a reason to die. Is Wexler claiming the pregnancy is evidence of suicide?"

Locke frowned, but he didn't answer. Sam slid into Locke's embrace and put her face against his shoulder. In a low, sad voice, she said, "I'm sorry for snapping at you like this. I'm frazzled right now."

Sam's voice cracked. "I keep thinking—if only I had gone to her after I spoke with her on the phone. I could have prevented it."

Locke pulled her even closer and kissed her hair. "Sam, you couldn't have known what would happen, and if she was murdered, you could have been as well."

Sam looked up at him. "So you're not so sure it was a suicide, either?"

"I have no bias either way. But people are not always predictable. Anyone of us could have a moment we can't take back, in spite of how we might normally think or act." Locke paused. "But at the service today, I talked to Joe Vargas from the Sixth District. He mentioned that he saw Wexler arguing with AJ the day before she was found. She was leaving the pistol range, and he stopped her. The argument was pretty heated." Locke waited. "Sam, there is something else. AJ had been drinking, according to the toxicology report. You know she was upset. Liquor makes people do things they might not do if they were sober. She told you she could only handle one drama at a time. A lost love, trouble with her job, and a baby? Was it too much?"

"I don't know, Greg." Sam sighed and looked into his eyes. They stood in a silent embrace for several minutes, and then Sam said, "Do you remember when I asked Hogan why they call you G-Man and he said it was because everyone thought the college man with the JD should have become an FBI agent? I asked you why you chose local law instead of the FBI, and you told me that your hero was Melvin Purvis, the G-Man who got Dillinger, but that the FBI defamed Purvis by officially reporting that he committed suicide. The local coroner had an alternate theory that Purvis had died in an accidental shooting. I wondered then if you were in denial because you couldn't accept that your hero would have done something viewed as a weakness."

"So now?"

"Now, I need to consider that I may be in denial. Life can be hard. We see that more than most people. This job is hard too, especially for a woman struggling for acceptance and respect. I guess I need to admit there are moments of despair."

Locke, surprised but relieved that her mind-set was moving toward acceptance, nodded in agreement. "For the record, I made that answer up," he admitted. "I didn't go into the FBI because my father died, and I didn't want to live too far from my mother. The FBI won't guarantee an assignment to an agent." He squeezed her again and kissed her forehead. "One more thing."

She sighed at him. "You are beginning to sound like Colombo."

"A caution, Sam. Wexler complained to Lieutenant Farrell that you and AJ were snooping around the Green Valley nursing home case. Lieutenant Farrell respects you, and he trusts me enough to let me know. I think because she's dead Wexler won't push it, and even if he did, Farrell would push back on Wexler. But, Sam, if you keep pushing him, one of these times he isn't going to hold back."

Sam shoved away from Locke and threw her hands into the air. "AJ wasn't snooping around anything, and I haven't been snooping either, ever since the time he put Internal Affairs on my ass. I haven't done a thing to him, but I refuse to be intimidated. He is all bluster. As long as I have a witness, he won't touch me—I've learned that much from our confrontations at the station. He is a coward and a grandstander. He'd only take a shot at me on the sneak. But I can't say that I wouldn't like to see him try to get me."

"That's what I'm afraid of, Sam."

"Oh hell, Locke." She waved him off. "What's it to you?"

Locke placed his hands on her shoulders and held her tighter than he intended. Speaking in a low voice, very slowly and through gritted teeth, he said, "How can you ask me that? Hell, Samantha. I can't do this anymore. I am crazy about you, and I know that is the last thing you want to hear, especially after a bad marriage. It's possible to rebound and have a solid relationship with someone. Please trust me on that. I love everything about you, except for how you torture yourself. You are taking years off of your life, and I want those years to be my years."

Sam blinked and swallowed hard. Barely able to speak and struggling to keep emotion from her voice, she said, "Greg Locke, no one has ever said anything to me quite so beautiful. I'm feeling unworthy." She swallowed again. "I guess I hold back because I've made so many mistakes in relationships that I'm afraid of making more."

"We are not a mistake, Sam. We are a perfect complement. I'll always have your back."

"I'm not sure I deserve—"

"Get that insecurity out of your head and call out of work tonight. The sergeant will understand," Greg said, tightening his hold on her.

Stroking his cheek gently and brushing the dark brown lock of hair from his forehead, she said, "I can't. I've agreed to meet with a complainant. She is an eighty-five-year-old robbery victim with no one who cares about her. She was walking her dog in Rittenhouse Square when three guys pushed her around, kicked her dog, and took her purse. I hate those types of cases. I'm on a mission to make sure they are caught before another old lady gets hurt. Can we pick up this conversation the next time we can spend some serious time together?"

Locke picked up her hand and kissed it. "Did I ever tell you about the legend of the kissing hand?"

"No," replied Sam.

Locke opened her hand and kissed her palm. "You open your hand like this, and I kiss your palm. And then, my kiss makes its way up your arm," Locke said as he walked his fingers up her arm, "and into your heart. And then your heart is filled with my love and your joy."

"Really?"

"My five-year-old nephew told me that story, so I know it's true," he said, smiling until the corners of his eyes crinkled.

"Your family is chock-full of romantics. We will talk more soon," Sam said as she walked toward the door.

The world won't get no better if we just let it be. You got
to change the world, you and me.

—Gene McFadden and John Whitehead

FOURTEEN

———————————•—————————————

THAT AFTERNOON, ALL OF SAM'S TOUGH-GUY COLLEAGUES
went out of their way to be uncharacteristically sensitive. She sat in
the squad room and focused on her typewriter, trying to avoid eye
contact with everyone. But the open-space squad room was the perfect setting for the relentless and clumsy efforts of both uniformed
officers and plainclothes detectives to offer a constant stream of condolences. Before it all became her undoing, Sam pulled on her black
trench coat, let the deskman know she would be back in an hour,
and grabbed the keys to the squad car so she could meet with her
mugging victim.

When Ruth Halverson answered the door of her ninth-floor
apartment, Sam immediately noticed the dark bruises on her face
and arms. Anger surged through her on behalf of the poor woman,
but she was careful to keep her reaction in check. Sam also noticed
that, at eighty-five years of age, Mrs. Helverson was well-dressed and
petite, approximately a hundred pounds, with coiffed gray hair. In
spite of her bruised, waifish appearance Mrs. Halverson was spunky,
articulate, and proud.

But she was also shaken after her experience in Rittenhouse
Square. For the next hour, Sam listened to Mrs. Halverson talk about

losing her husband and her ensuing loneliness—and now her fear of leaving her apartment. She had a son who lived in Flemington, New Jersey, whom she called occasionally but who never visited her, so she never got to spend time with her grandchildren. Mrs. Halverson broke down crying, and Sam felt uncomfortable. Should she try to comfort her somehow? Her police training wasn't much help to a woman who was opening up her heart. Sam waited for a moment as Mrs. Halverson politely sniffed into a handkerchief, and then she moved into more familiar territory: the crime. She asked Mrs. Halverson to describe her assailants and repeat the details of the robbery, and then she showed her a book of photos of suspects recently arrested for robbery. But Mrs. Halverson seemed to falter; she couldn't quite remember the details, and she second-guessed most of what she did say. Sam suspected that Mrs. Halverson might not be the best of witnesses, and she also decided she would find Mrs. Halverson's son in Flemington and make him visit his mother.

Finally, Sam had to ask the painful question for the police report: How much money had been stolen? The elderly usually barely got by on Social Security, and Sam knew that even if an arrest was made, she would probably not get her money back. But when Sam asked her how much money was in her stolen purse, Halverson looked at her as though she was naive. "There were just some tissues in the bag," she said. "I keep it as a decoy. My money is kept inside my bra." With a twinkle in her eyes, she pulled out a folded wad of dollars. A big smile of relief broke out across Sam's face. Those thugs were no match for a lady like her.

After leaving the apartment building, Sam strolled through the square, festooned with festive wreaths and Christmas lights. Most of the people around were over thirty years old. This was the fourth robbery of an elderly victim in the past week in a four-block area, all around the same time of day. The injuries to the victims were becoming more serious. *It might be worth it to call the stakeout unit and have a granny squad team make themselves the next victims before someone's grandmother is killed by these thugs*, she thought.

On the drive back to Central Detectives, she found herself reminiscing about the past nine years. When she arrived at Logan Circle, she found herself drawn to the cathedral and decided to park the squad car. A short walk later, she entered the Cathedral of St. Peter and Paul.

Sam sat in one of the back pews of the dimly lit church. She smiled, remembering Kate's wedding day. She thought it funny that Kate's wedding had been one the happiest days she had spent with her friends—one of her happiest days ever. Everything she shared with Kate, Jonesy, and AJ was outside her normal comfort zone, and she was surprised that it was the first time in her life she felt real joy—elation that wasn't tempered with the guilt or judgment that always seemed to be a part of any Kelly family gathering. The wedding and the days leading up to it had been a new experience for her. The days were happy and absent of conflict and judgment. Everyone was free to enjoy the planning and the actual wedding day without fear of criticism, reproachful glances, and cautioning lectures to dampen the mood.

That day, she realized a few things about herself. First, her friends loved her unconditionally, encouraged her, and pushed her to be the best she could be.

Second, she—and Jonesy—came to appreciate the girly pampering that came with the wedding. Kate, Carmella, and AJ insisted on tutoring them, recognizing that a girl who wore a uniform could also aspire to dress like a cover girl. "The world is changing. A woman needs to be multidimensional to keep pace with the change," Carmella had said. "She should be ready to roll in the mud or sway down a runway, depending on the circumstances."

Third, Sam learned that she liked to drink dirty martinis occasionally.

And fourth, as Kate and Ray tied the knot, she noticed a five-foot-ten, quiet, determined Philadelphia detective named Gregory Locke, who strayed from his deadpan stare that day and shared the most captivating smile she had ever seen.

It was a great day. It was the day that she chose happiness instead of an existence filled with guilt and regret.

AJ had told her happiness was a choice. At first, Sam's efforts to choose happiness drifted occasionally. Her life since 1976 had had its ups and downs, but her network of friends kept her on the track toward optimism. Her friends had been there when she was at the crossroads, guiding her to make the right turn. They were her safety nets. Now, AJ, the one who had encouraged her the most, was gone forever.

The church around Sam was empty and still, but words began tumbling from her like a prayer. "Oh, AJ! Was I a good friend? Did I tell you enough how much you meant to me? Did I appreciate the time we had together? Did I let you down at the end? Oh Lord, I'm sounding like a Willie Nelson song. Well, at least I'm thinking in songs. That should bring a smile to your face." Sam began to hum their theme song from the academy, "The world won't get much better if we just let it be."

Sam knelt forward in the pew and lowered her head to her hands. "AJ, are you talking to me?" She squeezed her eyes shut and rubbed her temples with her index fingers. Her conversation with Chaplain Harris popped into her head. "Maybe your father spoke for you. You always told me to trust my instincts and look for a little help from my friends, just like he said."

Her gaze settled on the altar, and she shook her head. "Why did I even come here? This is definitely not me. I guess you *are* still with me and trying to save my soul by getting me to church. No worries, girl. I have been in a church twice today, and you are responsible for both visits." Sam smiled and actually meant it for the first time that day. "I feel it, and I'm inspired. You always said there was nothing the four of us couldn't do if we put our heads together. And our numbers have grown with Ray, Walt, and Greg. They are part of the posse.

"So now it's a search for the truth. Wherever the truth takes us, I need to believe that we can handle it. I need to believe *I* can handle it." Sam's gaze wandered to the stained-glass windows brightened by the setting sun. She continued, "No matter what happens, I do know you brought a light to this world that can't be snuffed out by your death, and that will help me find peace. The rest is just a search for the facts."

PART II

Philadelphia, 1976

*God in his infinite wisdom created men and
women differently.*

—Joseph O'Neill, Philadelphia police commissioner

FIFTEEN

In the far Northeast Philadelphia, green fields and swaying weeping willow trees lined the banks of the Delaware River. The peaceful, picturesque scene stood in sharp contrast to what was happening nearby within the walls of the Philadelphia House of Corrections and on the campus of the Philadelphia police academy.

At the academy, the first class of police-officer recruits, including women, were coming face-to-face with the brand-new physical training requirements. After a federal lawsuit against the City of Philadelphia, its police department consented to hire one hundred women to study their performance as patrol officers. The study would last for two years. The goal of the police department was to prove that women couldn't handle a grueling training regimen to become uniformed patrols.

Recruit Sam Kelly Evans, in her second week at the academy, leaned against the six-foot chain-link fence in the parking lot, bent over with her hands on her knees, and tried to catch her breath. Her face showed the disappointment that coursed through her: she had missed the timed mile-and-a-half run by forty seconds. Fellow recruit A. J. Harris noticed the defeated expression and couldn't resist a jibe. "Are you going to quit over being a little slow?"

Sam, still struggling for breath, looked up and shook her head. "I'm not a runner. I don't think I'll ever make the time requirement."

Kate Dominic and Michelle Jones, standing nearby, said in unison, "Me either."

"Oh, we have three quitters?" asked Harris.

Kate was the first to offer her excuse. "The PT requirements are part of the police commissioner's strategy to set women up for failure. You know, 'God in his infinite wisdom created men and women differently.' They know we can pass the coursework, so they'll get us instead on the obstacle course and a timed run. Did you know that they never required recruits to pass a physical training course before?"

Michelle nodded and said, "They have done everything they can to discourage us." She ticked each item off on her fingers. "We had to cut our hair short to make us look like little boys. We are wearing men's clothing, including men's shoes. Now they are going to make us finish a run and an obstacle course that has never been a requirement in previous classes. Most of the male recruits are military veterans who are used to physical training. We're definitely not the Olympic hopefuls of the group. The PD brass clearly has a plan."

"Wah, wah, wah, you sound like crybabies," AJ said dismissively. "If you haven't noticed, I'm a woman, and I made the time. I'm also one of those veterans. I hate to be the one to tell you this, but you are defeating yourselves before you've even finished the training. I don't doubt that the brass has a plan, but you can have a plan too. You can do this. You have a choice. Either blame the police commissioner and give up, or make sure he doesn't win."

Sam responded quickly. "I didn't say I wasn't going to try."

"I get it. We need a counterplan. Any ideas?" asked Kate.

"You want a plan? I'll give you a plan," AJ said, clearly enjoying this. "I can whip the three of you into shape in no time. But I need commitment, and I need you to do as I say. You ladies in?"

"I'm in," said Sam as she stood at attention and saluted.

"I'll give it a go," Michelle said, shrugging.

"I'm in, too," Kate said with a smile. "I can never resist a good plan."

"Good," AJ said, and she lowered her voice and got serious. "I'm an army vet, and in the army, we ran and then ran some more. I'm willing to kick your butts into shape. Of course, you need to know up front that no matter how hard you work, you'll never be a better athlete than me or, by the way, look as good as me while you're doing it." OK, there was a smile creeping into the seriousness. "My dad is an army chaplain, and he likes plans too. His favorite quote is from General George S. Patton: 'A good plan today is better than a perfect plan tomorrow.' We haven't been planning as long as the brass, but we'll have a good plan and we will beat them at their game."

"I think your dad and I would get along," said Kate. "And I have an idea of my own. I'm sure this won't be the only time we need to come up with a counterplan. I think we should stick together and work as a team whenever we see a potential stumble through the academy. Agreed?"

All four recruits nodded to each other, and AJ said, "Get some sleep. Tomorrow you start your real basic training. You will run by day at the academy and run by night at the A. J. Harris boot camp."

The next day, after class, the four recruits met at the track and football field of Northeast Philadelphia High. AJ pointed to the bleachers, and the other three women took a seat.

"OK, we're here. What's the strategy for turning us into athletes?" asked Kate.

"It's a five-step plan," AJ said confidently, standing before them. "First, we agree to meet here every weekday to train. Second, we pick our theme song. Third, I teach you to stretch. Fourth, we stretch again. Fifth, when I think you are ready, we run the track, jump the obstacles, climb the fence, and sing our theme song. Finally, I will keep time, and I won't share those times until I'm sure you can finish the run and obstacle course under the limit."

All three nodded, and Sam asked, "What's our song?"

AJ stooped down to the duffel bag at her feet and pulled out a tape recorder. "I've been thinking about it. I thought we should rely on Philadelphia talent to motivate us, and I thought our song should be relevant and inspiring." She hit the play button. "I think I found the perfect song," she said over the tune of "Wake Up Everybody" by Harold Melvin and the Blue Notes.

"The perfect inspiration!" Sam said, beginning to sway and sing along. "Wake up everybody, no more sleeping in bed…"

"I never feel inspired by songs," Michelle said doubtfully.

"You need to listen and ratchet up the passion, Recruit Jones. This song could be about us. By the way, seems like Sam can carry a tune. Anyone else?"

Sam laughed. "Does that make me a Blue Note? Will you be Harold Melvin?"

"No, not Harold Melvin. Teddy Pendergrass. I thought you knew music. Teddy sings that song."

"Really?" Sam said. "I always thought Harold Melvin was the lead singer."

"Yeah, you're not alone," AJ said.

"OK, sounds like we have a theme. Can we make it official?" Sam said, offering an outstretched arm. "In the words of d'Artagnan, 'All for one and one for all.'"

"So, the plan is singing songs and quoting a dead French writer?" Michelle said. She rolled her brown eyes, shrugged her broad shoulders, and pushed a strand of short brown hair over her right ear.

"Have faith, Michelle," Sam said. "Give it a chance. You might enjoy it along the way."

AJ laughed. "Sam wins this round. We are musketeers, and our song is 'Wake Up Everybody,' and you should practice being a Blue Note."

Michelle looked at her classmates thoughtfully. "We are an interesting social experiment and definitely an unlikely friendship. Under any other circumstances, I am not sure I would like any of you."

"You're not my friend yet, Michelle," AJ said, but her voice was light and teasing. For the first time, she wondered whether that might change—whether she wasn't meant to be alone, as she'd felt the past few years. She straightened her shoulders and slipped back into boss mode. "And we are very different. We have Sam, the optimist; 'we need a plan' Kate; 'every man is out to get us' Michelle; and I am the person who will keep you grounded. We have all the bases covered. Now let's do this."

On Wednesday afternoon of the fourth week, the four women met as usual at the high school track. They stretched to "Wake Up Everybody" and then jumped hurdles and climbed fences. As they ran the two-mile stretch, AJ sang selected verses from their theme song, with Sam singing backup. Occasionally Kate joined in, too. Jonesy—at some point, all of the women had slipped into calling her that—stayed resolutely quiet, but now she smiled at the other women as they sang the now-familiar song.

After completing the run, AJ announced, "OK, ladies—a celebration is in order. All three of you will beat the time!"

The three recruits began jumping, hugging, and high-fiving.

"Sam!" yelled a man leaning against the chain-link fence. He was in his early thirties, slightly built, and had curly blond hair.

Startled, Sam looked over her shoulder and fell as still as a statue. "Jeff, what are you doing here?" she asked in a flat voice.

"I wanted to know if I was going to go another night without dinner," Jeff shouted at her, slurring every other word. He was drunk. Again.

Sam spoke slowly and softly, hoping to defuse his hostile tone. "Jeff, let me introduce Kate, Jonesy, and AJ."

Kate, Jonesy, and AJ said hello, but Jeff didn't look at them or acknowledge them. "I asked if I was going to get dinner tonight," he demanded.

Sam kept her voice emotionless. "You will need to work it out yourself, Jeff. I won't be home for another couple of hours. I'll see you later."

Jeff glared at her but said no more. He turned and walked back to his car. When he sped off, he made sure the wheels of the car screeched.

Sam turned to her friends. "I'm sorry about that. The schedule has been rough on Jeff. But I don't want this to dampen the celebration. How about a quick meal and a glass of wine?"

At the Old Philly Tavern off Roosevelt Boulevard, the ladies sat at a corner table and ordered dinner. They tried, with little success, to regain their celebratory mood. No one knew how to relieve Sam of the humiliated look on her face.

Finally, Kate offered a toast to their success: "We now have no obstacles to our success," she said. And then, because she was Kate, she went on to outline the next stage of their plan. "We just need to pass firearms instruction, and we can declare victory. But I don't see that being a problem for any of us. The firearms instructors seem very fair-minded, and they've gone out of their way to be helpful."

As the four women clinked their wine glasses, Jonesy couldn't resist a sarcastic comment. "Only because they're afraid we'll shoot them."

Sam choked on her wine as unexpected laughter escaped her. "Jonesy, I can't figure out what I want most." Sam tapped her index finger to her pursed lips. "Let me see. Do I want to have your sharp tongue and quick wit—God knows I could use it—or to convince you that every man in the world isn't out to sabotage us?"

The four women laughed.

"This is one time I concede to you, Pollyanna," Jonesy said begrudgingly. "The instructors at the pistol range are good guys. They're not trying to sabotage anyone. They are, however, the exception, not the rule. After meeting your husband, I think we can agree on that, right?"

Sam said nothing, and the four sat silently for a full minute. Whatever ease and joy had reentered the room vanished with Jonesy's words.

Kate finally broke the silence. "Well, ladies, I have a long ride to South Philly, and we have an early morning ahead of us."

"Yeah, I need to get back to Manayunk and do my wash," said Jonesy.

Jonesy and Kate left, but AJ and Sam lingered at the table. AJ reached over and gently took Sam's left hand in her own. "Sam, I know the bruises on the thumb and wrist are from shooting with your weak hand at the barricade, but what about the bruises you try to hide on your arms and neck?"

Sam said nothing, but her eyes glistened, and she broke away from AJ's gaze. AJ persisted. "Look, my father's been counseling families for years. Spousal abuse is something he saw frequently, so I got to see it firsthand. If tonight is any indication, your husband is a nightmare. Brutality is unacceptable under any circumstances, but you have a special obligation to make sure that you don't tolerate it. You took an oath to protect and serve—remember? Protect yourself. You are a cop even if you are still a recruit. You can't be a victim."

"I know," Sam finally said in a half-whisper.

"So, what's the story? What are you doing with him?"

"The story isn't fascinating," Sam said with a joyless laugh. "I met Jeff, we dated, he showered me with gifts, he asked me to marry him. I thought it was the logical next step in my life. But then I realized even before we got married that it was a mistake. We don't— we don't really bring out the best in each other, I think. I tried to break it off, and he threatened to commit suicide, so I married him because I was afraid that he would hurt himself because of me. After we were married, though, he decided I didn't make him happy. He reminds me of it every day. I'm not sure I love him the way I wanted to be in love with another person, and at times I struggle even to *like* him. It seems like we have nothing in common—another thing he reminds me about constantly. But we made a commitment, and we need to figure out how to make this work. I'd hoped if I contributed more than a receptionist's salary to the bank account, it would help. He seemed happier at first, and we were starting to get along." Sam shrugged a little. "Turns out it was just more money for him to spend on alcohol. When he is very depressed, drinking makes him aggressive. The thing is, he's always sorry the next day. Some days I hate him and want to leave, and other days I just feel sorry for him." With her right thumb, Sam absently stroked the dark bruises blooming along her collarbone. "When he hit me the other day, I told him I was going to get a divorce. It just made him angrier, and he hit me again. He's Catholic, and my family is also very Catholic." She sighed.

"Divorce is not an option. He knows it, and I know it. Once I graduate from the police academy, I'm going to focus on our marriage. Things will settle down between us then."

AJ's hands still grasped Sam's left hand gently, but her words probed. "That's the best excuse for staying you can come up with?" she asked. "Even if you are Catholic—this is the twentieth century."

Sam's cheeks reddened. "My relationship with Jeff is complicated, and it might look bad, but it's my fault, too," she said. "I've been distracted by the academy. We will work it out." When AJ gave Sam a dubious look, Sam adamantly bobbed her head and said, "We will. I can make it work."

"You are a smart girl, Sam. Much smarter than you let on—even to yourself. Deep down, you must know that you can't ignore the violence. He is not fixable, and this thing you two have is not going to end well."

Sam looked down at the table. AJ watched her for a minute, sighed, and continued, "I don't share the story of my life with anyone, so consider yourself special. I was married and divorced. David and I were married for five years. I thought we were in love. Turns out, I was and he wasn't. David is not a one-woman man. He cheated—several times. At first, I tried to convince myself that David loved me but turned to other women because I lacked something. He seemed sincere in his apologies. In his own way, I think he was sincere, but his sincerity didn't change who he was. I was grasping for something that would never make me or him happy. It took me a while to realize it, but we were never going to be happy together."

AJ swallowed but kept going. "It was a blow to my life, and, more specifically, my self-worth. You know what my biggest fear was? It was not living up to the example that my parents set. My mom and dad were a love match and are still very happy together after thirty-five years. I thought my parents and family would see me as a failure. At one point, I thought about walking into the Pacific Ocean—for good.

"My father realized what I was doing to myself, and not because I willingly shared how I was feeling. He didn't press me to talk, but he talked to me. He told me that relationships were like shooting dice. You get very lucky sometimes, and other times, through no fault of your own, the dice go against you. After the divorce, Dad encouraged me to leave the military and Hawaii, where David is still stationed. He told me I should start over and follow my dream to be a model in New York. Modeling was my dream when I was eighteen. I wasn't sure that I still wanted it, but I was on my way to New York when I stopped in Philadelphia, and I decided I liked it here. I heard about the police test and found out I would have a ten-point advantage for my military experience. I decided to go for it because I thought it was an opportunity to make a difference for women in general and black women specifically.

"I reinvented myself. My ego and confidence are real, but I hide some insecurities. I always have to remind myself that I am deserving. I'll never fall into the trap of convincing myself I am unworthy to be loved and admired. But that part is beside the point. The difference between your story and mine is that I was in love and you clearly are not. And David never laid a hand on me." Under AJ's gentle hands, Sam's fingers knotted, an unconscious reminder of the ways she had been hurt. "I'm telling you all this for two reasons: First, I know how easy it is to lose your sense of self-worth in a lousy relationship. Second, I want you to know that your prison is self-imposed. I met Jeff for five minutes, and I know you will never be happy sticking by him. He humiliates you, and your bruises tell me that he is dangerous."

Sam couldn't meet AJ's gaze head-on, but her tone was resolute. Sam was a determined woman. "I'm humiliated that we are having this conversation and that I've given you a bad impression of Jeff," she said firmly. "Look, I appreciate your concern, but you're wrong on this one. I'm not a victim, and Jeff isn't as bad as I've made him sound. I know that I need to find a way to work it out, and I will."

"Sam, that's another bad habit you have. You blame yourself constantly. *You* didn't give me a bad impression of Jeff. Jeff did."

"I can work things out between us. I just need some time."

"Sam, please don't wait too long. It won't get better, and I predict it will get ugly."

The future belongs to those who believe in the
beauty of their dreams.

—Eleanor Roosevelt

SIXTEEN

THE FIRST CLASS OF FEMALE PATROL OFFICERS GRADUATED from the Philadelphia police academy in 1976 without fanfare or even acknowledgment by the police commissioner or police department commanders. All of them completed the run and the obstacle course with plenty of time.

"So, this is what graduation from the police academy feels like," Kate said afterward, sighing as she brushed her hair and adjusted her uniform in front of the full-length mirror in the ladies' room at the academy. Her friends already knew her well enough to know that the sigh wasn't wistful—it was angry. AJ paused behind Kate for a moment to admire how well her own tailored uniform fit her five-foot-seven, 121-pound frame.

Sam watched Kate admiring her reflection, and she smiled. "Your parents did a great job on the uniform, Kate. You look amazing. You too, AJ—did you have your uniform tailored, too? I'm jealous of both of you."

"The look is important," Kate said. "You don't get a second chance to make a good impression." She turned from the mirror. "Not that we had anyone to impress. This graduation debacle is another strategic decision by the police brass to diminish us. We are the first group of women to graduate from the Philadelphia police academy for work patrol, and we have been snubbed by the city brass. This fiasco hardly resembles a graduation ceremony."

Jonesy, never one to miss an opportunity to make an acerbic remark, said, "The brass is pathetic, but I can't say that I'm surprised. Actually, I feel lucky there was no fanfare. I'd hate to be overshadowed publicly by PD Barbie One and PD Barbie Two here in their tailored uniforms."

"This is serious. It's not funny," Kate said. "We are the first class of women to graduate from the police academy and be assigned to patrol. This day is historic, and it's being ignored."

"We all understand your disappointment, but we have bigger problems," Jonesy said. "We won't be assigned training officers when we hit the street. In the highest crime areas in Philadelphia, I might add."

Kate knew she was right, but still she raised an eyebrow. "Not to mention that you and Sam can't go on the street in those uniforms. You could use help from my father's tailoring shop to make those uniforms fit."

"No thank you, Bitchy Barbie," Jonesy shot back.

"Hey guys, we should be celebrating, not picking at each other, right?" said Sam, an anxious blush deepening on her cheeks.

Jonesy rolled her eyes, never willing to back down. "Pollyanna, just admit that not only have we been dissed by the clothes and the graduation ceremony, or lack thereof—we're also being sent out on the streets without anyone training us."

"I admit they are trying to discourage us," Sam said. "I just don't want to lose sight of the fact that we won round one. We just need another plan."

"We definitely need a plan," Kate said. "But first things first. I insist you go to my parent's tailor shop so we can do something about how you look." She waved her hand up and down Sam's and Jonesy's general appearance.

"And you accuse me of being insensitive in my delivery," Jonesy said, scowling.

Kate ignored Jonesy and continued, "In the meantime, we look for an unsanctioned training officer."

"I've got it covered," said Jonesy. "I know a retired beat cop. His name is Lou Korman. I met him at my barbershop. He volunteered to help me even before O'Neill's new scheme to make us fail. I'm sure he wouldn't mind helping all of us."

"You go to a barbershop?" asked Kate.

"Why not? Keeping my hair short through the academy made haircuts expensive. Barbers are cheaper than hairdressers—just one more inequity for women." She cut her eyes back toward Kate. "Again, what's with the bitchy remarks today, Kate? You aren't the only one who didn't get her graduation ceremony." Jonesy never liked to let on when something like this was bothering her, but it was clear she was also disappointed by the day.

Kate shrugged but said nothing, so Jonesy continued, "Anyway, Lou worked the Twenty-Fifth District. His beat was 2700 Germantown Avenue—Germantown and Lehigh. He loves telling war stories, and he's been sort of a cheerleader for me through the academy. He offered to answer any questions that might come up along the way. I can invite everyone over to my house, and if we click, we can continue to meet at my house. He can be our training officer. I'm sure if we buy him a beer and feed him a burger, he'll be happy to help all of us. He is a good guy, very supportive, and he's been like a father figure." As she spoke, Jonesy's voice lost its signature sarcasm, and she became almost earnest in her enthusiasm. It was a side of her that the other women had rarely glimpsed before.

"Wow, this major," Sam said. "We definitely have to meet this guy. This is the first time I've heard you say positive things about a man. A retired cop, no less. I'm sure General Patton would agree that while not perfect, it's a good plan for us."

"He is a talker and a storyteller," Jonesy said. "He strikes up a conversation easily. I guess that's part of being a beat cop. When I told him that I had been accepted to the police academy, he congratulated me by saying, 'Welcome to a front-row seat to the greatest show on earth.' I think he genuinely thinks women will be an asset to the PD."

Kate said, "So we have our training officer plan. What do we need to do to fix Sam's blushing?"

"My blushing?" Sam said as she blushed even deeper.

"Precisely what I mean. You owe it to womankind. You can't blow this for us. We have an image to establish. We can run, jump, and shoot, but we need a good reaction and decision-making skills. This goes well beyond cutting our hair short and wearing men's clothes." Kate saw the confusion turning to defensiveness on Sam's face, but still she pushed on. "You're not a social worker, you're a cop. You need to toughen up, and you need to drop the nun routine. Blushing every time someone curses around you is embarrassing to all of us."

"Kate, did I do something to offend you today? Why are you being so mean? Blushing doesn't disqualify me for police work," Sam said.

"Pretty close to it. What will happen if you need to handle a sex crime if you can't stop blushing when you hear a curse word?" asked Kate.

"That's not fair, Kate. None of us are fully developed on all the skills we need to be successful on patrol. That's why we are talking about a training officer. In my defense, I ranked in the top 5 percent of the class, with the highest score of all the women. I think that could offset the blushing."

AJ, who had been quiet for the whole discussion, jumped in. "Good for you, defending yourself," she said before Kate could reply. "It's nice to see you push back once in a while. Take Kate up on the offer to have her dad tailor the uniform. The blushing is a temporary condition and one which I am best able to help you solve."

"How are you going to help me with the blushing?"

"I am going to teach you how to curse like a sailor."

"Oh, I'm not so sure." Sam looked doubtful.

"Not to worry, Sam. The easiest way to stop blushing is to become comfortable using the words. Before you know it, 'what the fuck' will become a standard expression in your communications repertoire. You might actually find that those words feel right on certain occasions."

Sam didn't look convinced.

AJ laughed. "I'm not saying you have to cuss to your mother or the nuns who taught you in high school. But trust me, I'll have you cursing like a sailor."

"Isn't that disloyal to the army?" said Jonesy. "I thought you would have her cussing like an army ranger."

"Rangers take profanity to a new level—I would need more time," AJ said, laughing. "I'm going for the basics." She flung out her arm as if unsheathing a sword. "All for one and one for all?"

The four graduates touched their fingertips together, as if clashing swords. Sam and Jonesy said their goodbyes and walked toward their cars.

"Kate, you have a minute?" AJ asked as soon as the other two women were out of earshot.

Kate nodded. "What's up?"

"Don't you think you were being a little harsh with Sam?"

"I wasn't trying to be. I want her to be successful, but sometimes I think she might be a little soft for this job. It's like she lives in a vacuum."

"Or maybe you thought you were the smartest of us because you graduated magna cum laude from Temple, and Sam threw you a curve by beating you in the class rankings?" Kate didn't say anything. "Kate, the four of us have developed a tight friendship through the academy. I know things have to change now that we are going to our assignments, but I hope we can still work with and help each other. I predict that with your confidence and natural leadership skills, you will rise through the ranks and we will be proud to see it happen. Just don't underestimate the rest of us—especially Sam. Don't assume the Pollyanna thing is anything more than her way of dealing with difficult situations. Sam has experienced her share of real life and has some major decisions coming her way. We all will have to confront how this job will change our lives, but I think Sam will be the first to face her future. The job will be a blessing for her because she'll be making enough money to support herself, but she has a responsibility to herself and the job to make sure she doesn't allow herself to become a victim. When she needs us, I hope we are all there for her."

Kate listened intently and then nodded in agreement. "How did I miss it? I knew her husband was a strapper, but I didn't realize he was even worse."

"Strapper? Is that a South Philadelphia insult?"

"It's more of a description of a big loser. What should we do for Sam, AJ?"

"Nothing yet. We focus on supporting each other. We made it through the academy, but now comes the real test. We won't have many cheerleaders to make our transition into patrol. We need to be honest with each other, but we should make sure that our honesty doesn't translate into condescension. Sam's a smart girl. She is a sponge for advice and knowledge, and in the end, she may be a rock star."

"You're right. As I think about it, I was being harsh to both Sam and Jonesy. I think my frustration with the police department made me lash out at them. Truth be told, I'm afraid we won't be able to come up with enough plans to best the O'Neill plan. Men's uniforms, men's haircuts, and an obstacle course, compared to being assigned to the highest-crime areas in Philadelphia without training officers. I wonder if the veteran officers are even allowed to talk to us." Kate blew out a deep breath. "I think I'm a little afraid about what is going to happen to us. Thanks for letting me know that I'm being a jerk. I'm sorry, and I'll apologize to them."

"Don't worry about it. I'm sure Sam and Jonesy know what you are thinking, and it's water under the bridge. We've all been through a lot in a short time, but this is only the beginning. I think we will all take turns in…what does Sam call the Philadelphia Flyers penalty box? The sin bin."

Kate laughed. "Yep. I also think we are going to need the grit of the Broad Street Bullies to survive our tests yet to come."

"And Kate—I think we are all a little afraid about what's going to happen to us," AJ said.

Kate walked over to AJ, hugged her, and said, "All for one and one for all?"

AJ nodded, smiling. "See you at Jonesy's."

Safety doesn't happen by accident.

—A Wise Person

SEVENTEEN

MICHELLE JONES'S STONE-FRONT ROW HOUSE ON BAKER Street in the Manayunk section of Philadelphia was furnished with hand-me-downs from relatives. Jonesy's personal touch was decorating her walls with the watercolors she used in her painting hobby.

"Shame your address isn't 221 Baker Street. You know... Sherlock Holmes's address. That would be fitting, wouldn't it?" Lou Korman said, sipping his Rolling Rock beer and alternately brushing his gray mustache and thinning gray hair with his right hand.

The doorbell rang, and Jonesy ushered in her friends. "Lou, meet Kate Dominic, A. J. Harris, and Sam Kelly. Kate and I have been assigned to the Twenty-Fifth District." Kate, AJ, and Sam offered Lou handshakes.

"I am A. J. Harris, and this is Sam Evans. We're assigned to the Thirty-Fifth District."

Lou smiled. "I can see the PD got better-looking after I retired," he joked.

Jonesy affected a stern look. "Don't disappoint me by flirting with my fellow officers, Lou. I told them you were a father figure to me." Heading into the kitchen, Jonesy said, "I'm making steak sandwiches for lunch. Is there anyone that doesn't like cheese or onions?"

Kate surveyed the head shakes and called into the kitchen. "Jonesy, as they say at Pat's Steaks: everybody wants 'one cheese wit.'" She turned back to the rest of the room to get started. "You know, we have been corny about everything else," she said. "Let's give our group a name."

Jonesy immediately popped her head out of the kitchen to offer one. "We can call ourselves the Baker Street Five."

Sam raised a bottle of beer to toast. "And so begin the monthly meetings of the Baker Street Five."

Lou took a swig of his own beer. "It's nice meeting you ladies. I'm sorry I retired before I could work with any of you. Let me begin by telling you that I've worked both the Twenty-Fifth and the Thirty-Fifth Districts. I can tell you about the bosses, and I know many of the cops assigned to each district. I'm working part-time for a limousine company now, but I can be pretty flexible if you want to meet regularly." He paused. "I am always happy to answer any and all questions and to share any war stories you might want to discuss, but I thought we might start with a talk about safety. The longer you work in districts as busy as the Twenty-Fifth and Thirty-Fifth, the more you will find that your reaction time, senses, and instincts will develop. It's always important to stay alert, but rookies—more than anyone—need to appreciate that it might mean the difference between staying alive and getting dead."

"OK, Lou," Jonesy said, snorting a little in good humor. "I think we all agree that safety is a good place to begin."

"OK, good. Get used to hearing this, because at the beginning of every shift, your sergeant will say it, too. Stay alert to stay alive. Repeat these words to yourself constantly. Focus on your surroundings. Make sure you switch up your routes, including where and what time you might stop for coffee or get something to eat. I know that you think Commissioner O'Neill intentionally sent you to the busiest districts in North and Northwest Philadelphia in the hopes that you fail. That may have been his intent, but you should look at this as an opportunity and take advantage of it. You will learn faster, your instincts will develop sooner, and you will fine-tune the skills you pick up along the way."

Three hours later, as the Baker Street Five said goodbye, Sam said, "This was great, Lou. As Bogey said in *Casablanca*, 'Louie, this could be the beginning of a beautiful relationship.'"

"You really need to work on originality, Sam," Jonesy admonished, but they all laughed.

Lou chuckled all the way home. Ever since he'd been forced into retirement because of his heart condition, he'd felt useless. As he drove his red Buick Regal home, he felt for the first time in a long while that he still had purpose. He would help these women stay alert and stay alive.

Apples, peaches, pumpkin pie.
Who's not ready? Holler "I."

—*Jay & the Techniques*

EIGHTEEN

WORKING THE MIDNIGHT-TO-EIGHT SHIFT IN PHILADELPHIA'S Twenty-Fifth District had one upshot: there was little chance of falling asleep on duty. The Twenty-Fifth District was the busiest district in Philly—one of the reasons it had been nicknamed the Badlands.

Kate Dominic and Michelle Jones were assigned to Emergency Patrol Wagon 2502. As they inspected the vehicle for equipment at the beginning of their shift, Kate and Jonesy engaged in their usual banter about Commissioner O'Neill and his decision to send all of the female rookie officers on patrol without training officers.

"The rumor is, O'Neill is hoping the women will be so intimidated that there are no training officers and men are not allowed to work with us, that we will all request transfers to the Juvenile Aid Division," Jonesy said. "I won't be loving any female officer who requests that transfer."

Kate, the driver, advised police radio they were in service. Jonesy was starting the shift log when dispatch assigned them to a disturbance at the parking lot of Temple Hospital's emergency ward.

Kate confirmed the assignment, hung up the radio, and then returned to the O'Neill rumors. "Even if they told me that a promotion came with it, I wouldn't take a transfer, just to spite him," Kate said as she leaned over to the rearview mirror and kissed it.

Jonesy paused writing and cocked an eyebrow quizzically. "What are you doing?" she asked.

"I'm kissing my ass goodbye!" Kate laughed, and Jonesy joined in as they pulled out of the parking lot and headed to Temple. They arrived within a few minutes. Jonesy was still working on the paperwork when she heard Kate exclaim, "What in the world?"

Jonesy lifted her gaze to see a completely naked three-hundred-pound woman with a broad smile standing in the parking lot of the emergency ward. A security guard approached the driver's window. Kate rolled down the window and said, "What's up?"

"What do you think is up?" The security guard knitted his eyebrows, pointed to the smiling woman, and said, "You need to do something about Lady Godiva here. It shouldn't be much trouble for you. She didn't bring her horse today."

Jonesy shook her head. "No way, we're not taking her. She is obviously a mental health commitment. Why wasn't she taken to the hospital catchment center?"

"The catchment center is closed. They're overflowing, all over the city. The Thirty-Fifth District dropped her off, but the center is closed, so you need to take her back with you."

Kate sighed and slipped the gearshift into park. She rummaged through the back seat for the sheet kept on hand in every patrol wagon. Kate tried to wrap the sheet around the woman, but the woman kept dropping the sheet and waving to every onlooker like she was walking the Hollywood red carpet.

Meanwhile, Jonesy tried to fill out an incident report form. "Ma'am, could you give me your name?" she asked.

The woman stared at her first and then said, "Peaches."

Jonesy narrowed her eyes. "OK, Peaches, I need your full name. What is your full name?"

"Apples, Peaches, Pumpkin Pie," the woman retorted merrily. Kate was still trying to wrap a sheet around her, and her shoulders shook with laughter.

Jonesy turned back to the security guard. "This is ridiculous," she said. "She should be a three-oh-two commitment. I am not arresting her. Who do I need to speak with?"

Kate escorted Peaches to the back of the wagon and closed one door to afford some privacy while trying to coax additional information from her about her family, her street address, and any other potentially useful information—like a real name, for starters.

In the meantime, the security guard led Jonesy to argue in vain with the hospital staff over Peaches needing to be admitted. She walked back to the patrol car and asked police radio for the location of the closest open catchment center. The dispatcher responded that all centers across the city were closed, just as the guard had said. Peaches, for her part, was comfortably settled in the back of the wagon; she seemed to like being in police custody.

Jonesy and Kate looked at each other, unsure of what to do next. Jonesy said, "I refuse to take her into the district and hand her over to the turnkey to put her in a jail cell without clothes. But we can't leave her."

Kate said, "She told me she lives with her brother on Seventeenth Street. She couldn't give me an address or cross street, but she couldn't have walked a long distance naked like this. I called the operation room in the Thirty-Fifth. There was a report of a hospital case turned in by the wagon crew from the four-to-twelve shift—the complainant's name was 'Peaches.' No address, but she was picked up at Seventeenth and Tioga."

"That's out of our district," Jonesy said.

Kate nodded. "Maybe we should call the sergeant and ask for his advice?"

"No way," replied Jonesy. "That would be opening us up to criticism."

"Well, then. Do you have any other ideas?"

"Let's drive around and see if we can find her home. We can start at Seventeenth and Tioga. Maybe her brother, if he really exists, is out looking for her."

"You are afraid to call the sergeant, but you're not afraid to drive out of the district without permission? May I remind you that if we get caught, we will get a trip to the Front, and we could even get fired!" The Front was the police disciplinary board, and the threat of "going to the Front" was instilled in them at the police academy and continued to be reinforced by the brass when the recruits arrived at their assigned districts.

"Let's give it a couple of hours to figure this out. I couldn't sleep at night if I had to leave her in the district cell, in the state that she's in, for anyone to make a joke out of her—even if she doesn't seem to realize it." Jonesy's voice didn't give away the plea, but Kate understood. They had to be better than the patrolmen who had left her at the hospital; Peaches was in their care, and she was their responsibility now.

As if on cue, police radio crackled to life. "2502 Wagon, are you in service?"

Jonesy responded. "2502 in service."

"2502, take the robbery in progress on the corner of Broad and Hunting Park Avenue."

Upon arrival at Broad and Hunting Park, Kate and Jonesy found that the "robbery" consisted of two drunken friends arguing.

Their mutual friends promised that they would safely deliver the combatants to their respective residences. Kate and Jonesy notified police radio that the robbery was unfounded and they would be back in service. Before the Twenty-Fifth District Sergeant resumed patrol in the command vehicle, he walked toward their wagon to sign their patrol log. Kate and Jonesy knew that if he noticed the naked woman sitting in the back, they would have a lot of questions to answer. They held their breath and prayed that Peaches would remain silent in the back of the dark wagon. She did.

Peaches accompanied them all night while the officers responded to assignments from police radio. In between radio calls, they drove up and down streets west of Broad, occasionally opening the back of the patrol wagon to ask Peaches if she recognized where she was.

At about six in the morning, Jonesy opened the doors to the wagon once more. A woman riding by on a bicycle stopped and asked, "Why did you arrest Peaches?"

Kate's response was quick and excited. "You know Peaches?"

The woman nodded.

"Can you tell us where she lives?" Jonesy asked.

The woman pointed to a house about forty feet from the wagon and said, "She lives with her brother, but he's at work. He doesn't come home until 7:30 a.m.."

"Can you get us some clothes for her?" Kate asked.

When the woman agreed, all three women were surprised when Peaches blurted out, "I want size 4 panties, a 32B bra, and a small top." When the officers finished dressing Peaches in some very tight clothing accessorized by the white sheet, Peaches looked down at herself and said, "I can't walk the streets like this. I'll get raped or even something worse."

Jonesy turned back to the Good Samaritan and said, "I'll pay you $20 if you keep her with you until her brother comes home."

The woman nodded and brought Peaches into her house for a hot breakfast. Officers Dominic and Jones drove back to the Twenty-Fifth District and reported off duty.

∾

That weekend, the Baker Street Five met for their training class and a BBQ. The August air was thick with heat and insects, but no one seemed to mind. Everyone contributed food and drink, including Lou, who volunteered to do the grilling.

Kate and Jonesy were organizing place settings on Jonesy's wooden picnic table when AJ and Sam opened the screen door and swept into the small backyard. With beer bottles as microphones, AJ and Sam started singing "Apple, Peaches, Pumpkin Pie" by Jay & the Techniques. They swiveled their hips and danced dramatically. Lou, Kate, and Jonesy started laughing.

Lou said, "If the police thing doesn't work out, you two might be able to make a career in entertainment. I get the impression that the song is an introduction to an interesting war story. Am I right?"

Kate recounted the legend of Peaches, with Jonesy occasionally interrupting to highlight specific details—like the panic they felt when the sergeant was signing their log.

"Can you believe our luck that all the catchment centers in the city were closed?" Kate said. "As my mother used to say, if we didn't have bad luck, we wouldn't have any luck at all."

Sam jumped in, unusually animated. "The wagon crews in the Thirty-Fifth were complaining about that as well. Apparently, a federal court decision forced the shutdown of Byberry, the psychiatric hospital. So all of the local hospital catchment centers are overloaded. They can't handle the volume." Sam paused. "That said, why didn't you call for a supervisor?"

Jonesy shrugged. "Sergeant Bell was not warm or friendly at roll call. He was pissed off at all of the car accidents the rookies have had with the squad cars. He told us that he was tied up with paperwork and we shouldn't call him unless we needed him for homicide. And then I thought they would use it as a criticism of women."

Lou nodded, but he said, "The sergeant doesn't get to tell you that. Sam is right. You should have called for him. What would have happened if your wagon was needed to transport a prisoner or a hospital case? You put yourselves in a potentially bad position. Next time, call the supervisor." Jonesy started to interrupt, but Lou continued pointedly, "The men would not have hesitated to make that call. You shouldn't either. And by the way, I know Bell. He might come across as gruff, but he doesn't like how the women are being treated. He's your ally."

Jonesy pursed her lips and nodded. "OK, I guess you're right, Lou. I thought we were doing the right thing by solving the problem ourselves. I was afraid she would wind up in a cell. She didn't belong in a cell."

"The road to hell is paved with good intentions," Lou said. "You need to follow the process. It will protect you. Bell would have thought the same way and wouldn't have arrested her either. He would have fought with the hospital to admit her. It's his job to figure it out—it's not up to you to put yourselves on the line by disregarding protocol." Lou stopped for a second to wipe beads of condensation from his bottle, deep in thought. He continued, "You also prevented awareness of a real problem in the city by not escalating it to the right people. The issue is more significant than Peaches. People are suffering, and if it isn't fixed, they will continue to suffer. And cops will get blamed because the system is broken, and bad things will happen."

The women were silent. Lou cleared his throat. "On the other hand, I get why you didn't trust the system to deliver the right result. You believe that, for good reason, you are on your own to figure it out. Bell is a good man, but he is focused on dealing with poorly trained rookies and having women on the job for the first time—all under the watchful eyes of the brass, the media, and the public. He was wrong to make you feel like you shouldn't call for him, and I am sure he would regret it if he knew what happened."

After a couple minutes of thoughtful silence, Lou looked toward AJ and Sam. "Do either of you have any war stories you want to share?"

AJ raised her beer. "Yes, we do. Sam made her first felony arrest!"

Sam cringed, and AJ laughed and continued, "Sam stopped a car based on flash information. The victim identified them. Sam arrested two doers and recovered the gun and the complainant's wallet in the back seat of the car."

"Good job!" Lou, Kate, and Jonesy said in unison.

"Yes, it was all going great until she called for a wagon to transport the prisoners," AJ said, trying to keep her laughter in check. "Police radio asked her if she had an apprehension, and Sam said, 'Well, they said they didn't do it.' She heard clicks across the radio band for a good thirty seconds."

Sam lowered her head to her knees in a doomed attempt to hide her scarlet cheeks. "I was trying to be precise," she said, her voice muffled but clearly miserable. "I said too much. I'll never live it down. When I went into Northwest Detectives to process the arrest, they had already heard what I said. The interview with the detective there, a guy named Wexler, was more like a condescending lecture about compromising the case with my 'thoughtless words.' He asked me if I'd Mirandized the doers before taking their statements. I tried to explain that I never questioned them, but he just cut me off. And then Detective Johnson piled on." Sam lifted her head to parrot Jack Webb. "'The facts, ma'am, just the facts.'"

Lou laughed, despite Sam's clear distress. "If I know you, Sam, you're losing sleep over this. Don't worry about it. They will remember it for ten minutes and then move on to pick on someone else. You caught the bad guys, and a few jealous cops tried to distract from the fact that you made the pinch. Every cop has those moments. Your mettle is being tested."

"I am the one who distracted from the arrest. It was such a dumb thing to say. All my radio communications in the future will be less than one sentence," Sam vowed.

"Just chalk it up as a lesson learned," Lou said, still chuckling.

"Speaking of saying the minimum, how are the swearing lessons going? Are you still blushing?" Jonesy said, laughing.

"I've made progress," Sam said. "A few of those words ran through my head when I was in Northwest Detectives." She looked a little sheepish. "They just didn't come out of my mouth."

AJ smiled and explained, "Sam hasn't finished all of her homework yet. I gave her a list of curses. She is required to use at least one word per shift and in earshot of someone else. She still hasn't mastered the F-word. She can't bring herself to say it aloud in company, but we are getting there."

Lou laughed so hard, he choked on his beer. "The four of you make me laugh until my chest hurts," he said. "I really enjoy spending time with you ladies, but I don't think you are going to need me much longer. You will all make your mark on the Philadelphia Police Department, and it won't be a blemish or a smear. You represent progress that was a long time in coming."

All smiles, the Baker Street Five raised five bottles of beer. "Here's to police work and catching the bad guys!" Kate said. "We have only just begun!"

Jonesy raised her bottle in another toast. "My toast is more like a wish. Here's to finding a man like Lou who is secure enough in himself to like a female cop!"

AJ offered thoughtfully, "I'd just like to go out on a date with a guy who doesn't feel threatened by a woman who carries a gun. Except for you, Lou, there don't seem to be many around."

"Sorry, ladies, I am a married man and much too old for any of you. Don't despair. There are lots of men out there who would be proud to know you. Look at Sam. She has already snagged her Prince Charming." Lou nodded to Sam, who momentarily stared through him and then smiled thinly. AJ knew how much effort Sam's feigned smile took.

"And here's to your bride, Loretta, for sharing you with us," Jonesy said, raising her bottle once more.

Lou laughed out loud. "Loretta is grateful that you ladies give her an afternoon free once a month."

The months rolled by, going faster as the women dove deeper into their work. By November, when chill breezes swirled brown leaves through the streets, they were markedly more confident in their work—but they still worried about the ways the brass didn't take them seriously.

Kate and Jonesy were still on the midnight-to-eight shift in the Twenty-Fifth. At roll call, the sergeant called out patrol car, wagon, and foot beat assignments; Jonesy was on the foot beat at 2700 Germantown Avenue.

During the briefing, the sergeant reminded the second-shift officers that it was against police department procedure to take a personal car to a foot beat, and it was also against procedure for women to ride in a patrol car with a male officer or be transported to a foot beat by a male officer. If no female officers were available to provide transportation to the foot beat, he said, public transportation had to be used. He didn't address what they should do when many SEPTA routes ran infrequently or stopped altogether after midnight.

Luckily, that night Kate was assigned to a patrol car, so Jonesy hitched a ride to Germantown Avenue with her. When Jonesy opened her door to exit the patrol car, Kate said, "Wait—why are you wearing that blouse coat? You know it'll go below freezing tonight. You going to catch a cold."

"I haven't been issued a leather coat yet," Jonesy said, pressing her lips together. "I've been calling the clothing committee procurement unit, but they told me they should get it in in the next two weeks." She hunched her shoulders against a stiff wind.

"Geez," Kate said, exhaling. "How are you going to keep warm? All the businesses will be closed. Maybe hang out by a phone booth? I'll come by when I'm not responding to radio calls if I can, but this location is not on my sector."

Jonesy nodded. "I appreciate it," she said. "But I'll be OK. I'm tough." She squared her shoulders and shut the patrol door, waving goodbye in one brisk movement.

That night, the temperature did drop below freezing. Except for two visits from Kate, when she could sit in the warm patrol car for fifteen glorious minutes, Jonesy walked up and down 2700 and 2800 Germantown Avenue like a toy soldier. By the time the sergeant drove up to the curb to sign her shift log at 4:30 a.m., Jonesy was numb from the cold. Bell glanced at her over the clipboard and frowned. "Where's your leather coat?"

"I was never issued a leather coat, sir."

Bell stared at Jonesy for a minute but said nothing. He lifted the handle to the radio transmitter and called for 2512 patrol car to meet him at Broad and Lehigh Avenue. Within three minutes, Kate had pulled up to the corner and walked to the driver side of the sergeant's car with her shift log in her hand.

"Officer Dominic, you will have a two-person car for the remainder of the shift," Bell said briskly. "Officer Jones, you are assigned to 2512 for the rest of the shift."

"Yes, sir," they said in unison.

The sergeant nodded and put the car into drive. Jonesy jumped into Kate's car and said, "Turn the heat to full blast. I can't feel my feet."

Their squad had the next day off. Kate called Jonesy, who picked up on the first ring.

"Hey," said Kate.

"What's up," Jonesy answered, before covering the receiver to cough.

"Oh no, you're sick?"

"Yep. Chills, fever, sniffles. The entire package."

"I'm snapping out on the captain next shift. It's a disgrace that they didn't issue you a leather coat yet."

"Thanks. I'm too sick even to think about it."

By the next meeting of the Baker Street Five, Jonesy had been diagnosed with pneumonia. She still didn't have a leather coat.

"There is no excuse for this," said Lou, exhaling disgustedly. "I've never seen anyone leave the police academy without being issued their uniforms and all of their equipment."

"The captain seemed surprised when I walked into his office and complained," Kate said. "I understand he had the corporal survey every district in the study group to see how many rookies are still waiting for uniforms and equipment. Jonesy wasn't alone. He called HQ and gave them a deadline to make sure everyone has their equipment and uniforms." Kate lifted her shoulder in a half-shrug. "It's a small victory."

~

Winter blew through Philly and brought in its wake a tentative spring and then blazing summer. But at the fifteenth meeting of the Baker Street Five, more than a year after they'd first gathered here, no one felt like celebrating. The four women sat around the picnic table in Jonesy's backyard, the silence like an oppressive heat.

"I spoke to Loretta," Jonesy finally said, sadly. "We should have guessed that Lou retired for a reason. I think he would have been happy to be a beat cop for the rest of his life. Apparently, he and Loretta knew he was living on borrowed time because of his heart. Loretta blamed shift work." Jonesy swallowed hard. "She was charming. I don't think it's all sunk in yet. She thanked us for helping him transition through retirement. She said we made him feel like he was still on the job and had something to contribute." Jonesy's voice broke as she added, "Lou and Loretta never had children, and Lou thought of us as his surrogate daughters."

Kate squeezed Jonesy's shoulder. "I am not surprised I am crying, because I can blubber like a professional funeral crier," she said. "But I've never seen you cry before. I think you let Lou into your heart. For all your bluster, you actually found a man you liked. You thought of him as your father, didn't you?"

"No," Jonesy said, swiping a hand over her face. "My father was a mean drunk. Lou was a much better man than my father. I think… it was like he made up for him, you know? In many ways."

Kate hugged Jonesy. "We're all sad, and so sorry for Loretta, but we're even more sorry for your loss," she said, her throat thick with tears. "I can't imagine how I would feel losing my parents."

Jonesy nodded quietly.

"Speaking of parents," Kate said after a few minutes, "my parents want to have you all over for Thanksgiving and Christmas. I think it would be a good time. You would just have to put up with a little force-feeding and endure unsolicited advice about everything you wear. My mother has been asking me to extend an invitation to her Thanksgiving and Christmas tables for the past couple of years. I think it's a good time to make it a tradition, starting this year. You haven't lived until you've tasted authentic South Philadelphia cooking."

Whenever you are in conflict with someone, there is one factor that can make a difference between damaging your relationship and deepening it. That factor is an attitude.

—William James

NINETEEN

Sam yawned as she opened the door to the one-bedroom apartment in Northeast Philadelphia. The four-to-midnight shift had been a long one, as usual, and it was late now.

"I am going away for a few days," Jeff Evans announced from the sofa. There were four empty cans on the coffee table in front of him, and a fifth beer clenched in his fist. "To Cape Cod."

"Why?" asked Sam. "What is in Cape Cod? Have you ever been?"

Jeff waved an arm hazily. "I need to get out of here," he replied with a bite to his tone.

Sam wearily placed her badge and gun on the kitchen table, glanced at the empty cans in front of Jeff, and sighed. "I am too tired for an alcohol-induced argument."

"You are always too tired. And I can't stand the uppity 'tude," Jeff slurred. "You don't approve of my drinking? Are you going to lock me up, tough cop that you are?"

"Jeff, please. Let's not do this."

"Let's not do what? Let's not let Jeff drink to relax? You hate it when I enjoy myself."

"If you mean that I don't like to watch you drink until you are loud and obnoxious, you're right."

Jeff moved surprisingly fast; in seconds, he was standing up, his hands locked on her arms, pulling her roughly toward him until their faces were inches apart. Sam was frozen, stoic, unable or unwilling to acknowledge the pain. Jeff's hands moved up to her shoulders and then settled on her neck, his fingers circling her throat. He slowly enunciated each word. "I said that I need to get away. You at least pretend to be a smart girl. What is so hard to understand?" His breath was hot and stinking of beer, but Sam still couldn't move. When she finally spoke, her voice was quiet but firm.

"Take your hands off me, Jeff. I don't care where you go."

"What's the matter, not the tough cop now? I am not even squeezing as hard as I want to," he said through gritted teeth. "You got paid. Where's your check?"

"Why?"

"Why what? You're my wife. Your pay is my pay. Oh, but I forgot, you don't know what it means to be a wife. A *real* wife is supportive and doesn't question everything a husband does. Everything with you is an inquisition, now that you have that job and your lesbian girlfriends. If I could afford it, I'd be out of here."

"How much would it cost me for you to leave and never come back?" Sam asked, her voice level but her tone acidic.

Jeff released Sam's throat and threw her against the kitchen wall. He staggered back and noticed her gun on the kitchen table. He picked it up and hit her with it, once, in the head. He dropped the gun on the floor and grabbed her wrists, pulled them over her head, and punched her in the midsection. Sam winced instead of crying in pain, and it only made Jeff angrier. He pushed Sam against the wall and thrust his face into hers, whispering each word. "You are not getting off that easy. Besides, I'm not so sure Gene and

Kathryn's brown-eyed baby girl would ever want to upset Mommy and Daddy, or mess up her Catholic good-girl image, by walking out on her husband."

Resisting the urge to wince in pain, Sam wrested her hand free and said, "I am going to bed." She kicked her gun into the bedroom and slipped away from his grasp. Once in the bedroom, she shut the door and picked up the handgun. She glanced around the room before sliding it under her pillow.

Jeff gulped the remainder of his beer and yelled through the door, "I'll be gone before you wake up."

I hope so, Sam thought, but she said nothing. She eased herself into bed, the exhaustion that had coursed through her now replaced by adrenaline. When Jeff entered the bedroom, she pretended to be sleeping. She lay facing the wall with her hand on the gun under her pillow, wondering what would have happened if he'd decided to use the gun for more than a piece of pipe to her head. She couldn't trust him around a gun when he was drunk, she knew. *We won't make it to forty years old, much less forty years married, if we keep this up.*

These thoughts circled around and around her head all night. Finally, mercifully, she heard Jeff get up, but she still waited until the door slammed shut before she crept out of bed and got into the shower. When she passed the mirror after her shower, she saw the bruises on her arms, neck, and chest, and she felt the bump on her head gingerly.

Sam grimaced and thought, sadly, *AJ was right. This will end badly. I guess it's up to me to determine how badly.*

With a long sigh, she stared at her image and said, "OK, Scarlett O'Hara, we will think about this tomorrow. Get your butt in gear. We have work to do today."

A true friend is one who believes in you when you have
ceased to believe in yourself.

—*Anonymous*

TWENTY

SERGEANT POWELL'S LAST INSTRUCTION AT ROLL CALL WAS for Officers Harris and Evans. "After you fuel the wagon, see the turnkey in cell room. You have two prisoners to transport to the Roundhouse for processing."

AJ nodded. "Sure, Sergeant." Sam bowed her head in agreement and walked to the parking lot of the building to inspect the emergency patrol wagon's equipment.

Once they had secured the prisoners in the back of the wagon, they drove south on Broad Street from Champlost Street to the Roundhouse. As they stopped at the light at Broad and Erie, they saw a Twenty-Fifth District wagon coming in their direction. When AJ noticed that Kate and Jonesy were in the wagon, she signaled them to pull over.

"Hey," said Kate, "we were going to meet after our shift at Jonesy's house. There's a rumor that they might have promotional exams in the next year. Let's talk about a study plan."

Jonesy's house after the shift, with plenty of pizza and company, was exactly what Sam needed. AJ and Sam gave them the thumbs-up and continued down Broad Street to the Roundhouse.

AJ noticed that Sam was unusually quiet. She wondered if it had to do with the bruises she was trying to hide on her arms and neck. AJ knew Jeff Evans was a first-rate creep, but this was the final straw. She had been watching Sam ignore her situation for too long. Sam needed a push.

After the shift, Kate, Sam, and AJ made their way to Baker Street. Sam stopped off at her apartment in Northeast to change, found a six-pack of beer in her refrigerator, and was grateful to have a reason to remove it from the apartment. AJ picked up a pizza on her way. Jonesy had burgers sizzling on the grill by the time AJ and Sam arrived.

"Beer and pizza to add to the menu," said Sam, holding up the six-pack.

"Schlitz?" said Jonesy. "When did you start drinking Schlitz?"

"It's what I had in the fridge."

"Oh, you took Jeff's beer. Isn't that against marital rules?" Jonesy said cynically.

"I paid for it in more ways than one," Sam mumbled.

Sam quietly listened as the conversation turned to the promotional exams. Jonesy and Kate didn't allow for a moment's silence, sharing everything they knew about the upcoming exams and their thoughts about how to prepare for them.

The next several hours were spent identifying books, courses, and a schedule. Finally, Jonesy needed a distraction and put the radio on. An Abba song, "Dancing Queen," was playing. AJ picked up a beer bottle, nudged Sam and handed her a bottle, and began singing and dancing to the song. Energized by the music, Sam felt her mood lighten.

"The two of you really do sing well together," Jonesy said. "Lou was right. If this job doesn't work out, you could consider singing with a band."

Sam laughed. "I am just a backup singer to our own Ms. Diana Ross. My audience tends to be the shower walls."

Kate said, to no one in particular, "Ray says music heals."

The remark brought complete silence in the room. Everyone stared at Kate. Kate knew the next question, so she answered it before it was asked. "I, um, met a guy."

"We heard. His name is Ray, apparently," said Jonesy. "I worked with you all week, and you never said anything?"

Kate smiled. "I wasn't sure I would see him again. I met him at a fundraiser for Ernie David's family. Ray has a group. He sings, and he plays piano and sax."

"I didn't see that coming," said Jonesy. "A musician? I figured you were more the attorney type."

"Well." Kate swallowed and said quietly, "He is also a lieutenant in research and planning."

"Hmmm, slipping in the part where he is the enemy as if it were an afterthought. Have you become a traitor to the cause?" AJ joked, laughing.

"Does he know you are a uniform cop?" Jonesy asked.

"Yes, and so far, he doesn't seem to care that I'm a lowly cop. Just like I don't care he's a boss. He called me when I got home today. We'll see each other next Friday night after I finish the second shift. His group is playing a gig in Northeast, and I'm going to meet him there."

To break what seemed like an endless silence, Kate added, "I wish you three looked happier for me."

"I am happy," Jonesy said. "Just a bit jealous and a little shocked. Given your standards, I'm thinking he must be a nice guy. And I'd give anything to meet a nice guy. Either the uniform or job seems to put men off."

"I'm sure it isn't your razor-sharp tongue," AJ teased. "Kate might have cracked the code. Dating another cop. Some may hate us, but they probably understand us. We might have half a shot at a real relationship. I've concluded it must be the uniform or the gun. It can't be me. Who could resist this?" AJ said as she dramatically waved her hand around her face and form.

Jonesy turned to Sam. "What do you think, Sam? Does it bother Jeff that you're a cop?"

"I'm not the person to ask about relationships of any kind. My career choice has not enhanced my marriage," Sam said with a hint of sadness to her voice. "Not sure about dating other cops. It seems to me like they tend to be less than honest about their relationships, maybe because they or we see how tentative life can be and convince themselves that lying about themselves is OK." Sam shook her head. "You know how it goes."

AJ saw her opportunity. "How bad are things between you and Jeff? I'm thinking Jeff might be responsible for the bruises you're trying to hide."

"Bruises? What bruises?" Kate inquired.

Not giving Sam a chance to answer, AJ explained, "Jeff uses his wife as a physical and emotional punching bag whenever he remembers what a loser he is. Sam tolerates it because she has had a lifetime of Catholic guilt plus her family and Jeff chipping away at her confidence and self-esteem. He convinces her that she deserves to be treated like a mosquito that needs to be swatted. Don't go home to him, Sam," AJ begged.

"I hope you don't expect to get paid for that psychoanalysis, Dr. Freud. I'm not going home to him. He is out of town. At least for the weekend."

"Good, perfect time for a talk. You need to get out of that situation right away."

Jonesy and Kate looked at the two of them, still deeply confused.

"What are we talking about?" Jonesy asked.

"Let's start with the bruises," AJ said, her voice rising with emotion.

"Again, what bruises?" said Kate, trying to catch up to the conversation.

Sam ignored Kate and Jonesy. "AJ, I told you I would handle my marriage."

"Yeah, you told me that two years ago, and I've watched you implode," said AJ. "I backed off hoping you'd figure this out once you saw domestic abuse on the job. How many women have you heard use those words? *I can handle it. I can figure it out.* What is there to figure out? It can be rarely worked out, and you know it. You need to get out of the relationship. It's dangerous for you."

"It is more complicated than that. It is both of our faults."

Kate interjected. "Sam, it isn't that complicated. You can't let someone hit you."

"This is a private matter. AJ, I don't appreciate you sharing my private life like this. Kate and Jonesy, you wouldn't understand. You've never been married."

"You're right. Kate and I have never been married, but my father was a violent drunk, and I hated my mother for not saving us from him," Jonesy said. The room was perfectly still and quiet. "Are you going to wait until he can make your children victims, too? Our job is to protect and serve. That includes yourself. Trust me when I tell you, he is not going to stop. He is going to get worse."

AJ nodded. "You may not have admitted it to yourself, but we all can tell you that you don't love the guy. Why are you doing this to yourself? Take control of your life and leave him. Each day you stay adds more complications. You don't want to wind up pregnant or hurt even more seriously than you are now. You have a gun. He might catch you off guard and hurt you with it. On the other hand, if he raises a hand to threaten you, you could tell him that you will blow his fucking head off his shoulders."

"He would think I was bluffing." Sam's voice was quiet.

"We will practice being convincing." AJ knew she had to be brutally honest. "Sam, Jeff is a drunk, he is abusive, but what you don't know is"—AJ took a deep breath—"he is also the worst kind of cheater. I didn't want to be the one to tell you this, but I saw Jeff in a Center City restaurant with your sister Beth."

"So? He just gets along with Beth. As a matter of fact, he gets along with Beth better than he gets along with me."

"Oh, that's for certain. But not in a good way. By the way, it doesn't say much for your sister either. There is no doubt they are… close," AJ said. "I wouldn't be surprised if she is with him now."

AJ's last sentence hit Sam like a lightning bolt. Her mother didn't have a driver's license, and she'd called Sam that afternoon for a ride to a funeral. She'd mentioned that Beth was away. Sam's mind raced; she felt a range of emotions surging through her and knew she had to get away from everyone so she could process it all.

Sam raised her hand in a stop gesture, and in a defeated voice, she said, "It's late. I need to get home." She walked out the door.

I do not want a friend who smiles when I smile, who weeps when I weep; for my shadow in the pool can do better than that.

—Confucius

TWENTY-ONE

DRIVING HOME, SAM THOUGHT ABOUT WHAT AJ HAD SAID. She realized she wasn't even upset about the possibility that her husband was having an affair. Did she secretly wish he would give her a reason to walk away? If she was being honest, the answer was yes.

Was she surprised about Beth? Maybe, but in retrospect, it was all there to see if she hadn't been so distracted. Beth had always coveted her clothes, her friends, her relationships with their six siblings, and even the love of their parents. Sam always thought that Beth would outgrow what she thought was juvenile behaviors that consistently cause conflict with family and friends. Sam remembered the time when Beth went home from school and told Mr. and Mrs. Kelly that Sam was going to be excommunicated from the church because Sam questioned whether a loving God would send unbaptized babies to purgatory.

Sam's older brother Denny, a seminarian at St. Francis Seminary, had coincidently come home for a visit and was able to calm the fears of the Kelly family, assuring them that Sam was not going to disgrace the family with excommunication. Sam was grateful that the whole dilemma resulted in the disapproval of her remaining brothers and sisters, the relief of her parents, and her penance of being grounded; she was given the sole responsibility for the Kelly's housecleaning for two weeks. Denny privately teased Sam that he was becoming a priest to save her soul.

In another instance, Beth told one of Sam's friends that Sam had gossiped about her father losing his job. Sam felt guilty that she had told her mother that Sheila's father had lost his job, not realizing that Beth had heard and spread the news around the Catholic parish generating embarrassment for the McHugh church. No one believed Sam when she denied that she spread the rumor, and Sheila never forgave Sam. Even holidays were eclipsed by dramas that were created by Beth but somehow never attributed to her. Sam guessed that Beth would have preferred being an only child. She was never good at sharing anything: not a room, not clothes, and not their parents' love and approval. Even when Sam married Jeff, Beth created a family drama because Sam asked her older and closer sister Reagan to be her matron of honor. After her mother interceded, Sam and Reagan decided that for family peace Beth would be the maid of honor, because family peace was the most important thing for an Irish Catholic family. It turned out on her wedding day, Beth made sure she made a grand entrance to the wedding by being late for the ceremony.

Why hadn't Sam seen the signs? When Beth and Jeff seemed to click, Sam thought it was because Beth...what? "Be honest with yourself," Sam said aloud to the empty passenger seat of her car. "Jeff seemed happier when Beth was around, and that made it easier for you."

Rather than feeling devastated by the betrayal, Sam unexpectedly calm and in control for the first time in several years. "Time to confront your future, Sam. Affair or not, it's time to make a decision and act on it. You can't do this anymore. There is no going back."

At five thirty the next morning, instead of showering and dressing for work, Sam remained in bed, staring at her bedroom ceiling. The phone rang, and Sam answered, knowing it was Jeff calling. Sam was only half-surprised to hear that he sounded like he was still drunk. Jeff's words were slurred, and she could almost smell his bad breath through the phone as he said, "You there? I'm staying an extra day."

"Feel free to stay an extra lifetime, Jeff. Is Beth with you?"

Jeff sneered. "Well, well, well, Philadelphia's finest is finally catching on. Must be all that studying for the detectives' test."

In a controlled voice, she said, "So, how long have you and Beth been a thing?"

With anger in his voice, Jeff responded, "What's the matter, Sam? You jealous your sister has what you don't?"

Sam ignored his attempt to get a reaction from her. "If you mean you, Beth can have you. She gets the booby prize. I won't be here when you get back. We never belonged together, and the sooner we part ways, the happier we will both be."

Jeff's next words were a warning. "Don't be stupid. You are going to be there when I get back, or I will make sure you regret it."

Sam's voice was equally threatening. "Oh, but I can, and I will walk away, and without a second thought. Hear me, Jeff. We are done. At this moment, I want nothing from you but a divorce. This divorce can be painless or painful, but there will be a divorce. And if you think I am going to let you play your silly head games with me— think again. If you lay a hand on me again, one of us will die…and it won't be me. I hope your love life works out for you. Goodbye, Jeff."

Sam hung up the phone and slumped against the wall, her hands shaking and her stomach churning with nausea. She wondered if Jeff had heard any trembling in her voice.

Moments later, the phone rang and rang. She didn't pick it up. When the phone stopped ringing, Sam used it to call to the Thirty-Fifth District and notify the corporal she would not be reporting for duty. As she struggled to organize her thoughts, she remembered Kate's solution to every problem.

"You're right, Kate. I just need a plan," she said to the empty kitchen. She sat at her table, a cup of coffee in hand, and gazed out the window. To anyone who didn't know better, she would have looked the picture of peace and calm. But her mind was working rapidly, preparing herself for the ways Jeff might retaliate—and how she would respond.

When Sam didn't show up at work, AJ was concerned and called Sam's apartment, but Sam didn't answer. Just as she was about to leave the district to go on patrol, the corporal told her that she had a telephone call. AJ answered the phone and was relieved to hear Sam's voice.

"Hey, AJ. I wanted to let you know that I won't be into work today, but everything is fine. I took your advice and confronted Jeff when he called me early this morning. I think he was still drunk, but he understood what I was saying. I told him that I was leaving him. Oh, and you were right. He admitted that he and Beth…you know."

"You OK?" asked AJ.

"I think so. I guess I feel relieved. I know it will be short-lived, though. Jeff won't make this easy. I need to get out of here before he comes back, and I am not going to tell him where I am going."

"Did he threaten you?"

"We threatened each other. It may be bluster on his part, but I'm going to lie low until he cools off. It'll be bad for a time, but eventually, I think he'll run out of steam. No matter what, I won't change my mind. He can't say or do anything to make me come back."

"I won't let you. Let me know what I can do to help, and please promise you won't keep anything from us. Don't let your guard down. He is dangerous," AJ said.

"You have helped. You made me face my reality. You are all good friends, but I appreciate that you made me face my future. Thanks."

"You can stay with me until you can find an apartment or someplace else to go," AJ said.

"Thanks, but Jonesy told me that she was thinking about renting a room in her house. I'm going to ask her if she would be interested in having me as a roomie. That is, if she isn't afraid of Jeff showing up one day. I'll speak with her and Kate soon. I packed up what I want to keep, and I'm leaving the apartment now. I am going to the bank and taking half the savings account before he gets back, and then I am going to call the police radio for a meeting with Jonesy. I called the Twenty-Fifth, and she is working a wagon with Kate. Catch up with you later." But instead of hanging up, Sam paused for a moment. "AJ?"

"Yeah?"

"Thanks again. I don't make friends easily. I couldn't design a better friend than you."

"You too," AJ said, sounding a little choked up.

Sam replaced the receiver with a gentle click. She sipped her cup of coffee and looked around her apartment. She felt a little pitiful; she didn't want a single memento from this apartment or marriage. She grabbed her bag, locked the door, and slipped the key under the door. As she walked to her car, she wondered if Jeff had been right— that she was a cold wretch. She didn't feel heartbroken or even sad. Instead, she felt like an elephant had been lifted off her shoulders.

After stopping at her bank, Sam drove to the Twenty-Fifth District to talk to Jonesy and Kate. She met Wagon 2502 in the 3600 block of Germantown Avenue, where they pulled into a parking lot off of Erie Avenue. They both looked surprised to see her.

"Hey there," said Sam, propping her elbow on the lowered car window and leaning out to speak. "I wanted to apologize for my rudeness last night. You were all right, and I was wrong. I faced my inner demons....and Jeff. He was on the phone, so I had more courage than I would have had in person. I left him, and I am now homeless. I was wondering—"

Jonesy immediately pulled her keys out and said, "You have a room at my house."

As Sam accepted the spare key, she said, "I was hoping you would offer, but I do come with baggage. I have no idea what Jeff is going to do, and there is a good chance there will be a confrontation. Can you handle that?"

"Oh, that would be his mistake. Let him come and try to start something. It would make up for a lifetime of anger that I've carried for abusive men. If he is stupid enough to stalk a house with two women who know how to shoot a gun, he can bring it on."

"Uh, OK. I don't even want to think about that possibility. You know, you can be a little scary with that gunslinger talk, Jonesy." Sam half-laughed. "Anyway, we can talk about finances when you get back to the house today, but I appreciate the offer. I can give you the details after work. Can I take the blue room?"

"You mean the Lincoln bedroom? Of course," replied Jonesy. "And I do intend to interrogate you as soon as I get home, but for what it's worth—you look relieved."

"You deserve to know exactly what happened. I promise to tell the truth, the whole truth, and nothing but the truth." Sam held her hand up as if swearing on a Bible.

As she drove to Manayunk, Sam thought about Jonesy's comment. She did feel relieved, for the first time in five years. Why did it take so long to make the decision? In less than twenty-four hours, she had changed the course of her entire life.

During the next week, Sam managed to avoid Jeff, probably because he didn't know where to look for her. Sam had never shared Jonesy's address, and her address and phone number were not published. Sam spent time with her parents but said nothing about leaving Jeff. At twenty-five years old, Beth still lived with their parents, but when Sam visited her parents, Beth avoided eye contact and left the house whenever Sam was there. Sam couldn't bring herself to talk about leaving Jeff with her parents or her other siblings, but she guessed it was only a matter of time before Beth would share her version of the breakup with the family—and then the games would begin.

There can be no life without change,
and to be afraid of what is different or unfamiliar is to be
afraid of life.

—*Theodore Roosevelt*

TWENTY-TWO

A WEEK LATER, SAM'S BROTHER CALLED AND ASKED HER TO meet him for coffee. Father Dennis Kelly, Sam's favorite brother, was a Roman Catholic priest. Except for Denny and her oldest sister Reagan, Sam had always felt detached from her other siblings. After Denny and Reagan came Leana, Danielle, Francis, Michael, and Beth, whose entire personalities seemed to be predicated on negativity; Sam's thoughts and opinions never aligned with them. And as a younger child, she always felt like target practice for their disapproval, which only accelerated when she became a cop. Denny and Reagan were always supportive and complimentary—in stark contrast to the others. The remaining siblings did not approve of Sam's choices. She didn't expect them to support her decision to divorce either.

Sam agreed to meet Denny at a diner by the King of Prussia mall located in the suburbs of Philadelphia. When Sam walked through the door, Denny was already at a table, drinking a cup of coffee.

"How's the job, Officer?" Denny asked as he stood to hug her.

"I am learning many new things. Please bless me, Father, I think I have found my true vocation." Sam laughed as she pretended to bless herself.

"You know, you are a very disrespectful little sister. I'm not sure I can give you absolution because you are never truly sorry."

"Yeah, but you like me anyway. Seriously, the job is good, and there are days I feel real purpose. But it's also a window to a world of tragedy, need, and loss."

"When I was chaplain at Philadelphia General Hospital, I saw some things that gave me nightmares. PGH was a training ground for understanding the dark side of life. It tested my glass-half-full outlook many times. There were days that the glass didn't just look half-empty. It seemed completely empty. There's no going back to your days of being innocent once you see certain things. Are you sure that you want to lose your innocence completely, Sam?"

Sam looked down at her coffee cup. "I am not so innocent, and I'm guessing you know it. Are we here so you can hear my confession?"

"I am always willing to hear your confession, little Sister," Denny said, winking kindly. "But today, I'd like to talk about you and Jeff."

Sam said nothing, but she felt a moment of panic about what Jeff might have told him. She folded her hands and placed them on the table. Knowing his sister, Denny reached over and patted her folded hands.

"Don't look so uncomfortable. Jeff called me and told me you had left him. Thing is, he thought I already knew, and I didn't say anything to change his mind. He also thought I already knew he had hit you and that you caught him cheating on you. He told me he was sorry, that things will change, and he wanted me to tell you to go back to him." Denny cleared his throat. "I am surprised he thought you had told me. He doesn't know you very well, does he? As a matter of fact, if I were to describe the one thing least likely to change your mind, it would be for Jeff to threaten you with a very public and dramatic spectacle."

Sam held her breath for a second, expecting Denny to mention Beth, but he didn't. Sam looked up from the table and said, "Denny, I know as a priest you're supposed to tell me to go back to my husband. I am sorry to be a disappointment to you, but I am not going back to him, and nothing you can say would convince me otherwise."

"First of all, little Sister, you have never been a disappointment to me. You are a strong woman and an independent thinker. Second, I have no intention of asking you to go back to Jeff. Remember, I'm your brother, too, and I would never want my sister to be a punching bag for anyone. And we were just talking about my time at PGH. I learned enough about domestic violence to never ask you to go back. I asked you to come here because I want you to know that I'm here to listen. I told Jeff that I would recommend family therapy to help you both through this, but I was clear that I would not try to influence your decision. I think he was surprised that I wouldn't help him."

"To be honest, Denny, I'm surprised, too."

"Why's that?"

"I thought it was your job to tell me to go back to him and work it out. Isn't that what the church tells you to do?"

"Where did you get that impression?"

"Twelve-plus years of parochial education and our brothers and sisters. Have you noticed their interpretation of religion? Pass judgment and undermine women who don't know their place or accept their lot in life. My responsibility is to live with my bad choices. Don't upset Mom and Dad and the proverbial apple cart. Do I have it right?"

"That's harsh, Sam, but I do forgive you—without judgment—because I've seen them in action. However, they really don't matter. You need to decide what is right for you. Mom and Dad will understand. They see, know, and understand more than you think. They will be concerned, but they will also trust your decision and support you."

"Very understanding of you, big Brother. I should've known that you would have my back." Sam smiled. "Let's change the subject before I get too emotional. How are things in your life?"

"That's the other reason I wanted to talk to you. I am...not so good."

"What? What's wrong, Denny?"

"I was diagnosed with Parkinson's disease."

Sam inhaled sharply. "What can I do?"

"Pray for me." Denny patted her clasped hands on the table once more.

When Sam told her parents that she had left Jeff, Gene and Kathryn Kelly never asked for additional details and never brought the subject up again. But as Sam predicted, the rest of the family found out through Beth. A few days before their father's birthday dinner, Reagan told Sam that Beth was busy sowing sympathy and support for poor Jeff, the victim of an unappreciative wife who was leaving Jeff behind because she was joining the feminist movement.

The night of the dinner, Sam prepared herself to face the firing squad. She braced herself by practicing her stone face. As expected, her siblings all vied to dominate the conversation. But it actually made it easy to stay in the background and watch. No one mentioned Jeff or asked why he wasn't present. Beth, a nursing home office assistant without a degree in medicine, ignored Sam, for the most part, but made a point of taking Sam's car keys and moving her car, chastising Sam for parking her car too close to the intersection and causing cars to struggle making the turn onto the side street. Beth speculated aloud that Sam parked that way because she thought because she was a cop, she could ignore traffic laws. No one, including Sam, said anything, and no one but Denny even looked at Sam. Denny just rolled his eyes. Beth, preferring to remain in the center of attention, then moved on to sharing her "professional opinion" and medical opinion of Denny's prognosis. The conversation continued until Gene Kelly became aware of the conversation and said, "It's my birthday. I get to decide what we talk about. How about those Eagles! I think this is the year we are going to go to the Super Bowl. I remember walking to Franklin Field to see an Eagles game the last time the Eagles won a championship. It was in 1960. My friend and I walked to Franklin Field in a snowstorm. Eagles fans have always been gluttons for punishment." Everyone except Beth laughed and the conversation lightened significantly.

In the kitchen, Marie Kelly turned to Beth and said, "Why are you always angry at your sister Samantha?"

Beth glared at her mother. "Why do you always defend her?"

In the meantime, Sam's sister Reagan asked Sam, "Why do you always stay silent when Beth attacks you in front of the family?"

Sam looked at Reagan and sighed. "The only thing it would accomplish is upset Mom and Dad. You know they hate when their children argue. I try to diffuse it by not saying anything at all. I also feel sorry for Beth. I think she is unhappy because of me."

After dinner and cake, Denny cornered Sam and whispered, "You owe me one, little Sister. Except for your little parking infraction, which caused a bit of a stir, I single-handedly created a diversion from questions, left-handed comments, and anecdotes about working women and failed marriages. They are all on their best behavior. But, for the record, rumors of my untimely death have been greatly exaggerated."

Caught off guard, Sam burst out laughing, and Denny joined her. Their brothers and sisters looked disapprovingly at Sam. Sam pretended to glare at Denny and whispered, "I hope in my next life, I come back as the first son in an Irish family. They are never blamed for anything."

"You are Catholic. We don't believe in reincarnation," Denny said with wink.

"Just my luck," she said, still trying to control her laughter. As Sam hugged her brother goodbye, she whispered, "I do owe you, big Brother. You can cash that chit in anytime."

Character does not develop in ease and quiet. Only through experience of trial and suffering can the soul be strengthened, ambition inspired, and success achieved.

—Helen Keller

TWENTY-THREE

SAM WAS WORKING SOLO IN THE 3515 RADIO PATROL CAR. She'd just reported on day shift when she, along with another sector car and a wagon, received a call to meet Homicide at Broad and Rising Sun Avenue. When she arrived on the scene, Sam spotted a squad car, an unmarked car, and a stakeout wagon. She gave a quick wave to AJ, who had been working a patrol car in the adjoining sector and had also been directed here. Homicide detectives were sharing pictures and giving directions as Sam joined the briefing. A detective from Homicide, Joe Rice, handed Sam a photo.

"We have a warrant for this guy. He is wanted for two drug-related homicides. According to our snitch, the nine-millimeter he used is supposed to be good for two additional homicides. We expect to find him, guns, and drugs in the house. Stakeout is going in first." Pointing to the wagon crew, Rice said, "The wagon crew is taking the alley. Evans, you take Eighteenth Street north of the location, and Harris, you take Eighteenth Street south. Keep an eye on the alley and the rooftops. Take your hand-held radios and switch to H band. If you see anything, let us know."

Sam nodded to the other officers and drove a few yards to her assigned location. As the stakeout crew exited the vehicle with M

16s, a crowd started to gather on the street. Several minutes later, Sam followed the gaze of two teenage boys looking up, and she saw a man running across a first-story roof, two houses away from his hideout. Sam pulled her .38 revolver and pointed to the man, and all of AJ's assorted profanities flowed out of her as she demanded he jump down from the roof. The suspect hesitated. Sam yelled her command, and the curses, again. Finally, Sam hollered, "You have one second to put your arms up and jump off the fucking roof, or you are a dead man."

A teenage boy in the crowd yelled, "That crazy bitch is going to shoot him."

Sam maintained her eye contact with the suspect, but she had to bite the inside of her cheek to keep a nervous giggle from escaping. A moment later, the suspect jumped from the roof into the bushes below. At the same time, the officer leading the stakeout, Gannon, ran toward Sam with an M 16 in hand to help her handcuff the suspect and take him into custody. From the rooftop, Officer McDevitt raised an arm with a handgun in his hands and yelled, "I found the nine-mil."

Holding the suspect in one hand and an M 16 in the other, Gannon nodded to McDevitt and then helped load the suspect in the wagon that had just arrived to transport him. Gannon looked over at Sam, nodding to her four-inch revolver. "Good thing he dumped that gun before you raised that .38. You would have lost the gunfight."

Still trying to calm her racing heartbeat, Sam could think of nothing to say but "Right."

Gannon continued, "That was the damnedest thing I've ever seen. Why did he jump off the roof do you think?"

Sam shrugged. "I don't know. You would need to ask him."

Gannon walked over to the patrol wagon, reopened the door, and asked him. "Hey, why did you jump?"

The suspect responded succinctly, "Did you hear that crazy bitch yelling at me? She threatened to shoot me."

AJ walked up to Sam and said, "Are you the crazy bitch?"

Sam nodded. "Seems so."

AJ continued, "Was that you whom I heard cursing like a sailor?"

"Yep."

"And did I hear you yell the dreaded F-word?"

Sam winced and stifled a laugh at the same time. "Several times—and at no point did I blush."

AJ winked and patted her on the back. "Well done, girlfriend."

Sam whispered low enough so that only AJ could hear. "Lucky, you mean. Must be Lou watching over me. He wants me to live long enough to get that gold badge. Bad guy tossed the nine-mil before I saw him. I definitely would have been outgunned. I think he thought I was just crazy enough to start shooting at him. How lucky am I?"

"I don't think you were dealing with Professor Moriarty here. I also think we still have an advantage. Men haven't yet figured just how far we are willing to go to defend ourselves. We have the upper hand until they figure it out: we may be crazy bitches, but we are not trigger happy."

"I won't tell if you won't," Sam said with a relieved chuckle.

Over the next several months, Sam settled into her new life on Baker Street with relative ease. Jonesy was easy to live with, especially since they worked opposite shifts, and the study group was always at Jonesy's house. Sam was content to stay on Baker Street, and Jonesy seemed to be happy to have her as a roommate.

Sam actually found herself excited about the new stage of her life and her new mind-set. While everyone noticed the change in Sam, only AJ pressed Sam for more information.

"Sam, we all see how different you are. It's like a weight has been lifted from your shoulders. I have two questions: Why didn't you leave him after he hit you the first time, and did you out your sister with your family?"

"The answer to both questions is the same. I hesitate to do things because I recognize my own contribution to my mistakes, and I try to avoid making things worse. I am the one who made a series of bad decisions that brought Jeff, and trouble, into my life.

I never told you, but at one of my low points with Jeff, I had a fling with a married man. It was one night and a mistake. I couldn't look at him again, and he either got the message or felt the same about me. I thought I could do it without regret, but it only made my guilt complex much worse. So, you see, I can't throw stones. I didn't do the right thing by marrying Jeff, I didn't handle my marriage the right way, and, truth be told, only his affair with my sister gave me the excuse I needed to walk away." Sam took a deep breath. "Besides, what do I get for telling anyone anything? The one lesson in life that I've learned is that people think what they think. And when it comes to my family, it's a no-win for me. I'm going to hold my tongue and save my energy for a more important fight. My focus now is on the job—study for the detectives' test, get myself promoted, and live happily ever after."

"Sam, I know you will be promoted to detective. But, girl, you need to believe you are a priority in your own life. You worry about and fight for everyone but yourself. Fight for yourself. You should be willing to protect yourself as much as you are willing to protect everyone else."

"Believe me, I will. I've turned over a new leaf in life. The past is behind me, and I am different from the person you met at the academy. The next time I need to fight for the right side, my challenger will experience a shitstorm the size of Hurricane Hazel."

"You go, girl," AJ said, laughing.

Although she was content in her new life, Sam was still a little surprised that Jeff hadn't made more aggressive moves to find or punish her. Sam figured he had had no success swaying her brother or her mother to his side, and she began to feel confident that the worst of it was behind her. She still worried sometimes about violence from Jeff, but mostly she felt relief over breaking out of the virtual prison she had created for herself.

Just when Sam was feeling that Jeff would go away quietly, he showed up as she was leaving.

On the other hand, Sam had confirmed her black sheep status in her family. Beth pretended to have the inside track on Sam and Jeff's breakup—if only they knew!—and she worked relentlessly to portray Jeff as the victim of Sam's emasculation.

On a cold, rainy day in Philadelphia, Reagan asked Sam to meet at the Penrose Diner.

"Thanks for having lunch with me today," Reagan said, hugging Sam before taking a seat.

"No problem, Reggie," Sam said, but the casual words were a question of their own.

Reagan looked at Sam and then looked away. "Sam, you need to talk to the family about your separation from Jeff. Beth is throwing you under the bus with your brothers and sisters and Mom and Dad. You need to tell your side of the story. They are all gossiping about you—especially the sisters-in-law, and it's not flattering. Our brothers' gossipy wives are loving it."

"I'm sure they are, but you know they always have. It's their chance to feel superior. I don't have anything to say. If I said anything, it would get twisted. There is little point to it. "

"You need to confront this, Sam. Can you at least talk to me?" Reagan asked.

"Reagan, do you remember the gift they gave to Mom and Dad last year for their anniversary?"

"The book of memories?"

"Yes, the one that Beth, Leana, and Danielle made with a few of the sisters-in-law. As I recall, everyone had input except for you, and me."

"They were very proud of their creative, from-the-heart, homemade gift," Reagan said with a slight tone of mockery.

"Yeah. It was a little weird that they needed to memorialize their stellar characters for Mom and Dad, but it was very telling about the personalities in our family. Did you notice they described themselves as kind, nurturing, selfless, religious, and caring? They described me as stubborn and opinionated. Although I wear both labels proudly, it says a lot about the way they see me. The condescending barbs they shoot my way at every family gathering about my choice or careers tell me all I need to know about how much they would be willing to believe me. While I don't like shift work, you might have noticed that I do like using it to get out of or leave family functions early."

Reagan said nothing; she simply nodded in understanding. Sam forged on. "Bottom line, Beth has their ears, and nothing I say would change their opinion of me or of the truth. I'd be wasting my breath, and it's none of their business anyway. The truth is ugly on a lot of levels, and my best course of action is to forget the past and move forward."

Sam paused. "However, since you are the only sister who sincerely cares, I will give you all the sordid details." She glanced over at the waitress. "You'll need another coffee and maybe something stronger," Sam joked.

*Every stage of life is unique. At any age and
stage of life, there are obstacles and opportunities, trials
and triumphs. Never allow the negative bring to
you to a sudden halt. Make the most of the positive
opportunities and stay positive.*

—Lailah Gift Akita

TWENTY-FOUR

Philadelphia, 1984

AT ROLL CALL IN THE TWENTY-FIFTH AND THIRTY-FIFTH
Districts, the results of the civil service exams were announced. Kate
Dominic would be promoted to sergeant; Sam Kelly would be promoted to detective. AJ and Jonesy scored pretty well on the detectives' exam but were not within striking distance of being promoted
in the first round; still, they were happy for their friends and planned
a dinner at Ralph's Italian Restaurant in South Philadelphia. After
toasting Kate and Sam's promotions, Jonesy and AJ announced that
they had submitted transfer requests to other areas of the city. In
addition to expanding their knowledge of the city, they wanted to
move on to something new as well.

"Looks like we have a lot to celebrate," said Sam. "Including the
fact that my divorce is final, and I will start my new job as Detective
Samantha Kelly."

"Good for you, Sam," said Jonesy. "How about you, Kate? Any
name changes in the wind? You can't stop talking about Ray Rossi.
When are we going to be formally introduced to your lover boy?"

158

"Eventually. If he has any gigs coming up, I'll get you invited. Actually, I told him AJ and Sam could sing, and he'd like to invite them to do a song with the band."

"As long as I'm the lead singer," said AJ.

"My singing career is limited to Baker Street and, for the most part, the shower," said Sam.

As they were enjoying the meal, a waitress delivered a bottle of wine to the table. The waitress told them that the bottle was compliments of a gentleman at the bar—specifically, for AJ. AJ looked over and caught the eye of a tall, athletic-looking man in casual clothes and a brown leather jacket that brought out his blue eyes and sandy hair. He raised a glass to her.

"Excuse me, ladies. I think I need to thank our beneficiary," AJ said as she stood up and walked to the bar.

"Uh-oh. I know him," said Jonesy. "He's a cop. A burglary detail guy from the Twelfth District. I don't know his name, but his nickname is Pretty Boy, and he knows it."

"He looks like a womanizer," said Sam. "I hope AJ sizes him up quickly and walks away."

"Good instincts," said Jonesy.

"He's met his match. She'll give him a run for his money, and have fun doing it," Kate said, laughing.

"I hope so. I don't like him already," Sam said, looking down at the table.

"You jealous, or are you having one of your feelings?"

"A bad feeling, Kate. But I have a bad feeling about most men these days. Don't pay attention to me."

"AJ is more man-savvy than the rest of us. She can take care of herself."

Sam nodded her agreement, but she couldn't shake the sense of caution rising in her.

After a few minutes, AJ returned to the table. Sam did not like the starry-eyed look on her face. Sam leaned over to the right and murmured so only Kate could hear. "I think this will be trouble."

"Maybe, but there is no stopping it," Kate whispered back, and then she piped up her voice to make an announcement to all of them. "We need to plan a road trip this summer. We have never gone to the Jersey shore together. Let's plan a trip to Cape May in late June or July, but not later than early August. A girls' weekend. What do you say?"

"I've never been, but I have heard about Cape May. I hear that Atlantic City is also a happening place. Want to see a show? Maybe the *Temptations* or *Sinatra*—would that cost a fortune?" asked Sam.

"I'm in regardless of cost. Anyway, you're getting promoted, you have the money," said Jonesy. But then she added, "We can't let our new jobs and different shifts cause us to lose touch. We are still the Baker Street Four. Let's do it up. I know a great bed-and-breakfast in Cape May. In the meantime, since my house is still centrally located, if we can coordinate some girls' nights out, my house is still available for a quick pizza or burgers." Then Jonesy, in her typical direct style, asked the question that had been hovering in their minds. "Not trying to rain on anyone's parade, but did you see the newspaper today, Kate?"

"Yes, I did, and I got a call from staff inspectors. I already volunteered to take a polygraph to prove I didn't cheat on the sergeants' exam."

"We would all vouch for you," said Sam.

"Why did someone name you, do you think?" asked Jonesy.

"Somebody stirring up trouble with bullshit stories, or somebody trying to keep Kate from finally celebrating a graduation from the academy," AJ said. "If I had to vote, I'd vote on bullshit."

"I think a little bit of both. No one believes a woman could legitimately pass a promotional exam, and someone guessed that Kate would be mad if the Philadelphia PD brass decided to skip another graduation ceremony because of scandal."

They all laughed.

Always trust your gut; it knows what your head hasn't figured out yet.

—*Anonymous*

TWENTY-FIVE

———————————— • • ————————————

ON HER LAST TOUR OF DUTY BEFORE HER PROMOTION, SAM was assigned to a Thirty-Fifth District patrol car on the four-to-midnight shift. AJ was assigned to a patrol car in the adjoining sector.

The shift began with a radio call for Sam to respond to a disturbance at a nursing home on Williams Avenue—the one, she realized, where her sister Beth worked. AJ, assigned to the next sector, decided to back up Sam, who announced she was on the scene. Sam was about to notify dispatch that the call was unfounded when she was approached by two women in the parking lot of the facility.

The first woman, well-dressed and in her forties, introduced herself as Brenda Neal. She was obviously distraught. The second woman, Leighann Jordan, was about forty years old, tall, thin, and was wearing jeans and a blue down jacket. She seemed like a force to be reckoned with. Neal was too upset to speak, so Leighann was the spokesperson.

Sam and AJ listened intently as Leighann related concerns about the death of Brenda's mother and several other nursing home residents. She insisted that the residents were dying in a similar fashion and at an alarming rate. They claimed to have raised their concerns with the nursing home staff, but they'd been treated like hysterical women. They were requesting a police investigation. Leighann handed Sam a list of six residents who had died over the past five months. Sam thanked her and looked at the list.

"So, these are all potential victims? Do you have any additional information that would help us get to the bottom of this?"

"Brenda and I are here all the time. Between us, we are here five out of seven days a week, and we knew most of these residents. They were not on death's door. Not even close. I am a retired nurse. I worked in a nursing facility, and the death rate there, where people were very ill, was significantly lower than the one here."

"Can you provide documentation of that?"

Leighann bit her lip. "No, that's just how I remember it. But I'm sure you can find out the statistics on death rates."

"OK," replied Sam, a little disappointed that they didn't have more solid leads. "Is there any other information you can provide?"

"Yes, something I realized today. I think at least four of the victims might have had dementia, and they had outbursts at times before their deaths."

"Why would that matter?" asked AJ.

Brenda Neal spoke up, choking on her tears. "We think that someone is killing them because they don't like old people who complain."

Sam and AJ remained calm and empathetic, but they both wondered what they could do to help these women.

"Thank you, Mrs. Jordan and Mrs. Neal," Sam said. "We are going to interview the person in charge of the nursing home, and then we will turn the paperwork over to the detective bureau. They will contact you and work with you."

"You believe us, don't you?" Brenda asked.

"I believe that asking the detectives to follow up is the right thing to do. Thank you for your time."

"Officer, my father is in this facility," Leighann said. "I've tried to get him to come home with me, but he refuses. I am going to keep trying either to take him home or move him to another facility, but it's hard. Please help me make sure that he is not the next victim. Because there will be a next victim if we don't do something about this."

Sam locked eyes with Leighann. "Mrs. Jordan, we are here to do what we can to sort this out. Officer Harris is going to take your personal information while I speak to the person in charge."

Roger Lang, the shift supervisor of Green Valley Retirement Community, wore a short-sleeved yellow polyester collared shirt tight across his protruding belly and a plastic pocket protector with four differently colored pens. At first, he was polite and friendly.

"Unfortunately, the director of the community is on vacation, but I would be happy to speak with you," he said. "Please, have a seat, Officer."

"No, thank you, I don't expect to take up too much of your time," Sam replied. "Detectives will be in touch for an in-depth discussion."

"Why detectives?" Lang said, alarmed.

"Mr. Lang, there is concern that several patients have recently died, and the cause of death was the same or similar."

"Officer, old people live here. Most people die of old age, so yes, the cause of death would be similar."

"Can you tell me who signed the death certificates for this list of residents?" asked Sam.

"Who gave you this list? Was it Leighann Jordan? This is a violation of our residents' privacy! Leighann is nothing but a know-it-all, a troublemaker. She doesn't know what she's talking about."

Just then, A. J. Harris walked into the office and nodded at Sam.

"I'm just trying to collect as many facts as I can to resolve the complaint," Sam said. "Can you provide the name of the doctor or doctors who signed the death certificates? Also, were any of the bodies sent to the Philadelphia medical examiner's office for any reason?"

Lang looked agitated, but then he seemed to decide that the quickest way to get rid of Sam was to acquiesce. "I should be able to check. Give me a minute," Lang said, walking into another office. When he returned, he was holding paperwork.

"Officers, the paperwork indicates that two different physicians pronounced these residents. All died of respiratory failure—very common with the elderly." He softened a little. "Look, you need to understand how emotional a family member can become when a parent dies. I am not being dismissive of Mrs. Neal, but this is an emotional time for her. The retirement community will cooperate with any investigation, but there is nothing amiss here. Mrs. Neal is a daughter, distraught over her father's death. Her emotions are being fueled by a hysterical and irresponsible woman making unfounded accusations. The turmoil that Leighann is causing for Mrs. Neal is disgraceful." Lang was visibly disappointed when neither Sam nor AJ nodded in agreement.

"Could I get a copy of the paperwork you're holding?" Sam asked.

"I am not sure I can share these documents, Officer"—he squinted at her name tag—"Evans. It is a privacy issue."

"It would be helpful for my report."

"OK. I guess, given the serious nature of the complaint, the director wouldn't mind."

"One more thing. Can you tell me how many patients have died over the past year?"

"I don't have that information, but I will pass on your request to the director when he returns on Monday. I assure you, however, there is nothing at Green Valley that is the least bit out of the ordinary."

"Thank you, Mr. Lang. I appreciate your help in sorting this out."

AJ and Sam left the building, returning to the squad cars in the parking lot.

"I cringe when I hear you called Officer Evans. Lose that name tag, Sam. Make a clean break," AJ pleaded.

"I'm not having a new name tag made. I won't need a name tag when I'm a detective. I won't need to wear a uniform," Sam said pragmatically.

"What do you think about this complaint?"

"I think they believe something is happening, and they might be on to something."

"Based on what?"

"My gut instinct, my feminine intuition, my Spidey sense—whatever you want to call it."

"Oh, shame on me thinking you're referring to some sort of evidence that I missed.

Well, that should make for an interesting conversation with the detectives. Good luck."

"I never said that Northwest Detectives is going to be happy to see me," Sam said, chuckling.

AJ let out a sharp whistle. "Oh, lookie here, the day is getting better. Your sister Beth and her friend over there are watching us." Sam held still, resisting the urge to jerk her head up, but AJ followed Beth's path. "Now she's making her way over. How can she face you, much less talk to you? And it seems we're gonna get some attitude."

"What are you two doing here?" Beth spat at the officers. "Is this your way of striking out at me, Sam? It wasn't my fault you placed your job above your husband and marriage."

Sam said nothing, just stared at Beth.

"Now that was an interesting way of greeting your sister. Your conscience bothering you, Beth?

And for the record, we're here on police business," AJ said.

Beth raised her voice. "The police are not needed here. Leighann Jordan is a troublemaker, and she is manipulating Brenda Neal into making something out of nothing. End of story. You can leave."

"Now that you have voiced your opinion, you can continue on your way," Sam said in an even tone of voice without looking up from the form she had begun preparing.

"I know what you're up to. You and your friends always causing trouble!" Beth said, sneering and walking off in a huff.

"OK. That was just weird," Sam said. "What was with the grandstanding and the emotional outburst?"

"I don't care for her dramatic outbursts. Does she work here? What does she do?" asked AJ.

"She works here, but I'm not really sure what she does. I can't figure out if she is a secretary, a nurse's aide, or the physician in charge. She never went to college, but she has somehow convinced the family that she is a medical expert."

AJ pursed her lips and thought for a moment. "I think she has gone off the rails with paranoia. She's been wondering how you would strike back for her violations of the sister's code. You've driven her crazy, waiting. Now she thinks you will get her through her job. Honestly, if you look at it that way, you couldn't have planned a better revenge. You avoid one of those guilt trips you always take, and she thinks she has the devil at her heels. You win."

"A hollow victory. I can't help but feel that Jeff was the manipulator, and she was more of a victim."

"I might buy that explanation if I thought she was the least bit ashamed. Forgive me if I offend your sensibilities, but your sister is a greedy bitch. She went after him because she thought you wanted him. She hoped she could take him away, along with your self-esteem. Jeff went after her because he's a misogynist who got his rocks off boffing his wife's sister. Christ, I can see that she is just plain jealous of anything that you have. She hates Kate, Jonesy, and me because we are your friends. I think it's because you are happy when you are with us. She hates you being happy. You should tell your family the truth about what she did."

"To what end? For a moment of satisfaction? Truth be told, Jeff and Beth gave me the push I needed to see it all clearly—to realize exactly what I needed and wanted. Anyway, except for Denny and Reagan, I have nothing in common with the rest of them. Believe me, the whole thing would be used to trash my character even more. No, I'm not going there."

Twenty minutes later, Sam walked into Northwest Detectives to turn in her report to the deskman. Al Stinson, an older, plump, balding, ruddy-faced detective with glasses, smiled at Sam when she said, "Hey Al, I have an interesting one."

"Sam, all your reports are interesting. They're like reading a novel. What's up?"

As Sam was relaying the details, Detective James Wexler walked over to the deskman and ripped the report from his hand.

"I'm next up on the wheel, so this is my job. I'll handle this." Taking a moment to review the report, Wexler continued, "It looks like Officer Evans's promotion is going to her head. Trying to impress the brass with your detecting skills? This is just a make-work pile of crap, but now that you made a report, I'll need to follow up." Grabbing his coat and the keys to a squad car, he added, "Don't code this yet, Al. I'll interview the facility and the crazy ladies. I'll probably make this case an unfounded minor dispute."

Sam looked pleadingly at Stinson. "What did I do to him? Did I somehow offend him in a past life? This case is legit. Can't you assign the case to someone who gives a darn?"

Surprised, Stinson replied, "You know the process, Sam. Wexler is the assigned detective. He was up next on the case wheel. That's the way investigations are assigned. As far as what's up with him goes—he's just mad because you are getting a promotion. He thinks the women were given the answers to the promotional exams."

"I'm sorry he is an idiot. It's a shame Mrs. Neal will pay the price for his stupidity."

Wexler glared at her and snapped, "I'm done with you. Put your patrol car back into service, you uppity bitch."

Stinson froze, Sam glared at Wexler, and he glared back. But Wexler was the first one to flinch. Glancing away and walking out of the squad room, he said to no one in particular, "I'm going on the street to do my interviews."

Stinson puffed out a breath of air and said, "Sorry about that, Sam. If it helps you understand him, he has a sick child and a lot of medical expenses. He has been trying to get to Homicide for over a year now, hoping to make more money in overtime to pay his bills. He thinks a woman might be going to Homicide, and he'll lose another chance. You and your upcoming promotion are hot buttons for him."

"I'm sorry, Al, but that doesn't really help. I don't care what he thinks about me, but his personal situation should make him more empathetic to the complainants. I almost wish one of the men had received the radio call instead of me. Wexler has already drawn his conclusions before he's asked a question. He's just going through the motions now, and he'll close the case simply because he hates me. That is just wrong."

"If he thinks it has merit, he will work on it. Especially if it means he gets to impress Homicide."

"If he doesn't think it's an obvious homicide, he won't put any time into it, though, will he?"

"No, Officer Evans. He won't."

Two weeks later, the complaint against Green Valley Retirement Community was coded "unfounded" by Wexler.

Every experience, good or bad,
is a priceless collector's item.

—Isaac Marion

TWENTY-SIX

SERGEANT KATE DOMINIC REPORTED TO HER NEW ASSIGN-
ment in the Fourteenth District in the Germantown-Chestnut Hill
section of the city an hour early. Kate was eager to introduce herself
to the captain, the lieutenant, and the sergeant who would share her
responsibilities as a shift supervisor.

Dressed for the part and brimming with confidence, Kate held
her first roll call. After inspecting the squad as they stood at attention, Kate read the directives, white papers, and relevant flash information. Before dismissing roll call, Kate made her first mistake. She
paused and asked if anyone had any questions. From somewhere in
the back of the line, an officer yelled, "Is there any truth to the report
in the newspaper that you are one of the 'dirty thirty' that cheated on
the sergeants' exam?"

Caught off guard but quickly recovering, Kate responded, "In
the past five years, you guys wouldn't share a coffee. Why would anyone share the answers to a test with me?" The twenty officers standing at attention and the shift lieutenant all roared with laughter. "For
the record, I graduated magna cum laude from Temple University,
and I don't cheat."

Lieutenant Simpson, the shift commander, tipped his hat. "Nicely done, Sergeant Dominic. You will do fine." As the officers left roll call, most of them walked up to welcome her to the district.

In Center City Philadelphia, Sam showed up at Central Detectives at Twenty-First and Pennsylvania for her first shift as a detective. After meeting her new captain, Sam received a brief orientation from her supervisor, Lieutenant Mike Clark; her sergeant, Johnny Johnson; and the deskman, Mike Mullen. Clark told her that she would be partnered with a couple of experienced detectives until he believed she could handle cases on her own. An hour later, she got her first chance to prove her worth. Mullen told her that she and Detective John Hogan were assigned to the burglary of a restaurant on Race Street at Third.

Detective Hogan was in his late fifties, six feet tall, broad-shouldered, and with a nose too large for his face. The length of his nose was accentuated by the Stetson hat he wore indoors and out, and Sam thought she could smell the faint whiff of alcohol on him. He reminded Sam of a character out of a Damon Runyan novel. Hogan nodded to her when they were introduced, but he said nothing. Sam was happy with that; she didn't want to make small talk or discuss herself anyway.

Hogan kept up his silence during the fifteen-minute ride to the restaurant. At the crime scene, the manager showed them to a room where the safe had obviously been broken into.

Hogan turned to Sam. "Detective, what's your next step?"

"I'm going to call the mobile crime unit to process for fingerprints," Sam said. Hogan nodded. Sam then turned to the employees. "Look around. Is there anything here that you don't recognize?"

The employees, hovering in the doorway, scanned the room quickly. "Over there," said the barmaid, pointing to the floor about a foot from the safe. "I've never seen that briefcase before."

None of the others had, either. When Sam knelt and popped open the unlocked briefcase, she found a screwdriver, a sweatshirt, and a pair of sweatpants. She turned to the barmaid and asked for a brown paper bag from behind the register. As Sam lifted the pants from the briefcase, a laundry tag scratched against her arm. "Who has their sweatpants dry cleaned?" she said, not realizing she was speaking aloud.

"Good point," Hogan said. "What are you thinking, Detective?"

"Can laundry tags be traced? I'm sure a laundry would remember someone who dry-cleaned their sweatpants."

"I'm sure they would. Maybe you should look into it," Hogan said, and he smiled. Sam scratched a reminder in her notes to contact local dry cleaners.

When they returned to Central Detectives, Hogan introduced Sam to two of the detectives on duty: Greg Locke and James Wexler. Locke gave her a friendly smile, but Wexler barely nodded.

After they walked back to Hogan's desk to debrief, he asked, "You already know Wexler, Kelly?"

"Yes. Is he visiting from Northwest?"

"No, he was transferred to Homicide last week."

"Lucky me," she mumbled, barely audible, but Hogan heard her.

"So, you have a history with Wexler?"

"I wouldn't call it a history. More like a mutual disrespect."

"Is this going to get interesting?" Hogan asked, his eyebrows arching under the Stetson.

"Hope not," Sam replied, her lips pressed. She felt a tension headache beginning to build behind her eyes.

Sam grabbed the daily crime summary sheets for the past month and scanned the room, looking for a place to sit. She noticed something odd: the squad room didn't seem to have enough chairs or typewriters for all of the detectives.

She turned to the detective she'd just met. "Hey, Locke. Is there assigned seating?"

"First come, first serve. If you need to process an arrest or interview witnesses, anyone will give up their seat and typewriter, though. It's busy now because many of the detectives stay here and catch up on paperwork while waiting to be called to testify in court. It thins out as they get called to court."

Sam nodded and turned to the file room. She found a broken chair in the corner and made herself comfortable, reviewing the summary sheets and taking copious notes about several Center City restaurant burglaries.

An hour later, the deskman found Sam and handed her a police report. "You have a robbery arrest to process. Officer Grafton over there is from the transit police—he made an arrest on the Broad Street subway. The wagon crew left the suspect in room three."

Sam walked back into the squad room and saw an open chair in front of an unused typewriter with a folded newspaper lying atop it. She found another chair nearby and scooted it over for Grafton. They both sat down, and Sam slipped the newspaper to the floor so she could begin typing their interview. But only a few minutes passed before Wexler charged into the squad room and right up to her.

"Get out the fuck out of my chair and away from my typewriter!" he bellowed at Sam.

Sam was stunned, but she quickly recovered. "I believe the chair and typewriter belong to the City of Philadelphia, and I need to process an arrest," she said without rising from the chair. "If you were sitting here, it looks like you were reading a newspaper. I know you are new, too. I understand that it's first come, first served—unless you are interviewing witnesses or processing arrests, which takes priority. And that's what I'm doing."

The squad room was utterly silent. Greg Locke winced and hoped Sam didn't think he'd set her up.

Wexler put his hands on the typewriter as if to take it away, and Sam reached her arms around it to keep it in place.

"Get your fucking hands off my typewriter," Wexler said, his voice an undisguised threat.

"You get *your* fucking hands off this typewriter—which, as I said, belongs to the City of Philadelphia and which you are not using. I need it to process an arrest."

Wexler lifted his right hand from the typewriter and formed a fist, but Locke grabbed his arm. "The lieutenant just called for you, Wexler. He wants you in the front office."

Wexler glared at Sam and then walked out of squad room. Locke quickly picked up the phone and called the lieutenant's office. After hanging up the phone, he walked over to Sam. "I'm sorry, Kelly. Wexler just transferred in last week, and I didn't realize he would go this far. I wasn't trying to set you up or anything like that."

Sam shook her head, still trying to hold on to her bravado but trembling inside. "I know you didn't do it on purpose. I am very familiar with Detective Wexler. I'm guessing you might have saved a few of my pearly whites just now, so thank you." Sam paused a moment and then asked, "Did the lieutenant really call for him?"

Locke seemed to refocus his attention on a report. "Of course he did. Listen, Kelly, I'd steer clear of Wexler until his ego recovers."

As if nothing had happened, conversations picked back up in the squad room, and Sam continued interviewing the officer, the complainant, and then the suspect from the subway robbery. The suspect was eighteen but still in high school. As Sam advised him of his Miranda rights, she explained his adult status. To her surprise, the suspect—now the defendant—wanted to give a statement to her. He seemed to trust her. Sam listened intently, never breaking eye contact, and then she asked if she could type up his story so they could both agree to what he said. The defendant nodded.

A few feet away, Hogan turned to Locke. "She's interesting, isn't she?" he said in a low voice. "Looks like a kitten and acts like a tiger. She did an excellent job processing the burglary this morning, even if she's wasting her time trying to find burglars. Too many people crimes to worry about property crimes. She has good instincts, though, and she's gutsy. Maybe a little crazy for standing up to Wexler. He'll be gunning for her now. I can see the signs."

"Not on my watch, John," Locke said, his voice quiet but firm.

Hogan chuckled. "Agreed. I like her, too, and she has a nose for the job. I'll be damned if I see Wexler torment her."

The confrontation behind her, Sam focused on her work. Sam visited her local dry cleaner, showed them the laundry tag from the burglary, and asked if it was traceable. The owner recognized the tag type and told Sam that the tag distributor was based in New Jersey. When Sam called the distributor, she learned that they worked with one dry-cleaning shop in North Philadelphia.

Sam hung up the phone in the squad room and turned to Hogan. "I traced the laundry tag, John. Do you feel like going on a road trip with me to North Philly?

"Wish I could kid, but I have an arrest to process."

Greg Locke stood up. "I'm in. I've never traced a laundry tag before. I'd like to see how it's done."

"Oh," Sam replied. "Well, thanks. I appreciate the help."

Mr. Lee, the owner of the dry-cleaning shop at Twentieth and Columbia, was Korean and spoke little English, but he worked through the language barrier and pointed the detectives to a store-room filled with boxes. As Sam's eyes traveled over the forty boxes in the room, she turned to Detective Locke with an apologetic look on her face. Locke was chuckling.

"Ugh, sorry, Locke. I didn't think it would be this much manual labor."

"No problem, Kelly. This is why they call detectives flatfoots. You've got to pound the pavements for the clues."

"Is that true? I thought that's what they call beat cops."

"Does it sound true?"

"Not sure."

"Just go with it," he said as he took off his jacket and rolled up his sleeves. He pointed to some of the boxes. "I'll take this side of the room, and you take that one."

After three hours and a little conversation, Sam declared success. "I found it! I think this is it. I have a name and address."

"Where's the address?"

"Camac Street—not too far."

"OK, let's thank Mr. Lee and ask him to give us this paper-work. We can drive by and see what the place looks like. Then we can go to the records unit and see if we can connect the name with a criminal record."

When Locke and Kelly returned to Central Detectives, Locke was grinning. Hogan looked up. "I'm guessing that grin means that you two had a successful road trip."

"Kelly hit the jackpot. We connected the laundry tag to the dry cleaner, found a name and address, and connected them to an arrest record. And the cherry on top: the fingerprint unit gave us a tentative match on a print from a second job that matches our guy."

"So, there are other burglaries?" asked Hogan.

"Kelly searched the summary sheets and microfiche and identified thirty restaurant burglaries in Center City in the past nine months. This guy is a one-man crime wave. We had his picture printed up to show the employees at all those restaurants. This is going to be a nice job. The captain is going to be happy."

"Well, let's get him in here before the special investigations unit hears about it and takes credit. Need any help pulling together the affidavit of probable cause for the arrest warrant, Kelly?"

"I'll take any guidance you can give. This is a first for me, and I want to do it right."

"First thing tomorrow we'll type up the affidavit for a body warrant and pick him up as soon as we can. While you're getting the warrant for the two cases, I'll go show his photo at the other restaurants. This is good work. Been around a long time, but I've never seen a case solved with a laundry tag before."

As predicted, Captain Callahan was very interested in the case—so interested, in fact, that he requested special investigations take the case. They were experienced at taking confessions and clearing multiple cases, he said. Although Sam was fine with the captain's decision, Hogan was not. He managed to convince the captain that he could have a crack at a confession if the special investigations unit was unsuccessful.

James Butler, also known as the Epicurean Burglar, was arrested for two counts of burglary. Butler agreed to provide a statement to the detectives, but even after several hours of questioning the special investigations team was no closer to connecting him to the crime spree.

Hogan decided it was time to take over, and he sent special investigations on a break. "Kelly, why don't you offer our guest something to eat or drink?"

"Sure, Hogan." Sam opened the door to the interrogation room and said to Butler, "This has been a long day for you. Would you like a soda?"

"Yeah, I am thirsty."

Sam grabbed a soda from the break-room refrigerator and then settled down into a chair across from him. Locke followed her into the interrogation room and stood quietly in a corner with his arms folded.

"I was reading about you," Sam said quietly—more admiring female than Philly cop. "You have an extensive history of burglaries for your age. Did we ever recover the piece you stole from the Philadelphia Museum of Art?"

Butler smiled at her. "Nope."

"You must be good at your craft. Are you the best?"

"I think so."

"So, did you hide in the same place in all of those restaurants until they closed? That takes patience."

"No. Sometimes it was a restroom, sometimes a closet. I always looked for a drop ceiling."

"You are a real cat burglar, aren't you? Just like Cary Grant in *To Catch a Thief.*"

Butler laughed. "I guess so." Pointing to Locke, he said, "He doesn't look like Inspector Clouseau."

"No?"

"No, he looks like a serious detective."

"Yes, well, I think you're right." Sam glanced over at Locke, smiling. "I think he sees himself more as Cary Grant than Peter Sellers. Can we talk about all the restaurants you did?"

"Didn't I do that with the other detectives?"

, "You were being too clever for them. I think you frustrated them."

"Well, I gave them enough information to figure it out."

"I don't think we're as smart as you. We'll need more information to figure this out."

"Nope, that would make it too easy," Butler said, smirking. Sam said nothing; she just sat and looked at Butler thoughtfully, her head cocked slightly to the side—still playing at impressed. The room was quiet for a full minute, and Butler added, "Are you disappointed, Detective?"

"Of course, I'm disappointed. I've never met a cat burglar before, and I wanted to hear the whole story. I hoped you could tell us which ones you did and how you did them."

"I won't tell them which ones I did, but have your boys come in with the list, and I'll tell them which ones I didn't do."

"The ones you didn't do?"

"Yeah, you are right. I don't think you guys will ever figure it out unless I help you. I'll show them which ones I didn't do, and you can figure out the rest of the story."

"OK, I'll be back."

After leaving the interrogation room, Sam called to Hogan. "Your turn, John. Do you have the list of burglaries? He'll point out the ones he didn't do."

"What?" Hogan asked.

Locke shrugged his shoulders at Hogan and said, "Sam makes things interesting, and this is one for the books. He is willing to point out the ones he didn't do, and we get to figure out the rest."

Locke and Hogan walked back into the room with a list of burglaries. Hogan introduced himself and said, "OK, before we begin, I have one question. Why do you get your sweatpants dry-cleaned?

∾

The next morning, AJ met Sam at her car in the parking lot at Central Detectives. Grinning from ear to ear, AJ handed Sam a copy of the *Philadelphia Daily News*. "Kate will be proud of you. Nice photo!"

Sam looked at her, confused, as she looked at the paper. "What are you talking about?"

"Front page, girl. You and Hogan are Wonder Woman and Batman!"

Sam scanned the article quickly and winced. "How did this happen? How did they get my picture? It doesn't mention Locke. He's going to think he was cut out." On cue, she heard a voice behind her.

"Morning, Detective Kelly. I understand your press secretary brought you the front page."

Sam squeezed her eyes shut before turning around to face Locke. "Sorry, Locke, I didn't know anything about this. You should have been acknowledged in this article."

Locke laughed. "No, this was all your show, Kelly. I was happy to be along for the ride. Hogan has adopted you and wanted you to get the credit for the case. He knows all the reporters that hang around headquarters. I'm glad he did it—you made all of us look good. It's a good day for all, including the captain and the inspector."

Locke, knowing AJ from her interactions in Central Detectives bringing paperwork and prisoners to the Detective Division, turned to AJ. "Nice seeing you, AJ. How is business in the Sixth District?"

"The crime in Center City is very different from Northwest Philly. I hope I am there for only a short while. My goal is to follow in my friend's footsteps and get promoted to the detective bureau."

"Worthy goal, big shoes."

Sam blushed. Locke waved goodbye and walked away.

"I thought we had solved the blushing, Sam," AJ joked, and then she glanced over at Locke's retreating figure. "Locke is a nice guy, and not bad to look at, either. I think he likes you. Word on the street is that he is getting a divorce. You might want to consider—"

"Stop. Locke is a coworker. The last thing I need is another relationship that doesn't end well, and with a coworker would be the worst. Besides, 'getting a divorce' isn't the same as 'divorced.' Look, I need to get going. Thanks for the heads-up."

As Sam walked into the squad room, the deskman called to her. "Kelly, you have a call on line three."

Sam nodded and picked up the phone. "Detective Kelly."

"Hello, Detective Kelly, this is Leighann Jordan. We met several months ago. I thought your last name was Evans, and I've been trying to contact you. I saw your picture in the newspaper this morning and realized I couldn't find you because your last name is Kelly and you're a detective now."

Feeling awkward, Sam said, "I remember you, Mrs. Jordan. How are you?"

"First I wanted to tell you congratulations. Sounds like you broke a big case. I knew you were a smart cookie the first time I met you."

"Nice of you to say. Thank you."

"But now, you asked me how I am. My father died, and I think he was murdered."

"Why do you think that, Mrs. Jordan?"

"I made the complaint, and they wanted to get rid of me, so they killed him. I would like to talk to you about it, but I can't right now. Can we meet next week?"

"Mrs. Jordan, if you think there was a murder, I need to connect you with the Homicide Division. They will investigate. There may be evidence they need to collect, and the sooner they can figure that out, the better."

"I tried to tell them. They wouldn't listen. They think I'm crazy—that Detective Wexler convinced them I'm crazy. Please help me. I know I'm right. Would you please hear me out?"

Sam caught a glimpse across the squad room table at Wexler, who seemed to be eavesdropping on her conversation. She knew the risks of stirring the pot—she could be reassigned, or she could lose the job she'd fought so hard to get. But she'd wanted this job so she could help people, not so she could turn them away when they needed it the most. She couldn't push Brenda Neal's face out of her mind, the way she had looked that day in the parking lot. Sam thought about how it felt to have men tell you you're crazy, you're way off base, or you're overreacting.

Into the phone, Sam said, "Of course, Mrs. Jordan. When and where can I meet you?"

~

Sam paced back and forth across the squad room, thinking about her conversation with Leighann Jordan. Watching her, Locke said, "You could probably bend spoons with the intensity of your thoughts." Sam nodded but ignored the comment and grabbed her coat. Startled, Locke said, "I was kidding, Kelly. No reason to leave."

Sam shook her head. "I am going on the street. I want to do some research and thought I'd walk to the Philadelphia Main Library." Locke was intrigued and asked, "We did pretty good with the laundry tag investigation. Mind if I tag along?"

"It would be at your own risk. This case wasn't assigned to me."

"Sounds interesting. You can tell me about it as we walk."

As they walked to the library, Sam told Locke about Mrs. Jordan and her theory—and her frustrations with Wexler. Locke saw the determined look in Sam's face. She was on a collision course with Wexler again, and she didn't care.

When they arrived at the library, Locke asked, "So, what are we looking for?"

Sam pursed her lips, paused, and then said, "First, I want to understand the side effects of two drugs. The first drug is called benzodiazepine and the second is fentanyl. In particular, I'm looking for their effects on the elderly. When I spoke with Leighann Jordan this afternoon, she mentioned rumors that several doses of these medications have gone missing at Green Valley. Second, I want to research mortality rates to see if there are statistics to back Leighann's suspicions. Divide and conquer?"

"OK," said Locke as he looked through the card catalog. "There's something called the *Physicians' Desk Reference* that might help with your question about the drugs. I'll look it up. You take the easy part," he said with a wink, "the analysis of mortality rates. Happy hunting."

After several hours of research, the detectives walked back to Twenty-First and Pennsylvania from the library.

"Thanks, Locke," Sam said. "How did you know about the physicians' reference book?"

"Inside information. My mother works for a pharmaceutical company. Actually, I could give her a call. She might be able to provide some additional insights into the drugs."

Sam nodded. "What do you think, Locke?" she asked. "Do you agree that Mrs. Jordan might be right?"

"Tough call," said Locke. "I agree it might be worth a closer look, but we have a theory and no evidence. It's up to Homicide to make the case. If you are asking for my advice, I think you make your best argument and then let it go, Kelly. Holding on to it will only bring you grief. You can't expect to solve everything, and in a city this busy, you have to know when to move on to the next case."

Sam didn't respond. They walked back to the squad room in silence.

≈

Sam had spent a long day waiting at City Hall to testify in a robbery trial. When she arrived at Central Detectives, the on-duty lieutenant directed her to the captain's office. The captain looked irritated from the moment she walked in, and he slammed the receiver of his phone into the cradle.

"Kelly, sit down. I just got off the phone with Internal Affairs Staff Inspector Castro. Somebody made a complaint about you. Are you investigating an unfounded homicide case?"

"I received a call from a complainant whom I believe is very credible. I was going to follow up and provide any information or evidence I might develop to the Homicide unit."

The captain's bushy eyebrows knitted even closer together. "Detective, you are to focus on the caseload generated by Central

Detectives. Contact Lieutenant Farrell in Homicide to debrief him and take yourself out of it before you leave today."

"Yes, sir."

"Do you have an idea who made the complaint to the staff inspectors?"

"Not for sure, but I think it was Wexler."

"I don't want Internal Affairs investigations in my division. I can make this go away, but watch your back, and keep your nose out of Homicide cold cases. Do we understand each other, Detective Kelly?"

"Yes, sir."

∾

Sam was packing for their trip to Cape May when she heard Jonesy calling her name. "Sam, the district attorney is on the line for you."

Sam picked up the telephone on the second floor. "Hello, this is Detective Kelly."

"Detective, this is District Attorney Jon Schatt. Can you report to Eleventh and Winter immediately to testify at a preliminary hearing for defendant Ronald Jenkins? You took a statement from him."

Sam stiffened and said, "This is my day off, and I was on my way out of town."

"I know it's an inconvenience, Detective, but I'm afraid we'll lose the case at the hearing if you don't testify. Judge Kisner refused my request for a continuance, and the complainant didn't show up for court. I promise, you'll be finished by noon."

"OK, I can be there in a half hour if I leave now," Sam said reluctantly. "But I'm dressed for travel in a sleeveless dress, does that work for you?"

"I need you as soon as possible. I'll see you soon."

Sam walked downstairs with her suitcase as AJ strolled through the door.

"We need to detour to Eleventh and Winter before we pick up Kate," Sam said. "The DA needs me to testify in a case. I'll call Kate while you two pack the car, OK?"

The preliminary hearings at Eleventh and Winter were always jam-packed. When it was hot, the room was stifling. The police officers and detectives waiting to testify crowded into a small room, next to the hearing room, where they could observe the proceedings and hear their cases and names called. Sam couldn't help but think of it as the police lair, eternally fogged by cigar smoke. When she walked in, she almost tripped over Wexler, who took the opportunity to blow smoke in her direction. DA Schatt strode into the room and called for her.

"Thanks for getting here so quickly. You are on next. I'll signal you to walk to the bar of the court."

Sam nodded. In her peripheral vision, she saw Wexler puffing his cigar and showing off his pearl-handled nine-millimeter to uniform officers.

When Sam was called to the bar of the court, she made momentary eye contact with the defendant, who nodded his head at her. The defendant, the public defender, the district attorney, and the detective stood shoulder to shoulder at the bar. Sam couldn't help but feel the imbalance. The public defender and the defendant both had a good eight inches on Sam and even more on the DA, a woman who looked to be about four-foot-ten.

The courtroom fell unusually quiet. The public defender began his argument: the confession of the defendant could not be permitted because it was taken under duress. Surprised at the allegation, Sam turned to face the defendant, who lowered his head. But that wasn't the only surprise. The defendant held both hands up to interrupt his attorney and spoke directly to the judge.

"My mother didn't raise me to disrespect women. I never said the detective threatened me."

The courtroom broke out in laughter. The judge banged his gavel to return quiet to the chamber and admonished the defense attorney. The case was held for court.

As Sam checked out of court, Wexler made sure she was within earshot when he said to the room full of cops, "What a joke. Take good look, everybody—this is what the police department has come to. Midget DAs and detectives in sundresses." The officers laughed so loud, they were admonished by the court liaison.

Sam pretended she didn't hear the remark, but she walked as fast as she could to the exit. AJ was standing at the Eleventh Street door, talking to Locke. Sam hoped Locke hadn't heard Wexler, but she knew the chances were slim to none.

To AJ, she said, "I'm done. Let's hit the road." And then, pretending to just notice him, she said, "Oh, hey, Locke."

"Sam, ignore Wexler," Locke said. So he'd heard. "Nobody really listens to him anyway."

"Yeah, right. You must've not heard the roars of laughter."

Trying to change the direction of the conversation, Locke said, "AJ told me you have tickets to *Sinatra* at Resorts. I wish I were going. Enjoy!"

"Oh, we will definitely enjoy," said AJ.

Sam couldn't wait to put the morning behind her and have some fun. "See you next shift, Locke."

Locke smiled at her. "Nice case, Sam. I've never seen a defendant actually defend the detective. You always make it interesting."

∼

After the four women arrived in Cape May and checked into the Congress Hotel, Kate switched into tour-guide mode to show off the Victorian architecture of Cape May.

"I think one of these will be the subject of my next watercolor," Jonesy said, admiring the intricate cornices and unique colors.

By the time the sun set, they had walked the beach and the promenade, and Sam could feel the tension lifting from her shoulders.

The next day, Jonesy and Kate introduced AJ and Sam to the boardwalk in Wildwood a few miles away, and they ended the night with cocktails by the pool.

The third day, they left Cape May and drove to the Seaview Hotel on Route 9 in Absecon, New Jersey, for the last leg of the trip—and for a special introduction.

Before they left Philly, Ray Rossi had surprised Kate with five tickets to the Frank Sinatra concert in Atlantic City, a few miles away from where they were now staying. She was blown away by his thoughtfulness, and her three friends were equally excited to finally, formally meet him. Kate first met Ray at a police fundraising event where his band, Anti-Corruption, was performing. AJ, Jonesy, and Sam had been to similar performances since then, but tonight would be their first official introduction to the man in Kate's life. They insisted on treating him to dinner at the main dining room of the Seaview before they left for the show.

"Are you sure we won't be third wheels?" Sam was adjusting the waist of a royal blue sleepless short A-line dress and running her fingers through her curly brown hair as she looked into the reflection of the elevator. AJ was wearing a sleeveless black dress and a mauve lipstick that offset her green eyes and short black hair. Both Jonesy and Kate chose jumpsuits. Jonesy wore a pink-and-green floral with a white background, and Kate wore a white jumpsuit with silver strappy heels and silver earrings, which provided an elegant accent to her dark pixie-cut hair.

"Ray doesn't do anything that he doesn't want to do." Kate assured her.

"What will the scandalmongers say if they see the four of us with Lieutenant Rossi? It might ruin his career," AJ half-joked.

"I wouldn't be with Ray if he even thought that way."

Ray met them in the lobby. He was five-foot-ten, broad-shouldered, dark-haired, and fit-looking. His smooth, confident manner and pleasant smile instantly put everyone at ease.

At dinner, Sam brought up the hotel's connection to Philadelphia and Grace Kelly.

"Sure, the hotel is elegant," AJ said. "But the hallways upstairs remind me of *The Shining*." She shivered.

"Yikes, I won't get that image out of my brain tonight," Sam said.

They all laughed.

Kate turned to her boyfriend. "Ray, here's something I wanted to ask you about. Sam got this phone call from a woman who believes elderly people are being murdered at a nursing home. Homicide called the case unfounded, after barely looking into it. What would you do?"

Sam interrupted. "Kate, you haven't heard my latest update. I was called into the captain's office and ordered to cease and desist. I cannot do any additional work on the investigation, and I was told to turn my information over to Homicide."

"What!" exclaimed Kate. "How did that happen?"

"Staff Inspector Castro and Detective Wexler happened."

Ray looked from Sam to Kate and said, "Well, if you still want my advice—I recommend keeping out of trouble and doing as you were ordered. While I'm not a fan of either, there are good reasons to have one assigned investigator. You can undermine a case."

Sam nodded without saying anything, and the conversation soon swung back to happier topics.

Several hours later, after the concert and a drink at the bar, the five strolled down the Atlantic City boardwalk. The full moon shone on the white tops of waves pulsing against the shore. AJ watched a young couple dart out from under the boardwalk, and she began singing, "Under the Boardwalk" by the Drifters. Sam joined in, and by the second verse, Ray was singing, too.

When the singing stopped, Ray said, "That wasn't bad! You ladies should definitely come to our next gig. You could even sing with us."

"Was this our audition, Lieutenant?" asked AJ.

"It's Ray, unless we're on duty. Yeah, this was your audition, and you passed with flying colors."

"I'll be there. How about you, Sam?"

"I'm happy to go, but the stage is all yours."

～

Three weeks later, Anti-Corruption finished their set at a club in Northeast Philly. Bobby O, the piano player and drummer who also doubled as the DJ, put on the Donna Summer song "I Feel Love."

Local celebrities from a Philadelphia dance show took the center of the floor. "Discophonic Donna," wearing a short white dress and three-inch heels with long platinum hair loose and tumbling down her back, took Bill's hand as they both dipped into a series of tricky disco dance moves.

AJ, Sam, Kate, and Jonesy watched from the sidelines.

"I couldn't do that on my best day," said Kate. "I only know the mashed potato and the Bristol stomp, while these two over here are a modern Astaire and Rodgers."

"I've been too busy learning jujitsu and dragging two-hundred-pound men across the floor," Jonesy said sarcastically.

After another set of elaborate moves, Sam exclaimed, "Jiminy crickets, I need a few dance lessons."

AJ, Kate, and Jonesy turned their heads toward her in unison.

"Oh no, Pollyanna is back!" Jonesy said. "We can't let you regress." She took on the deep, measured intonation of a priest. "'Jiminy crickets' is unacceptable language for a police officer. For your penance, you must say two Hail Marys, five Our Fathers, and twenty-five What the Fucks."

"I volunteer to teach you a couple of dance moves," offered AJ. As the four women laughed, the next song, "Always and Forever" by Luther Vandross, started to play.

"Look who's heading our way," Jonesy said. It was Jack Nathan, walking across the dance floor with his eyes set on AJ. To their surprise, AJ scooted off her barstool and accepted his invitation to dance.

Sam watched with narrowed eyes and called out, "Don't go far, AJ. Ray is expecting you to debut your talents soon."

AJ rolled her eyes as she walked away. "Got it, Detective Kelly."

Sam turned to Jonesy. "Why is it so easy to identify losers except when you're involved with them?" she said. "She's gotta know he's a short-timer."

The boundaries between life and death are at best shadowy
and vague.

—Edgar Allen Poe

TWENTY-NINE

———————————•—————————————

SAM SPENT THE DAY IN CITY HALL COURT AND DIDN'T GET
home until 5:00 p.m. After a quick meal and a hello to Jonesy, she
fell into bed for a couple of hours before getting up for work again at

9:30 p.m. She was the "early man" for the "last out" shift, starting at 11:00 p.m. and finishing at 7:00 a.m.

It was a Wednesday night in autumn, and the cooling weather
seemed to slow the pace of criminal activity. Sam was hoping for a
quiet night, but she feared the full moon would work against her.
If her coworkers were any indication, she was in for it. A beat cop
called out to Sam in the squad room, "Hey Sam—it's kiss a cop day.
How about you plant one?"

"Sorry, Edwards, I think that would constitute a conflict of
interest." Edwards's partner laughed while he pretended to pout.
"Anyway," said Sam, "I believe you've collected enough kisses today.
Saw you on Action News this morning! Very impressive. I would
vote for you as the pride of the PD."

Edwards clutched his chest, winking. "Alas, my heart is broken, but I realize you have a reputation to maintain."

Just then, the phone rang. Sam answered, "Central Detectives,
Detective Kelly speaking."

A hesitant voice on the other end of the line said, "Um, hello, uh…I work at the desk of the Drake Apartments at Thirteenth and Spruce Streets. I was just reading the *Philadelphia Gay News*, and there is an article about a guy wanted for murder by the Loudoun County police in Virginia. The article included a picture, and…it looks just like a guy who lives in this building."

"I appreciate the call, sir. Could you tell me a bit more?" Sam probed.

"Yeah, OK," replied the caller. "The article said this guy, William Brown, is wanted for murder in Loudoun County, Virginia; and in Washington, DC; and Baltimore."

The caller had Sam's attention. "Sir, do you have a fax machine to send me the picture? Could you also tell me the spelling of your name and give me your number?" she asked.

"My name is Joseph Kozlowski, and my number is LO4-1235. I can fax the article as soon as you give me the number," he replied.

They hung up, and Kozlowski faxed the article to Central Detectives. Kelly pulled the printout off the fax machine, read it, and called Kozlowski back.

"Mr. Kozlowski," Sam asked, "how sure are you that the man is William Brown?"

"I am 99 percent sure. He's using a different name, but the guy looks exactly like the picture in the newspaper. I'm good with faces. It's my job to recognize people."

Sam told Kozlowski she would be in contact with him after she verified the warrants and made some additional inquiries. Next, she contacted the Loudon County police after finding a warrant in the NCIC database to confirm the arrest warrant was still active. She put the call on speakerphone so she could use the computer at the same time.

"Sergeant Griffiths, Fairfax Police Department," a man's voice, with a slight Southern accent, announced.

"Sergeant Griffiths, this is Detective Kelly from the Philadelphia Police Department. I'm calling to confirm a warrant for William Brown."

"Did Philadelphia pick him up?" Griffiths asked, and Sam could hear the excitement in his voice.

Sam responded, "Well, no, not yet. But we have received information that could potentially lead to his apprehension."

Sam explained the call from the deskman of the apartment building, and the sergeant confirmed that two detectives from Fairfax PD had been to Philadelphia and had the suspect's photo published in the *Gay News*. Brown's modus operandi was to insert himself into the gay community and develop relationships with gay men before killing them. He would take their cash, pawn their valuables, and move on to the next community. Fairfax detectives speculated Brown was making his way up the East Coast, using similar schemes in Washington and Baltimore.

Sam thanked the sergeant for the information and promised to keep him advised of the outcome of her inquiries.

Sergeant Griffiths interrupted her. "Hold on there, darling. Can I speak to the detective in charge?"

Sam's comeback was quick. "Sergeant, you are speaking to the detective in charge."

After a brief, awkward silence, the sergeant said, "No offense, darling, but could I talk to a male detective? This guy is dangerous, and he has slipped through the fingers of some of the best detectives I know."

Hogan and Locke, who were walking into the room to report for their shift, stopped dead in their tracks and waited to see how Sam would respond.

Sam's voice was professional and monotone as she thanked the sergeant for his concern and quickly added that she had not yet met the "best detective;" she hung up the phone without giving him an opportunity to respond.

Hogan turned to Locke. "I've seen that look before."

Locke responded, "Oh, she is on a mission from God."

"And I thought it would be a slow night," Hogan said, chuckling.

By midnight, when Mike Mullen, the squad deskman arrived at Central Detectives to assume the duties of deskman, Sam had already ordered photos of the suspect, who had several aliases, to include in a photo arrangement, and she'd contacted Homicide, who said they were too busy to follow up on the call. Locke, overhearing Sam's debrief with the lieutenant, offered to go with her to Thirteenth and Spruce.

At the Central City apartment, Kozlowski immediately picked William Brown (also known as Willie Carter, according to the police database) out of the photo array. Kozlowski repeated that he was nearly positive the man lived in the apartment building. He drove a school bus, Kozlowski said, and he usually left for work around four thirty in the morning. Sam didn't think she had enough time to make a case or complete the paperwork for a warrant before then, but she also didn't want a potential serial killer out driving a school bus.

So, she devised a plan to stop him.

Locke reluctantly agreed to Sam's plan. He knew the sergeant from Fairfax had pressed her buttons with his "darling" and "best detectives" remarks. And Griffiths was far from done. When the detectives returned to the squad room, Lieutenant Clark immediately walked up to them. He'd received a call from Griffiths, who expressed doubts that she could successfully handle the follow-up required.

"Yes, sir," Sam said. "I received that message loud and clear from Sergeant Griffiths in my conversation with him."

Lieutenant Clark smiled at Sam's moxie. "Detective Kelly, I confirmed that Homicide is too busy. Follow the leads where they take you tonight. Write it up to turn over to Homicide in the morning."

Locke, meanwhile, began planning for a stakeout team to back them up when they confronted the doer. He had already contacted the on-duty team for a 4:00 a.m. rendezvous. While Sam waited on the corner of Broad and Spruce Streets to stop Brown, Locke and the stakeout team would be in an unmarked chase car a few yards away. An emergency patrol wagon would be stationed around the corner to transport the suspect once they apprehended him.

Sam changed from her suit into a sweater, jeans, and boots. The stakeout team arrived at Central Detectives to debrief the details and coordinate the plan. Sam fit her two-inch .38 Colt Detective's Special snugly inside the waistband of her jeans, under her sweater. A stakeout cop teased that her Colt was useless, and he would lend her money to buy a "real gun."

At 4:20 a.m., Sam was in position at Broad and Spruce. She watched a shadowy figure leave the apartment building a block away. Sam walked toward the silhouette of the man and recognized his face from the picture. She was about twenty feet from him when she called to him, "Hey, Willie!"

He looked at her for the briefest moment and then broke into a run. Sam chased him through a small parking lot, saying, "Police, stop! Police, stop!" She knocked the suspect into a car, and they both fell to the ground. Locke and the stakeout team were there immediately to pull the kicking and punching suspect from Sam. They pushed the suspect against a nearby brick wall.

"Settle down, Willie. You don't want to make it worse by messing with the police," whispered Locke.

"The police are messing with me."

"Let me give you a little friendly advice since you're an out-of-towner, Willie," Locke said, exuding a calm he did not feel.

"What's that?"

"Don't tug on Superman's cape, don't spit into the wind, don't pull the mask off the Lone Ranger, and don't fuck with the Philadelphia police. Especially female detectives. Now settle down, and things will go much smoother."

Locke shoved the suspect toward the wagon crew and offered his hand to Sam, who was still on the ground. As he pulled Sam up, he asked. "Are you OK?"

"The only thing that hurts is my pride. Send him directly to the PAB to be printed, so we know who he is for sure," she replied.

"It's him," Locke responded.

Back at Central Detectives, Lieutenant Clark advised Sam and Locke that two detectives from Fairfax County had already started driving to Pennsylvania. Sam had a moment of panic because the fingerprints had not yet confirmed they had the right suspect.

"What if he just looks like the man in the picture?"

Lieutenant Clark and Locke both laughed. "I told you, it's him," Locke said. "I know from talking to him."

Lieutenant Clark smiled and told Sam that she had done an excellent job. "Your instincts, as usual, were on target," he said.

William Brown arrived at Central Detectives at the same time the Philadelphia identification unit positively identified him as wanted by Fairfax County. Brown continued to insist they were mistaken.

Sam was working on the arrest paperwork when Detective Wexler arrived at Central Detectives. Sam could hear him complaining to the captain that she had overstepped and should have referred the case to Homicide. Fortunately, Sam knew, Lieutenant Clark had briefed Captain Callahan already. Wexler didn't realize that Callahan had been the one to update headquarters about the arrest. Callahan ordered Wexler out of his office.

Sam went to the restroom in the hallway, and suddenly she heard Wexler's voice on the other side of the door.

"...a fucking bitch who gets away with her shit because she blows Captain Callahan, Hogan, and Locke," Wexler was saying. "Locke only gave her credit for this and the other arrests because he walks around sniffing up her skirt."

Sam opened the door and just stared at him. She knew she couldn't find words hurtful enough to respond, so she decided just to keep staring, her eyes locked with his. The uniformed patrol officer and two other detectives scattered as quickly as possible. Sam was determined that she wouldn't be the first to look away, and soon Wexler broke contact and strode away.

As Sam was leaving the building and walking to her car, Locke caught up with her. He saw the stressed look on her face—which only grew worse when she noticed Wexler staring at them from a squad car.

"Seriously, is he the only detective in Homicide?" she fumed.

"Well, there will be at least one more. I've been transferred to Homicide."

Locke thought he saw a flash of disappointment on her face. It vanished immediately, but her voice seemed tight and controlled. "Congratulations, Locke. I know you worked hard to get that transfer. It has been a pleasure. I hope our paths cross again sometime."

"I'm not leaving the city, Sam. It's just a transfer."

Sam's entire demeanor was stiff as she offered her hand to shake. Confused by the sudden change in her, Locke said, "Well, it's been an experience working with you, Sam. You always make it interesting. You are one of the best detectives I have ever worked with."

Sam smiled, but she replied dismissively, "I think your nose is growing, Pinocchio. I'd say knock them dead in Homicide, but I think that would be in bad taste. Best of luck to you."

Locke took a step forward, but Sam moved back. "I need to go," she said as she looked past his shoulder, staring narrowly at Wexler, still in his squad car.

$\sim$

Kate was working as the day shift supervisor in the Fourteenth District when she decided to back up a squad car, responding to a silent bank alarm. When she arrived at Girard Bank, Kate took position outside the front door and directed the patrol officer to follow. At first, nothing seemed amiss, and she assumed the alarm was accidently tripped. Then she saw the face of the security guard on the other side of the door. Kate told the other officer to contact police radio and confirm the robbery was in progress. Just then, the robbers burst through the doors with a bank bag and two nine-millimeter handguns. One of the gunmen got off a shot, wounding Kate in the shoulder. The second gunman panicked and set off the exploding dye pack in the bank bag, creating enough distraction for Kate to get off two shots and injure both men. Within seconds, police radio broadcasted a citywide "assist officer" alert. One gunman was down at the bank, but the second escaped on foot with the patrol officer in pursuit. Within minutes, additional gunshots were heard. Police radio announced they had received calls from civilians that two police officers were dead.

AJ, who kept a police scanner in her apartment in Chestnut Hill, had heard Kate go in on the call, and then she heard the radio updates. She immediately called Jonesy and Sam.

"Jonesy, I know Kate went in on the radio call, and I haven't heard her on police radio since the 'assist officer.' The last report is that two cops are dead. They are being taken to Chestnut Hill Hospital. I'm on my way. Meet you there."

AJ and Sam rushed to Chestnut Hill Hospital. Jonesy drove to Kate's parents' house, but a squad car had already arrived to drive them to the hospital.

The police commissioner, several other commanders, and Ray Rossi were already at the hospital when Sam and AJ arrived. For the first time since they had met him, Ray was not cool, calm, or collected. His face was ashen and dead serious. As AJ and Sam walked through the door of the emergency room, AJ called to him, "Lieutenant?"

Ray looked at them and said, "One officer dead, one in critical. I don't know…" That was all he could get out. Jonesy arrived then, and the other two women shrugged and shook their heads, implying *we don't know anything yet.*

After a few minutes that felt like hours, Ray and the division's inspector were able to speak with the hospital staff. Kate was in surgery to repair a gunshot wound to her shoulder. Ray relayed the news to AJ and Sam, and he was already regaining some of his composure. When Carmella and Len Dominic arrived, Ray stuck to them like glue through introductions to the commissioner and commanders. When the surgeon came out of the operating room and reported that Kate was in stable condition, everyone breathed a sigh of relief.

But nearby, Eddie Foster's wife collapsed when she arrived at the hospital and learned her husband had been killed in the line of duty. AJ, Jonesy, and Sam sat with Carmella and Len, and words failed all of them.

Within a few hours, they heard that Kate had done well in surgery and was now recovering. The doctors advised that they leave for a few hours to rest up. As the three friends walked out of the hospital in the early morning hours, their sense of loss was overwhelming.

"I know this should go without saying, but this is not something I'd like to experience again," Jonesy said.

"Unfortunately, I think this is what we signed up for," Sam replied.

AJ was sober and thoughtful. "We can't help Eddie, but Kate is alive," she said. "We need to help her face her future, even if none of us knows what that will look like." The other women nodded. "OK, let's meet back here about noon?"

The next day, AJ, Jonesy, and Sam were walking into Kate's hospital room when they were suddenly brought up short. Kate was awake, but all of her attention was absorbed by Ray, who was holding her hand and talking in a low, urgent tone. The friends quietly backed out of the doorway when they realized Ray was proposing. Instead, they walked to the cafeteria for coffee.

"He isn't wasting any time. Do you think she is still under the influence and can make a good decision?" AJ rambled. "If she says yes, we will be in the wedding, of course. I am one of those people who look great in bridesmaids' dresses, no matter what they look like."

Jonesy rolled her eyes. "Do you ever get tired of pretending to be a Barbie doll? I hope she says yes. They are good together. Ray is one of the good guys. As far as the wedding goes, I'm not sure I'll fit in as a bridesmaid—but if I know Carmella and Len, it will be the wedding of the year."

"You'll be her maid of honor." AJ insisted. "And Sam and I will be bridesmaids."

"I am just happy to be planning a wedding and not a funeral," Sam said. Suddenly overwhelmed, her eyes glistened with tears. "I'm sorry. My own words just hit me. I know cops aren't supposed to cry, but I can't afford to lose any friends." Sam put her arms around AJ and Jonesy and said, "God, I love you guys."

Just then, Sam looked up and saw Wexler. The disgusted look on his face said exactly what he was thinking, *Leave it up to women to turn an officer shooting into a crying session.* As he turned and walked away silently, AJ stifled her laughter in her hand. Sam's shoulders sank down. "What the hell? What is he doing here? I'm beginning to feel like he's stalking me."

"Is that the infamous Wexler?" asked Jonesy. "If he's the assigned, he'd better not give Kate any grief. I'll shoot him."

"Don't worry, girl," AJ said. "Wexler thinks his superior investigative skills have landed him a juicy bit of gossip. I'm guessing that before your next tour of duty, the word on the street will be that he saw you with your lesbian lovers."

Just then, Ray walked into the corridor and toward them, a smile on his face. "She's having a good day," he said.

"Nice. Are you having a good day, Lieutenant Rossi? Did she say yes?" asked AJ.

Ray smiled. "I'm having a great day. In fact, I am the happiest guy alive. Pretend to be surprised when she tells you, though. Your turn to visit. She was asking for the three of you. I'm going for coffee. Len and Carmella should be here soon, so get in and get out before she gets too tired."

Kate was staring at the ceiling when they entered the hospital room.

"Was Wexler in to see you?" asked Sam.

"No, I'm not sure I know who he is," replied Kate. She squinted at the black band across the badge of AJ's uniform. "Isn't it a little premature for that? Based on what the doctor tells me, it seems I will survive this gunshot wound."

The three friends stared at Kate in silence for a second before realizing. "Of course, you don't know," Sam said. "Eddie Foster didn't make it."

Kate winced. "Oh, no." She lifted her hand to wipe an errant tear, and the ring on her finger flashed into view.

In an effort to change the subject quickly, Jonesy said, "That ring is gorgeous. Where did you get it?"

"Ray gave it to me," Kate whispered. The pain in her voice was obvious.

"And you said yes," Jonesy said. "We are all ecstatic for you, but don't strain yourself, girl. Save your strength for wedding planning."

"Thanks for being here." Kate's smile was sincere, but they could see the pain on her face.

"You get some rest," said Jonesy. "We will talk later. Call us if you need anything."

"Wait," Kate said. "You will all be in the wedding, right?"

"Of course!" they said in unison, heads bobbing in agreement.

∾

Four days later, after AJ visited Kate at Chestnut Hill Hospital, she stopped by the emergency ward to thank one of the nurses and saw a wagon crew bringing in a DOA. There was a man accompanying the crew, and AJ was sure she knew him from somewhere; he was young, maybe early thirties, with the stature of a football player and an Eagles tattoo peeking out under the sleeve of his scrubs. With a jolt, AJ realized he was a health-care worker she had seen at Green Valley Retirement all those months ago when she and Sam first took the report from Leighann Jordan. Maybe Sam was getting into her head. But what were the odds that there'd been yet another death?

AJ walked up to the guy as he was walking out the emergency room door. "Hi," she said. "Remember me?"

"Yeah," he said, "I remember you."

AJ forced him to make eye contact. He seemed a little nervous. "Can I buy you a soda or a cup of coffee?"

"I'm not sure. I've got to go back to work."

"A quick soda. What could it hurt?"

"Uh, OK. I guess I can have a quick one."

AJ ushered him to a corner table and brought him a can of soda. "Your name is Terrance, right?"

The man nodded yes. AJ got right to it. "Seems like there's a steady stream of residents of Green Valley who die, doesn't it?"

"Green Valley is for old people. They all die eventually," Terrance said.

"Maybe. But do you ever wonder if they should die when they do?" AJ looked straight into his eyes.

"Dunno, maybe, sometimes, dunno," Terrance mumbled, breaking eye contact to stare down at the table.

AJ swung for the fences. "Terrance, I need you to tell me everything you know about the drugs missing from Green Valley."

~

Everyone was relieved when Kate was discharged from the hospital and was recovering quickly. The holidays were around the corner, and the Baker Street Four (plus Ray) planned to spend Thanksgiving and Christmas with Kate and her parents.

Working hard through the weeks leading up to the holiday season kept Sam from dwelling on the sick feeling in her stomach when she thought about how Thanksgiving dinner would go with her family. On the other hand, she was looking forward to the dinner at Kate's parents' house. Sam decided to use shift work as an excuse to show up late for the family meal and excuse herself early, in order to make a break for round two. But even her careful strategizing couldn't keep the nausea at bay. When the day dawned, Sam wondered if she'd be able to eat anything at all.

The main topic of conversation was, of course, Beth. She had left her job at Green Valley and was looking for a new job. Sam knew Beth would probably lie about the real reason for leaving, but she wasn't surprised to hear her blame it on Sam. With exaggerated emotion in her voice, Beth shared her carefully crafted story. By the end, poor Beth had lost her job because of Sam's abuse of authority as a cop.

Her parents tried to ignore the obvious tension between the sisters, but Sam could see the pain on their faces. Her mother made several attempts to change the subject, but some of the other siblings and their spouses piped up to commiserate over poor Beth's predicament.

Seated next to her, Reagan rolled her eyes at Sam and muttered, "I can't believe they fall for her stories."

"Oh, I think it's less what they believe about her and more what they want to believe about me. It's a play to make Mom and Dad think less of me." Sam pushed at her uneaten mashed potatoes listlessly. "Do you ever feel as much of an outsider with this family as I do, Reagan?"

"Yeah," said Reagan. "Sometimes."

Sam decided to make her exit before the family tradition of sharing what they were most thankful for. As Sam made her way to the front door, Denny hugged her and teased Sam about leaving. In response, Sam whispered, "My hypocrisy has its limits. They wouldn't appreciate what I actually feel grateful for, and I am past the point of pretending."

The minute Sam showed up at Carmella and Len Dominic's home, AJ recognized the sadness on her face. AJ swung the door open wider and said, "We were waiting for you. Ray is playing the piano, and I thought we'd sing Christmas carols."

It only took a few carols for Sam's mood to lighten. AJ then asked to do a solo with Ray at the piano. Sounding like an angel, AJ performed her own rendition of "Hallelujah."

Everyone clapped enthusiastically, and Sam said, "You've been practicing, girl!"

"I love that song. Sam, promise me you'll sing this song at my funeral."

"Me? Sing at a funeral? I don't think so," replied Sam, but she was struck by the earnest look on AJ's face. "OK," Sam relented. "I don't intend to outlive you, but I will honor your request if I do. In return, you have to promise to sing Sinatra's 'My Way' at my funeral."

"You've got a deal," AJ said. The friends shared a smile that spoke volumes.

Len cleared his throat. "All this funeral talk when we're supposed to be celebrating our baby's miraculous recovery, and her upcoming nuptials with this gentleman!" He clapped his hand on Ray's shoulder, and Ray merrily plowed into the next carol in his sheet music.

Later, when Sam and AJ had a quiet moment to themselves while washing dishes in the kitchen, AJ said, "So how did it go?" Sam told her about Beth.

"Beth is blaming you for losing her job?" asked AJ, her brows knitting together in confusion.

"Seems so," responded Sam.

"The only one way her manager would've known you were related is if she told them. You don't look alike, and you were still wearing your Evans name tag that day. She needs to get a life and stop trying to steal yours." AJ paused, her hands still submerged in soapy water. She wasn't surprised Beth had crafted a story to undermine Sam. But she wondered if there was more to the story. Even for a jealous sister, this was taking spite to a whole new level. "You know, I have a new friend who works at Green Valley. I can verify her story."

"Don't waste your time. I'm sure she's lying. She can't help herself."

AJ reached out to pat Sam on the arm before she realized her hands were still covered in bubbles. "Don't let her get you down, Sam. My father once gave me a framed quote by Eleanor Roosevelt. It inspired me to take control of my self-esteem, and I'm going to bequeath it to you."

"What is the quote?"

"'No one can make you feel inferior without your consent.' Don't give Beth consent. You are a fighter. Fight back."

Carmella saw their serious expressions and decided to bring smiles back to their faces. Gesturing at the kitchen table, she said, "Ladies, let's get down to business. We have a wedding to plan. There's no time like the present to begin talking details."

"We can make this really easy for you Carmella. Whatever you say."

The next several months were filled with instructions from Kate and her mother. After the first two weeks, the friends bequeathed Kate and Carmella the title of wedding wardens. AJ loved the fuss, but Jonesy and Sam were out of their element, feeling like they were attending charm school. Carmella laid out a plan for fittings, waxing, and hairdressers. AJ laid out the fitness plan. After several pep talks, Sam and Jonesy decided to enjoy the ride.

Carmella and Kate had a complete grasp on the personalities of the three women and organized activities accordingly. Sam and Jonesy disliked shopping, so Carmella, Kate, and AJ shopped for the bridesmaids' dresses to be ordered from a store in New York. They picked a black full-length evening dress with a low back and straps leading to a bodice glittering with tonal crystal. Kate thought the ruched and wrapped bodice would flatter all of their figures. The final touch was a slit almost to the knee. While AJ was delighted with the choice, Sam and Jonesy were hesitant about wearing some-thing so form-fitting and fancy. Carmella stepped in and convinced them it was the perfect dress for all of them. She also said she would design matching jackets to wear in the Cathedral of St. Peter and Paul, where the ceremony would be held. Kate asked them to select shoes from three options—all strappy, black, patent leather shoes with three-inch heels. Jonesy rolled her eyes and insisted that she couldn't wear any of the shoes for one hour, much less an entire day. In the end, they found a similar pair of heels with a two-inch heel.

The wedding reception would a black-tie affair in a ballroom at the Four Seasons Hotel, across from the cathedral in Logan Circle. Carmella and Len were sparing no expense. As Kate and Carmella shared the details for an elegant evening, Sam and Jonesy exchanged increasingly nervous looks.

Jonesy finally interrupted. "I thought this was going to be a gaudy South Philly wedding and that we'd be wearing pink or purple gowns that Kate would love and that we would hate. This feels a little too main line for us. I'm not sure that we're up to the challenge."

Sam remained silent, but Carmella didn't miss the quiet nod of agreement or the look of uncertainty on Sam's face.

Carmella said, "Ladies, please trust me. We will make sure you are totally ready for this wedding. I have a plan."

AJ, Sam, and Jonesy looked at Kate and burst into laughter.

"Where do you think I get it?" Kate said, joining them.

When they calmed down a bit, Sam spoke up. "I'm just not sure I have the social skills to fit in," she said. "Ray's uncle is the chief of the detective bureau. I hope we don't stand out in the wrong way."

Jonesy turned to AJ. "I'm going to need tutoring on how to walk down the aisle."

AJ responded, "Lessons start now. But—"

"Yeah, we know," said Jonesy, snorting with laughter again. "No matter how hard we try, we will never look better than you."

Happiness often sneaks in a door you did not think
was open.

—John Barrymore

TWENTY-NINE

GORGEOUS AZALEAS BLOOMED AT THE PHILADELPHIA Museum of Art, and the wind blew neither too chilly nor too humid for a brief moment in time. May was the perfect month for Kate and Ray's wedding.

The wedding wardens, Kate and Carmella, treated the trio of bridesmaids to a full day of glamour at Toppers Spa in the Bourse Building at Fifth and Chestnut. Jonesy remarked that she had spent more time and money on her appearance in one day than she usually would in a month. But even she had to admit they looked amazing. AJ had driven them all a little crazy with her workouts over the past three months. Sam and Jonesy had gone along with them willingly because they knew Kate was trying to get back in shape after her shooting injury. That afternoon, the black strapless dresses looked great on all three of them, but AJ looked like she was walking the runway of the Miss America pageant. Jonesy turned to Sam and said, "Let's get lots of pictures. We will never look this good again."

After a beautiful, heartfelt ceremony, the wedding party left the Cathedral of St. Peter and Paul and made their way to Boathouse Row behind the Philadelphia Museum of Art to take pictures. Sam smiled, admiring the bride and groom as they posed for their photos.

Jonesy was almost giddy as they sipped champagne nearby. Just then, a police wagon drove by. One of the cops recognized Sam and AJ and yelled, "You ladies clean up nicely. You give the term 'Philadelphia's finest' a new meaning."

AJ bowed, and Sam smiled. Jonesy didn't respond to the man, but she said to her friends, "We get to be PD Barbies today, and it's not so bad. I don't think Walt will recognize me, but I do know he'll love the black underwear."

"You still dating Walt? Why didn't he come to the wedding?" asked AJ.

"He's a widower with three kids and uses his vacation time judiciously," Jonesy said, shrugging. "He was scheduled to work, but he'll join us after the reception for the after-party."

AJ said, "I'm glad I'm not the only one with a boyfriend but without a date." She tipped her chin toward East River Drive. "Speaking of boyfriends. Look who's here."

Sam turned around and was surprised to see Detective Greg Locke jogging toward them along the path. Sam hadn't seen him in months.

"Wow," he said, coming to a stunned stop. "The three of you give the term 'Philadelphia's finest' a new meaning."

"We've heard that one," said Jonesy. "Do all cops have the same pickup line?"

But Locke didn't hear her; he had eyes only for Sam. She found herself staring back.

"Long time no see, Sam."

"You jog here?"

"I live in the neighborhood. I have an apartment in that building," he said, pointing across the street. Suddenly realizing he was dripping with sweat, Locke wiped a hand across his face and said,

"I'm sorry I'm sweaty, but when I saw you, I wanted to say hello. You look great, Sam."

"Thank you. You look good as well. It's great to see you again. It's been a while."

"I know. The last time we spoke, I wasn't sure you ever wanted to talk to me again."

"Sorry, you know how Wexler pushes my buttons. I was being an idiot."

He smiled and repeated, "You look great." He squinted and motioned behind her. "I think the photographer is calling you. But it's nice to see you again, Sam. Don't be a stranger. Stop by Homicide whenever you're in at the PAB. I'd like to buy you a coffee and talk cases."

"I get the impression he wants to talk more than 'cases.' I never noticed that Locke had a dimple in his right cheek," AJ said, watching him jog away.

"Neither did I. He doesn't usually show his full smile," Sam said, not realizing she had spoken aloud.

"Gottcha—you like him," said AJ. "Let's get back to this wedding business."

Take a chance! All life is a chance.
The man who goes farthest is generally the one who is
willing to do and dare.

—Dale Carnegie

THIRTY

IT WAS A LITTLE BEFORE 11:00 P.M. WHEN JONESY ANNOUNCED to Sam and AJ that Walt was on his way to pick them up and take them to a club on the Delaware Riverfront. Sam was in a wandering mood, and she asked Jonesy and AJ if they wanted to join her in a walk across the street to take in views of the Benjamin Franklin Parkway. At the fountain in Logan Circle, Sam paused to point out the parkway's strange allure.

"Isn't that beautiful?" Sam mused aloud. "The parkway is like a red carpet to the Museum of Art, which has its own carefully lit landscapes. I can't imagine that the Champs-Élysées is more elegant or beautiful."

"I'll let you know how it is when Walt takes me to Paris for my birthday," replied Jonesy.

"Walt is taking you to Paris?" asked AJ.

"He doesn't know it yet, but yes. That's why I want him to save his vacation," Jonesy said with a smile.

AJ and Sam laughed.

"What? Allow a girl her dreams."

As Sam reached into her small purse to pull out a penny to throw into the fountain, she noticed three teenagers walking toward them, whispering.

They crossed Race Street and approached the women. Sam sized them up as trouble and began to regret the excursion. She motioned to AJ and Jonesy, saying, "This could get awkward if we end the night in Central Detectives as complainants."

"Don't worry," said AJ. "I'm packing."

"You are? Where?" Sam asked.

AJ smiled. "I'm always ready for a good fight."

As the boys advanced, the three women made eye contact with them. The silence was broken when one of them said, "Hey—they're five-oh. Let's get out of here." The boys turned and ran. The three women looked at each other and laughed.

"Anybody recognize them?" Sam said. "How did they know we're cops?"

A familiar baritone voice said from behind them, "It might be the 'make my day' looks the three of you gave them."

Sam's heart missed a beat as she recognized Locke's drawl. She spun around quickly and smiled.

AJ cocked her head and said, "Detective Locke, so nice to see you again. Out for a midnight jog?"

Locke never took his gaze from Sam. "Finished my shift. Is this a closed party, or can anyone join?"

"I'd invite you to join us, but apparently, you haven't noticed me yet," AJ said dryly. "We're on our way to the riverfront. A club by the name of PJ's."

Just then Jonesy spotted Walt's car and waved him over. "You are welcome to join us if you want," yelled Jonesy as she rushed to Walt's car.

"It would be my privilege to join you. Anyone need a ride?" asked Locke. Without speaking, Sam walked toward him.

"Thanks for the offer," AJ said, "but I'm going with Jonesy." AJ looked at Jonesy and said, "I definitely don't want to interrupt whatever that is. Are they still staring at each other?"

"No, Locke took Sam's arm to cross the street and is helping her into the front seat of his Rivera," Jonesy said as she glanced back.

"This day is getting better and better," AJ said. "Kate snagged the love of her life, and Sam is actually spending time with a real man."

"Slow down. Locke's recently divorced. What if he's just looking to get laid?" asked Jonesy.

Walt spoke up. "Locke isn't that kind of guy."

"I think and hope you're right," AJ said.

On the drive to the riverfront, Sam talked about the wedding nonstop, and Locke listened quietly. He glanced over several times, thinking she looked more relaxed than he had ever seen her, and he'd never heard her talk so much. She suddenly stopped talking and glanced over at him.

"When did you start wearing glasses, Locke?"

"And the always inquisitive Detective Kelly is back," he said, purposely avoiding a direct answer.

"I wear them when my eyes are tired, especially at night. You wouldn't have noticed because you never looked at me before," Locke said.

"Ouch, that hurts! For the record, I noticed you, Locke. Anyway, you look good in glasses."

Sam tilted her head and knitted her brow. "What does that mean?"

"When I saw you at the art museum today, I thought Detective Kelly was on hiatus. You let your guard down, and you were pleasant and engaging—almost flirty. I'm kind of hoping Detective Kelly stays on vacation."

Sam stared at his profile and considered his words as he drove down Market Street.

Sam leaned into his ear and whispered, "I gave Detective Kelly the day off. Hi, my name is Samantha. It's a pleasure to meet you, Greg."

Locke smiled. "The pleasure is all mine, Samantha."

"If you don't mind my boldness, you smell good, Greg Locke." Sam closed her eyes and breathed in, adding, "Mm-mm, Old Spice suits your rugged, handsome stature and your quiet, slightly gruff, stone-faced demeanor."

"Really? So, how much have you had to drink today, Samantha?"

Momentarily surprised, she said, "I'm high on life today, but feel free to buy me a dirty martini at PJ's."

When Sam and Locke arrived at the riverfront, they found a parking space immediately. He opened Sam's door and offered his hand to help Sam out of the car. As they walked to the club, Locke didn't relinquish her hand, and she did not try to pull it away.

"Do you think we beat them here?" he asked.

"I'm not sure. If they are here, you can bet they found a table in a corner, with their backs to the wall and a clear view of the door."

Locke laughed as he opened the door to the club and let her walk in first. Sure enough, Jonesy and AJ were already positioned at a table in a corner with a direct view of the entrance. They were already sipping martinis, and AJ raised up the one they had ordered for her as they neared the table.

"What are you drinking, Greg?" asked Walt.

"Scotch, but I can get it. Anyone else need a drink?"

"We're good," said Jonesy.

The live band was taking a break, so the loudspeakers began playing "Dancing in the Street" by Martha and the Vandellas. AJ was the first on the dance floor, with Jonesy right behind her. Once the song was over, the band, which included a brass section, came back to do another set. The lead singer began singing the Frankie Valli hit, "Can't Take My Eyes Off of You."

Locke took Sam's hand and led her to the dance floor. He spun her and led her to the beat of the music in a combination of swing and slow dance. She was surprised to find he was a very good dancer, and she was even more amazed she could follow him. He controlled their movements perfectly and was totally in sync with the music. They said very little but never broke eye contact through the dance. As the song was ending, he pulled her close and said, "OK, get ready for a big ending." Then he dipped her.

She laughed. "Wow, I didn't realize you were multitalented. You actually have skills beyond police work."

As the band transitioned to "You Belong to Me," Locke pulled her to him and whispered in her ear, "Stick around, kid. I have several skills you've never seen."

Watching them from the corner table, AJ said, "Have they stopped staring at each other yet?"

"Not really. He occasionally whispers in her ear," replied Jonesy. "How can they dance that well together? Has she been keeping something from us?"

When they arrived back at the high-top table, Jonesy said, "OK, Fred and Ginger, where did that performance come from? How many times have you two danced together?"

Sam laughed. "First time. Beginner's luck, I guess."

Locke smiled like a Cheshire cat, but admitted, "I hate to tarnish my new image, but I only have the moves my sister taught me when she forced me to be her dance partner."

Jonesy skipped right to the point, fixing a glare on Locke. "You better treat her right, Locke, or you will answer to us."

Sam looked at them wide-eyed and blushing. She lifted her martini glass to cover her mouth and leaned toward AJ and Jonesy to whisper through clenched teeth, "While I appreciate the solidarity, ladies, it was just a dance. Keep it up, and you'll scare him away."

AJ looked around Sam. "Locke, could we scare you away from Sam?"

Locke raised a brow, a mischievous glint in his eyes. "Not a chance."

AJ nodded. "Didn't think so."

Locke continued to smile as he sipped his scotch and watched Sam's face turn beet red.

AJ shook her head slowly, side to side. "That is believable you've never danced with each other before. I do, however, take credit for teaching Sam how to dance the hustle."

"Speaking of the hustle—who invited him?" Jonesy asked. The air shifted suddenly. Jack Nathan had just entered the bar and looked around before noticing them. He had promised to escort AJ to Kate's wedding, but backed out at the last minute. He seemed to be free now, though. He went to the bar to order a drink.

Noticing the change in energy, Locke took Sam's hand and pulled her again to the dance floor. As the singer began his rendition of "When a Man Loves a Woman," Locke pulled Sam into his embrace and looked down at her face. "You don't like Jack Nathan?"

She frowned. "I'm that obvious?"

"You wouldn't make a good poker player."

"It's AJ's life, not mine, but I don't want her to get hurt. She deserves better than him. She is a good friend and has a pure heart. He seems like a player and self-centered to boot. Tell me I'm wrong, Locke."

"You're right. He is a player. I wouldn't want him dating my sister." Locke paused. "The four of you are very close friends, and you really care about each other. I have to admit, I'm a little jealous."

Sam raised her eyebrows and said, "Jealous? Why, Greg Locke, there is no need to be jealous. I have room in my heart for one more friend." Sam winked up at him and then closed her eyes, leaning against his chest and breathing in Old Spice. She savored every note of music and every second of the dance.

Locke was surprised Sam seemed so relaxed. Until today, his interactions with her had been limited to cautious conversation and occasional glimpses of humor. He hadn't seen her for months, and when they parted ways, he had tried to convey he was interested in keeping in touch. But he got the impression she wasn't even interested in exchanging a phone call. When he saw her this afternoon, though, something passed between them. She looked stunning, and she seemed different than he had remembered. Tonight, she was looking at him, laughing with him, dancing with him like they had known each other for years. She was flirting. While he liked the new Samantha, he wondered if alcohol was playing a role. Sam didn't seem drunk, but the change was dramatic enough to wonder.

A little after 1:00 a.m., Jonesy told Sam that she and Walt were leaving.

"Could you take the long way home?" Jonesy asked. "Walt's mother is staying at his place with his kids, and we'd like a little time to ourselves.

Sam nodded. "Of course," she said, and Jonesy and Walt left the club. For his part, Locke was happy to extend the night with Sam. A few minutes later, Sam noticed that AJ was gone, too. Locke saw the puzzled look on her face and asked her what the matter was. "Have you seen AJ?" she asked.

"AJ and Jack Nathan left when you were in the ladies' room. They seemed to be having an argument."

"Oh. Then I guess it's for the best that I'm not a third wheel. Could you give me a ride to my car, Locke?"

"Sure, where's your car?"

"In Manayunk."

"Sure, I can drive you to Manayunk."

"Jonesy asked me to take the long way home. Is that a problem?"

"No problem at all."

They were driving down the Benjamin Franklin Parkway when Sam said, "Pull over, Locke." Locke pulled over in front of the Museum of Art, and Sam jumped out of the car, saying, "Come on. Let's do the Rocky run up the museum steps. I bet I can beat you!"

"So, you think you can beat me in heels and a gown?" he drawled.

"I grew up in Manayunk and climbed the iron steps from Lower Manayunk to Upper Manayunk every day to and from school. AJ has been whipping us into shape for the wedding. I have the stamina—and the well-developed legs, I might add."

Sam kicked off her shoes and hiked up her gown. "See?"

"Yes, there is no denying your legs," Locke said with an admiring shake of his head.

"I'm getting a head start," Sam said, dashing up the steps two at a time. Locke stayed behind her intentionally and smiled the entire way.

At the top of the steps, Sam raised her arms in victory and jumped. "I win, I win!" she said as she turned around to see Locke nearing the top of the steps, smiling. "You let me win!" she accused.

"Sorry, I had such a good view, I couldn't bring myself to take the lead," he said, winking.

"So much for my stamina. I'm completely spent," she said, putting her hands on her knees. "You're not even out of breath."

"Allow me to assist you," Locke said as he encircled his arms around her and pulled her back to his chest. She leaned back against him, and he kissed her head lightly, making his way down to her neck. Sam rolled her head back and looked up at the sky.

"This has been a magical day, Locke."

Locke responded, "Uh-huh. Hmmm, Chanel Number Five."

"Yes, it is. Do you like my perfume?"

When Sam didn't pull away, Locke trailed light kisses down her neck and said, "Uh-huh."

"Aren't the parkway and the art museum some of the most beautiful sites in Philly? This was such a wonderful day, start to finish. I feel like Grace, not Sam, Kelly."

Locke stopped kissing her hair and shook his head. "No, you are not like Grace Kelly. You are more like Maureen O'Hara. You have spunk and fire, and you are not afraid to fight back."

"OK, so if I'm Maureen O'Hara, who are you—John Wayne?"

"I could be John Wayne."

"No, not Wayne," said Sam. "You're more like Atticus Finch."

Locke looked at her quizzically. "Atticus Finch?"

"Yes, in *To Kill a Mockingbird*."

"I know who he is. I went to Catholic school, too. But why am I Atticus Finch?"

"You are a paragon of honor and virtue in a less-than-honorable world."

Locke laughed. "How many martinis have you had?"

"Detective Locke, do you think I didn't notice the times you saved me from myself and discreetly prevented me from taking a punch from Wexler? Even tonight, you're struggling to be honorable and save me from myself."

"How so?"

"You're afraid to kiss me because you think I am drunk."

"Maybe a little, but I am more afraid that tomorrow you won't forgive me."

"I am pretty sure I'm going to like you tomorrow."

"That is good to hear, because I am pretty sure I'm going to be crazy about you for the rest of my life. So, could we at least be in the same movie?"

Sam placed her finger to her mouth and tapped her lip, thinking, and then she said, "Yes, you could be John Wayne. He was rather dapper and lawyerly, and he starred with Maureen O'Hara in *Miracle on Thirty-Fourth Street*. Does that work for you?"

"It could, but to the disappointment of many, I didn't go to law school after college. I'm just a cop."

"Just a cop, you say? Nothing could be further from the truth. You are a unique detective. Very different from a typical cop. Why, you don't even have the standard-issue Philadelphia police mustache."

Sam laughed, and then she and Locke stared at each other for several quiet seconds before Sam whispered, "I want this day never to end. What do you want, Locke?"

Locke spun her around to face him and placed his hands on her face. "I want everything, Samantha Kelly," he said, staring deep into her brown eyes.

"Everything is a lot," she replied slowly as she tried to process what he meant.

"Uh-huh," he murmured, and then he kissed her, releasing the passion that had been building through the night. Sam, breathless from his unexpected tenderness, relaxed against his five-foot-ten frame. Locke picked her up in his arms and carried her toward his car.

"What are you doing?" she asked.

"I don't want you to step on something, walking in bare feet."

"Oh, but I don't want you to break both our necks by falling down the steps. Let me walk," she said, wrapping her arms around his neck and giving him butterfly kisses on his neck and earlobe as she slipped to her feet.

After settling Sam on the passenger's side, he slid into the driver's seat. She stared at him with big brown lusty eyes, and he leaned over to pull her to him for one last kiss. Locke then drove around the circle and down the East River Drive toward Manayunk, wondering how Detective Kelly would feel about their kisses when the sun rose in the morning. There was only one way to find out; he had to ask her. He pulled his car over. Sam gave him an uncertain look, but she put her arms around his neck and began to bite his earlobe. Locke grabbed her shoulders and moved her away. "We need to talk, Samantha," he said in a low voice.

Sam felt like the wind had been knocked out of her. She'd thought she was reading him well, but oh God, how embarrassing. She must've been moving too fast for him, and now he thought she was a slut. *How do I save face?* she thought.

"OK, Locke, I get it," she said with bravado. "No need to put me on notice. You're trying to tell me it was a nice night, and we had a good time, but there will be no next time. No need to feel guilty or tell anyone about this—right?"

Locke arched his eyebrows. "That is exactly what I am not trying to say," he replied.

"Oh?" she said slowly, looking down at her hands, which were now on her lap.

"Sam, I've always liked you. I liked working with you, even though you kept a wall between you and your coworkers. I understood the wall, but I couldn't figure out why you never lost eye contact with suspects but rarely looked at your coworkers. When I saw you today, you took my breath away. When we spoke, I felt like I was meeting a different person. I sensed you were ready to make contact, and I was right. We haven't stopped looking at each other. I like it, but I want to know: what happens tomorrow after the alcohol wears off? Will I be reintroduced to Detective Kelly or still get to know Samantha? While I liked working with Detective Kelly, she always kept her distance. I would much rather continue to get to know Samantha."

Sam expelled a deep breath and laughed. "Locke, for the record, at no time have I been under the influence of alcohol. I had a little, but I am not drunk. When we spoke in the azalea garden before the wedding reception, I had a sip of champagne. During the reception, I had half of a martini. And you were with me for three hours at PJ's, where I nursed a martini to be polite but never finished it. I have always had my wits about me. I have never enjoyed my friends or a day like today—I mean, yesterday—so entirely. Kate and Ray have a special relationship. And Kate went out of her way to make sure we shared this day with her. Jonesy and I were convinced we'd hate the wedding and the wedding planning. We called Kate and her mother the wedding wardens, if you can believe it. We whined through every step of the way, but we actually found ourselves enjoying the whole thing. The workouts, the waxing, the spa, and the makeup were different but fun. Special. Then, when you came jogging down the trail and we saw each other, something happened. You connected with me, with one look. I can't explain it, but I don't want to lose it.

"This family of positive people and feeling good is new to me. This...regard...I have for you is new to me, and the sense that you feel it too is exhilarating for me. It's not alcohol—it's bliss.

"Kate and Ray are great role models for a relationship. Kate is a strong personality, and Ray isn't the least bit threatened by it. He is in fact proud of her. The wedding was flawless. I didn't think the day could get better until you showed up at Logan Circle. It was like I conjured you up. And then—"

Locke laughed and put a finger on her lips. "I'm glad quiet Detective Kelly has taken that hiatus, but I need get in a word edgewise. Samantha, this is the best day I've had in a very long time. It will be a setback for me if you have second thoughts about spending time with me after tonight. I need to know that you will let us continue to explore these feelings."

Sam smiled. "And I thought you were letting me off easy." Just then, the radio began playing "That's All." Sam closed her eyes, smiled, and said, "Ray sang this song to his bride at the wedding."

"Ray is a good man," Locke said.

Sam said, "It's a great song. I'd like a song."

"I believe God put me on this earth to please you. A song you shall have, and the record will be your possession, the minute you choose. How about one of the songs we danced? 'When a Man Loves a Woman' or 'Can't Take My Eyes Off of You?'"

Sam kissed his cheek. "Possible contenders, but I need to make a perfect choice."

Locke pulled her to him and said, "Sam, I don't want the day to end. How about I take you home, you change, and we get some breakfast and spend the day together."

Sam looked at him and said, "I have a counteroffer. How about we go to your apartment, get comfortable, and I make you breakfast?"

Locke's pulse started to quicken, and he said, "OK, what would you like?"

Sam bit his ear and whispered, "I want it all, too, Locke."

Locke smiled, remembering her comment. "All is a lot, Sam!"

"Yep," she replied with a nod of her head and a twinkle in her eye. Locke drove them to his apartment with his heart pounding in his chest.

Sam woke up the next morning to the smell of coffee brewing. As she walked over to the patio door, her thoughts about the events of the last twenty-four hours were interrupted by the vision of the Philadelphia Museum of Art, lit by a beautiful sunrise. She walked to the credenza and looked through Locke's stereo LPs. She found an album of Nat King Cole's greatest hits. She turned on the turntable and played "Unforgettable." Locke walked up behind her and pulled her into his chest. He swayed them to the music and whispered, "Maybe this could be our song."

Sam laughed. "Hmmm, maybe." Locke walked back to the kitchen as Sam continued to stare at the skyline of the city.

Eventually, she made her way to the kitchen, where Greg was placing the finishing touches on a plate of creamed chipped beef and hash browns. "It's not Melrose Diner quality, but at least you don't have to share half a booth with strangers," he joked.

"The only problem is, I promised to make you breakfast."

Greg ignored her and changed the subject. "I was thinking, how would you like it if I transferred to your squad?"

Sam panicked. "Wexler works two-squad. Do you think that's a good idea? He is such a dick. If he found out about us, he would torture you."

Locke raised an eyebrow and turned her to face him. "You know you excite me when you curse, but what do you mean *if* he finds out about us? I don't intend to court you in secret. I don't care who knows about us. I'm good with the whole world knowing."

Sam looked down at his chest. "Please, Locke," Sam pleaded, "I am a private person. I hate gossip, and I hate being watched or judged. For the time being, I want to keep you and me a secret. I want to keep this good."

"I can handle Wexler and anyone else who has something to say," Locke said reassuringly. "Wexler can be a jackass in general, and I admit he does have a hard-on for you. But you let him win when he gets to you. I never openly interfered because you wouldn't have permitted it and because I didn't have the right to get in the middle. That was before. Things have changed."

"Locke, please don't ever get into it with him or with anyone because of me. I would never forgive myself if you were hurt over me. That would be the supreme humiliation for me, and our friendship wouldn't survive it."

Locke took her hand. "Well, I was thinking of something more than friendship, but I'll take what I can get. You have your terms. Private it is, but can we renegotiate this agreement in six months?"

～

In Manayunk, Walt was fixing his tie as Jonesy poured his coffee. Walt took a sip and said, "When you see Sam, please thank her for giving us time alone last night. I think she and Locke were happy to be alone, too. They seem to like each other."

"I hope so," Jonesy said. "Sam used to accuse me of having a jaded view of men, but these days, I think she has taken on the role. Locke is a good guy, and he's obviously smitten. I wonder where she spent the night. Do you think we can tease her about being a Lockette now?"

"From what I observed, that is a distinct possibility. Speaking of weddings, what do you think about our future, Jonesy?" asked Walt.

Jonesy kissed the top of his head. "I wasn't speaking of weddings. Don't start getting honorable with me," she said. "You and I have something nice here. Let's not rock the boat. You have the kids to raise, and I would just complicate things, especially with the girls—we are a demanding lot."

"OK, babe. If that changes, let me know. I am all in, but it's your call," said Walt.

～

At AJ's Chestnut Hill apartment, the conversation was less amicable.

"Look, AJ, I'm sorry I missed the wedding. Can't we get past it? That's why I got threatening vibes from your friends, right? I think they make any conflict between us worse. You need to start living your life without those hags."

"Those hags are my sisters. They care about me, and they think you are just jerking me around. Quite frankly, I am beginning to feel the same. You bailed on going to the wedding but show up at the after-party and want to make nice. Where are we going with this, Jack?"

Jack ran a hand through his hair.

"This is why I don't like your friends. They make you think this way."

"No, if the tables were turned, I would be the one telling my friends they were stupid to put up with this. Our relationship has been one-way: You ask, and I give." AJ sighed. "Look, I'm tired, and I don't want to argue and say something we can't get past. Decide what you want and who you want. I'll be waiting. Goodbye, Jack."

"I want you, AJ. I just need to work some things out."

"Goodbye, Jack."

Jack grabbed his jacket and left. AJ shook her head and said aloud, "Why would I fall in love with a jerk like him? I'm not taking my own advice."

*Far and away the best prize that life has to offer is the
chance to work hard at work worth doing.*

—Theodore Roosevelt

THIRTY-ONE

WHILE KATE AND RAY WERE ON THEIR HONEYMOON IN
Tuscany, Captain Callahan asked Sam if she was interested in a
transfer to the Homicide Division.

"Thank you, Captain, but I am happy here in Central
Detectives. I'm curious, though—why?" asked Sam.

"I think the chief thinks it's time for a female homicide detective. Your track record for investigations leads the division, and I
understand the chief asked about you after Ray Rossi's wedding. You
know his sister is Ray's mother. I'm happy to hear you want to stay,
but does your decision have anything to do with Jim Wexler?"

"No, Captain. I admit I wouldn't look forward to working with
Wexler, but he isn't the reason for my decision. Division work crosses
all types of crime, including homicide. I'm not ready to focus on
a specialty."

When Sam arrived home after the day shift, she told Jonesy
of her discussion with the captain. "Jonesy, I know that you are new
to the detective bureau, but if you have any interest, you should put
in for a transfer as soon as possible. The PD brass wants a woman in
Homicide, and it might be a good opportunity—especially if you feel
awkward about working in the same division as Walt."

"I'm interested because it's Homicide, but I don't have your hang-ups. I don't care who knows that Walt and I date. He is in a different squad. I don't attract controversy like a magnet, like you do. But maybe if you would just stop pushing when you're challenged, they'd leave you alone."

"What do you mean?"

"Don't tell me you're surprised to hear that. Sam, when we were in the police academy, we worried you were too complacent. Now we worry we created a monster. Except when it comes to your family, you refuse to back down."

I know that God will not give me anything I can't handle;
I just wish he didn't trust me so much.

—*Mother Teresa*

THIRTY-TWO

"OK, Reagan, I'll be there." Sam hung up the phone, nausea creeping into her stomach as she contemplated the family meeting that afternoon to discuss Denny. Sam had noticed that Denny was looking more fatigued lately, and she was afraid of the news.

When Sam walked into Leana's home, all their siblings except for Denny had already arrived. Sam made eye contact with Reagan and immediately saw her distress.

"What's the matter, Reagan?"

"I'm sorry that I'm here. I didn't think it would be an ambush, Sam."

"What do you mean?"

"There was a pre-meeting, and Beth and Leana already convinced our brothers and their wives to gang up on Denny."

"To what end?"

"They have a list of restrictions for him."

"Why?"

"Doctor Beth over there is determined to revoke his driver's license, and she has a whole list of other demands. She said she's doing it to protect Mom and Dad from additional stress. They worry about him driving." Reagan's voice was both bitter and sad.

"Even if that were true, this is all out of line. I'm not going to be a part of this."

"Leana and Beth knew you wouldn't. That's why you weren't invited to the pre-meeting."

"Reagan, are our brothers too gutless to stand up for Denny's rights and his dignity?"

"Seems so, Sam."

Just then, Denny walked through the door. Beth immediately launched into the list of family demands. Denny was to give up his license and his car, but he was also not allowed to talk to their parents about his health issues. Finally, Denny shouldn't visit their parents on days he wasn't well, Beth proclaimed, because it was too upsetting to see him like that.

Denny looked shocked and hurt. Sam didn't hold back. "Denny, let's get out of here. This is bullshit." Sam turned to face her siblings. "How dare you make demands! And how dare you represent Mom and Dad this way? This is beyond controlling. It's sick. You are all despicable."

Reagan spoke up. "Sam's right. This fiasco is beyond belief. I'm outta here too."

As Sam, Denny, and Reagan turned to leave, Beth spoke up, her voice following them out the door. "If there is a tragedy, it will be on your conscience."

Denny regained his composure as they walked toward their cars. "I'm glad to have such strong sisters. That felt like a trap, and I wasn't prepared," he said. "I'll circle back with them when I'm not so off kilter. I'll talk to Beth next week when I'm visiting Mom and Dad."

~

AJ was the first to hear the news over the police radio, a week later. A fatal car crash on the East River Drive; the car was registered to Reverend Dennis Kelly. AJ rushed to Central Detectives so Sam could hear it from her.

AJ drove Sam to the crash site. In addition to her brother, her parents were pronounced dead on the scene. The accident investigation division determined that the weather was not a factor in the accident, and it was a single-car crash.

Sam couldn't breathe. It had taken only a week for Beth's prediction to come true. This was all her fault.

AJ read Sam's thoughts. "Sam, the East River Drive has many winding and potentially deadly turns. That's why there are so many single car crashes on this road. This is not your fault."

"Yeah, sure," Sam said, already feeling numb.

The funeral of Kathryn and Gene Kelly and their son, Father Dennis Kelly, was well attended. Sam was touched by the significant police presence. Locke agreed to remain in the background, but he stayed close.

The service was held at a small church in Manayunk. The rift between Sam and her siblings had become more pronounced as the funeral details were finalized. She overheard her gutless brother say that his parents and brother were dead because of petty infighting among his sisters. As Sam walked away from the grave site, she realized that she had nothing in common with her siblings and little desire ever to see them again. Reagan was the only sibling Sam wanted in her life.

Could my life get any lower or more depressing? Sam thought. In one year, she ended a marriage, saw her best friend almost killed on duty, and lost three of the most important people in her life. *Will the pain ever subside?*

PART III

Present Day

*I love those who can smile in trouble, who can gather
strength from distress and grow brave by reflection…they
whose heart is firm, and whose conscience approves their
conduct, will pursue their principles unto death.*

—Leonardo da Vinci

THIRTY-THREE

"SAM, ARE YOU OK?" JONESY ASKED. SHE WAS STANDING NEXT
to Sam's pew in the cathedral where Kate and Ray were married. "I
got a call from John Hogan. He said you reported on duty and then
walked out of the division hours ago, and no one has heard from you.
Hogan and Mullen are covering for you, but they're afraid you're out
on a ledge somewhere. I figured you wanted to be alone to think, but
I thought I'd look for you before they put together a search party. I
don't know why, but I knew I'd find you here. You OK?"

Sam shook her head as if to clear it from the fog of memories.
"That would have been a fitting end to a sucky day. But thanks for
saving me from myself. I'm OK. I came in here to think for a minute,
and I lost track of time."

"Did it help you get your head on straight?" asked Jonesy.

"I think so. This is really the first time since AJ died that I've
been able to sort through my thoughts. I think I can take a step back
and be objective now. I am ready for one of Kate's grand plans to
prove it."

"Kate's on it, and I'm right with both of you. Before Hogan
called me, Kate called. When she and Ray were at AJ's apartment, she

found something. Kate wants to meet and talk about it. She hasn't even told Ray about it yet. How about you report back to the division to let them know you didn't jump off the Ben Franklin Bridge and then make your way to Baker Street?"

Sam nodded and then replied, still feeling a little dreamy, "The last time we were here, it was a great day. We were all so happy and so…together. I was hoping this place would make me feel better, and hoping AJ would send me a sign. I think she did. At least, my head is clear."

"After years of listening to your arguments over the value of religion, I guessed that you would try to tap into AJ's spirituality out of desperation. She might make a believer out of us after all. I stopped by a church this afternoon, too."

"I think I am trying to muster some of AJ's determination. I'm not going to give up until I'm satisfied I know what happened to AJ. We owe it to her, Jonesy."

Jonesy offered Sam a high five and replied, "We gotta wake up everybody." She paused. "We owe it to her, but we also owe it to each other, Sam. Get back to Central, and wrap it up for the night. See you at Baker Street."

Several minutes later, Sam took a deep breath and walked into Central Detectives, stone-faced. 'Hey Mullen, Hogan," she said, nodding at them. "Sorry I was gone so long. Did I miss anything?"

"Jack Nathan is in the back room," Mullen said. "He's asking to talk with you, Kelly."

"Really?" replied Sam.

"Do you want me to get rid of him, Sam?" asked Hogan.

Before Sam could answer, Jack Nathan walked in. Hogan and Mullen stayed close but said nothing.

"Sam, I need to talk with you. I can see you're angry at me, but it's because you don't understand. Can we go somewhere and talk?"

"Jack, are you here to confess to AJ's murder? If so, I'm interested. If not, we have nothing to discuss at this time."

"I want you to know I loved AJ and would never do anything to hurt her."

"You would never do anything to hurt her?" Sam asked incredulously. "Jack, if you came here to lie to me, I'll remind you that I carry a gun."

"AJ always said you were a good listener. If you would just sit down and listen to me, I could make you understand that AJ was a victim of love and not of me. You need to believe me. I can't come to work every day thinking you, Kate, and Jonesy hate me and hold me responsible for AJ's death." Jack was good—very good—at convincing women they should give him a second chance. But Sam wasn't AJ, and she wasn't having it.

"Well then...I guess you better get a new job, Jack." Sam enunciated each of her next words with bone-chilling clarity. "Let me be clear, you lowlife excuse for a man. If you're looking for absolution, think again. From this day forward, I'll be on your heels looking for an opportunity to make you pay for what you did to her."

"Are you threatening me?" Jack said in disbelief, looking to Hogan and Mullen for support. He saw only loathing on their faces.

Sam turned her back on Nathan, and Hogan and Mullen followed in her wake. She strode toward the squad room to collect her computer and files so she could leave for the day. Hogan said, "Wait for me, Sam, I'm leaving with you."

As the two detectives walked down the long, gray corridor at Central Detectives, Hogan said, "I think you made him cry."

"He deserves to shed more than his tears. Why would he come to a detective division to talk to me like that?"

"I think because he wanted witnesses in case you decided to shoot him."

Sam laughed. "Thank you, John. That was funny. I guess I surprise myself when people believe my don't-mess-with-this-crazy-woman act. I needed that laugh. Thanks."

"I'm glad I could make you laugh. Yes, you are very convincing—it didn't look like an act. And after three wives, I never take a woman's threat for granted."

Sam turned and hugged him. "You're one of the good guys."

"Yeah, that's what all my ex-wives told me, too."

Sam laughed again.

"Good night, Sam. Take care of yourself."

"All is good, John. Thanks for covering for me. See you tomorrow."

≈

At Baker Street, Kate, Jonesy, and Sam sat in a circle. They all wore sweatpants and sweatshirts and drank beer. The room was lit only by the burning log in the fireplace.

"You were right, Sam, when you said today sucked. Except for your singing."

"Jonesy is right. Sam, you were amazing! Ray couldn't stop talking about you. Did you work things out with Locke?"

"Yes. We went back to Greg's apartment, and he made me a sandwich. He was kind, I started blubbering, and then, of course, he went out of his way to comfort me, which made it worse. I'm still angry he wants me to believe AJ committed suicide, but I didn't want to fight with him."

"You're not alone," said Kate. "Ray and I can't talk about it without arguing. I found some papers in AJ's apartment, and I didn't tell Ray because I thought he would be dismissive."

"They're idiots, including Walt. They don't understand that we're not in denial," said Jonesy.

"Jack Nathan was waiting for me at Central Detectives. I think I threatened him. John Hogan told me I was convincing."

"You are scary when someone is on your shit list," Jonesy said.

Sam laughed. "Greg cautioned me about how scary I sound when I refer to my 'hit parade.' Now I know what he means."

"Locke is an idiot, too," Jonesy said.

"I wouldn't characterize him as an idiot. He is protective, and he cares. They're all being protective, even if it is misdirected."

"That makeup session you two had today must've sent you to the dark side if you're defending him," Jonesy said as she rolled her eyes.

Sam smirked at Jonesy and turned to Kate. "What do you have, Kate?"

"As I was packing some of AJ's things, I found a notebook. It looked relatively new because it was blank for the most part, but I noticed from the spiral binding that someone had ripped out pages. There was a receipt tucked inside with a date stamp from a few days before. I thought if she had ripped them out, I'd find the pages in the trash. I looked around but didn't see anything. I picked up the book and threw it in frustration, and it opened to a page with writing. Here it is. It's not much information, but it's interesting. It probably wouldn't have caught my eye if you hadn't said AJ was going to tell you something about Wexler. Then again, anything about Green Valley piques my interest."

Kate handed the paper to Sam and Jonesy. There were only four lines scrawled in AJ's familiar handwriting:

Fentanyl and Benzodiazepine

Wexler and Green Valley

Sam and her sister

10/8: Terrance Owens

"OK, I can explain the first three lines," Sam said. "I don't get the fourth line, but I think we can surmise she was meeting Terrance Owens on October 8. The question is, who is Terrance Owens? A resident, a relative, an employee?"

"What do the first three lines mean?"

"Fentanyl and benzodiazepine were the drugs reportedly missing from Green Valley when Leighann Jordan asked me to reopen the case. Wexler was assigned to the original case and declared it unfounded. My sister, who worked there, accused me of getting her fired."

"Do you think this is even related to AJ's death?" Jonesy asked. "Let's take a step back and review all that we know and list the potential suspects. What about Jack Nathan, his wife or girlfriend, or a stranger? Can we dismiss them as suspects?"

"OK," said Kate, "I'll scribe. Let's list the facts we know, our suspects, and the potential theories." Kate wrote short statements as she repeated them. "AJ is found dead in her apartment. No forced entry. The only other keys to the apartment belonged to Jack, Sam, and maybe the apartment manager. The weapon used was her service revolver. Jack Nathan called 911, but he reported a hospital case, not a homicide. The paraffin test confirmed Nathan had gunshot residue on his hands. Nathan's polygraph was inconclusive. Anything else?"

"Yeah. Jack, the gutless wonder that he is, came to Central Detectives tonight to try to convince me he didn't kill her. He is definitely afraid of something," said Sam.

"He should be terrified," said Jonesy. "He knows we hate him, and we all have weapons. But why would he want to talk to you in a police station?"

"Hogan thinks he's afraid I'd shoot him. But he's also a grandstander and would want everyone to hear him say he didn't kill her."

"What did you do?" asked Kate. "I'm thinking that you weren't in the mood to forgive and forget?"

"Let's just say I blew my chances of taking his confession if he did do it. I think he's going to avoid me like the plague from now on."

"That doesn't sound so bad," Kate said. "OK, is there anything else we should consider about Jack?"

"Yeah, he's a pathological liar. In the statement he gave Wexler, he said they met at one of Ray's fundraiser gigs. We all know he tried to pick her up at a restaurant."

"We will need to keep in mind that he lies even when he doesn't need to. It could send us down a dead end," Kate said. "OK, let's get organized. Where do we go from here?"

Jonesy said, "We have one witness who talked to AJ right before her death. It's you, Sam. I know you already told us, but let's go through what you know about that night."

Sam nodded and took a deep breath. "AJ called me from a pay phone at about twelve thirty in the morning. She was crying so hard I could barely understand her. She told me that Jack's wife and girlfriend had showed up at her front door around six in the evening.

They didn't waste much time with small talk. After announcing they were both sleeping with Jack, they talked her into visiting him to show him their matching bracelets. They drove in separate cars to his apartment in Northeast Philly. I think it's somewhere off Cottman Avenue. Got there around 7:00 p.m. They weren't sure he would be there, but AJ had his key. Turns out AJ was the only one of the three who had a key—I guess that meant she was at the top of his totem pole, so to speak. Jack walked in, and the three of them were sitting on his big brown leather couch, waiting for him. AJ said Jack's complexion went from pale to gray in about thirty seconds. For the first time in his life, he was caught so off guard that he didn't have his usual glib story line prepared. Lisa, the other girlfriend, and Betty, the wife, laid into him.

"AJ just listened, and all of a sudden she realized she was the only one who didn't know he was cheating. Lisa knew Jack was seeing AJ and Betty, and Betty knew Jack was seeing AJ. AJ quickly began to regret being there, participating in their assault on Jack, because they were as pathetic as he is. AJ left his apartment and drove around for a while. She was doing some soul-searching about why she is good at sizing up situations and men except in her own life. She finally pulled over at a phone booth and called me. I had just walked in the door after the four-to-midnight shift when I heard the phone ringing.

"We talked for a long time. She asked me to give her the same advice she had given me when I needed a kick in the butt to get off the self-destructive Jeff train. I struggled to say anything at first because I didn't think I could compare Jeff to Jack. I was never in love with Jeff, and she was clearly in love with Jack. Because I wasn't sure what to say, I did what I do best: I kept asking questions. Finally, she reached the same point I had on the night she'd told me about Beth and Jeff—when I realized I wasn't surprised. She said she knew Jack was a bullshit artist. She started recounting all of the lies she caught him in. We laughed about the time he tried to convince her that he was working, when AJ walked into him coming out of the FOP bar. She knew he was lying, but she felt so sure about his commitment to her that she didn't care. She thought that his fear over her breaking up with him showed that he loved her. When she told me how he bought gifts in triplicate, I started to laugh because I thought that if it were a Hollywood script, no one would believe it. I told her so, and she laughed with me. We spent about an hour talking about how to get Jack out of her life.

"I knew she was in a phone booth and it was raining. I asked her to come over, but she said she was due in court in the morning and needed to go back to her apartment for uniform and equipment. I told her I was also due for court, and she asked me to meet her after I checked in. She said she needed to talk about Wexler. I thought she was going to give me a lecture on not pushing his buttons, but when I tried to get her to tell me more, she said she could only handle one crisis at a time. When she used the word 'crisis' in the same breath as Wexler, I thought it meant trouble, and I didn't want to wait until the next day. But she insisted. And, although it's my greatest regret, I was tired, so I gave in. I thought it could wait. I'll regret that decision until the day I die." Sam's voice softened, and she stared into space as she continued, "When Locke told me AJ was dead, my brain went right to Wexler. I can't explain it, but I knew somehow he would be the assigned investigator. When I saw Wexler at Homicide later that day, he was as mean and obnoxious as expected. But what I didn't expect was his reaction when I baited him by making him think I knew more than I did. I definitely pushed a button. He looked afraid when I suggested that he should be interviewed."

Sam paused and squeezed her eyes shut. "Damn it, if AJ had told me more, or if I had driven to her apartment, we'd know more. Maybe we could have even saved her."

"Maybe," said Jonesy. "But if someone killed AJ and then you showed up, they might have killed you as well."

"Thanks for the vote of confidence." Sam countered. "You're assuming I would've been on the losing end of a gun battle. Locke said the same thing. To the contrary, I believe the two of us together, me and AJ, might have made the difference."

"Maybe, maybe not. Is there anything else you can remember?" asked Jonesy.

"Not the night she died. But there's something I have to tell you. When I was going through my drama with Jeff, she told me about her divorce from David when she lived in Hawaii. She said at one point, she was so low she thought about taking a walk into the Pacific Ocean. She never said that she acted on her thoughts, and I didn't ask. I was going to ask her father about it, but I decided it wasn't the time to bring it up."

"OK, so we're back to square one. Either Jack Nathan is a murderer, or AJ did commit suicide," said Kate.

"No, we're not. We have a list of possibilities—including a couple of angry women and Wexler. But let's begin with Jack," suggested Sam.

"Jack looks guilty, but you don't think he did it, do you, Sam?" asked Kate.

"No, I don't. Jack thought he could convince AJ of anything. He is a self-centered philanderer and a jerk, but I don't think he's a murderer. But we can't rule him out."

"What about the not-so-ex-wife and girlfriend?" asked Kate.

"We keep them on the list, but I think their target for revenge was Jack, not AJ. I would guess when she walked out of Jack's apartment, they were convinced their goal was accomplished."

"On the other hand," said Jonesy, "we think Wexler is guilty of something even if it's just being a misogynist prick."

"Yep." Sam agreed. "Wexler has always tormented me specifically, hiding behind his Internal Affairs buddy to make trouble for me whenever he could. But his current obnoxious behavior wouldn't be out of the ordinary except for the following facts:

"Fact 1: AJ made me think trouble was coming my way in the form of Wexler. It sounded bad because she referred to it as a crisis. Since I haven't heard anything yet, the crisis might have died with AJ. That is suspicious because Wexler never misses an opportunity to screw with me.

"Fact 2: I told you about Wexler's reaction when I pushed back at him. I was trying to match his callousness with accusatory malice. I was only fishing, but I think I snagged something. I'm not sure what it is yet, but there is something. And I think that he thinks I know more than I do. The thought occurred to me that I should avoid being alone with him—just in case.

"Fact 3: Wexler showed up extra early for first shift and maneuvered his way into becoming the assigned investigator for AJ's death.

"Fact 4: AJ's notes tell us she was snooping around the Green Valley investigation. I don't know why she didn't tell us, but I'm guessing she wanted me to have plausible deniability if she were caught. Wexler may have found out.

"Fact 5: He would have had the opportunity to rip the notes out of her notebook when he processed her apartment on the day of the shooting. Did he completely miss it, or didn't it mean anything to him and he had nothing to hide?"

Jonesy was sitting up straight. "My guess is that he has something to hide, and right now he is sticking needles in his Samantha Kelly voodoo doll. Wexler just reached the top of my hit parade of suspects. I'm in the best position to keep an eye on him, and I will watch every move he makes from here on out. Beyond that—what's our move?"

"It's finding Terrance Owens," Sam said. "We find out who he is and what he can tell us about AJ and anything else."

"OK, who takes point on finding Terrance Owens?" asked Kate, still taking copious notes.

"Me. l can contact Leighann Jordan. She might know Terrance Owens if he has a connection to Green Valley," Sam replied. "Jonesy, can you see if you can access any reports from Homicide, mobile crime, and the medical examiner? I'd like to see if there are any nuggets of information we might consider. And I'd like to try to zero in on the time of death as closely as possible. Maybe that will exclude some of our suspects."

"That's enough thinking for me, I need some sleep," Jonesy said, yawning. "Kate, are you staying or going back to South Philly?"

"I'm going home. Ray and I have been walking on eggshells with each other, and I don't want to add to the strain."

"You've changed. I never thought you would go out of your way to appease him!"

Kate rolled her eyes. "I'm not appeasing anyone. Ray is my husband. Oh, I'm tired, and I don't want to argue with you, too. Suffice to say, sometimes I think Walt is a saint."

Sam laughed. "Amen, sister. Our girl Jonesy keeps us on our toes. She defends Locke when I'm mad at him, but she gets mad when I defend him."

Jonesy shrugged. "I just don't get you two sometimes."

~

Sam met Ray Rossi at a Center City coffee shop the next morning.

"You look tired, Sam. I'm assuming the three amigas had a late night?"

Sam's eyes filled with sudden tears as she remembered the four musketeers were no more. Ray immediately knew what she was thinking. "I'm sorry, Sam, I didn't mean to upset you. I wanted to tell you again how beautifully you sang at AJ's funeral."

"So you said yesterday, Ray. What's up?"

"I was thinking about how we can help each other. I have an idea that I ran by the band. Sam, music is a healer. I think we all need healing, and you can help."

Sam stopped him. "I'm tired, brother. Where are you going with this?"

He smiled. "I'm trying to flatter you to pull you into my plan. The band is doing a holiday benefit to raise money for the families of fallen police officers."

"I'm not taking AJ's place with the band, and I'm not singing the national anthem at the Thrill Show, Ray," she said.

He put his hand up. "It's a holiday benefit at Palumbo's on December 29th. The Hero's Ball. And Kate told me that's Locke's birthday. If you sing, you'll get free tickets, and we can celebrate his birthday. God knows we need something to celebrate. All I ask is that we sing a couple of duets. How about it?"

Sam hesitated. "Ray, I'm flattered, but I haven't had formal training, I'm not that good, and I wouldn't want to let you down."

Ray was ready for that argument. He immediately countered, saying, "Perry Como never had formal training either. You can't deny his success."

She laughed and said, "I'm not sure that's a good analogy!" Sam rubbed her hand across her forehead. "What songs?"

"I'd like to sing 'The Impossible Dream' and 'Holding Out For a Hero' as a duet."

"OK, I get you and the 'Impossible Dream,' it's a classic. But you, singing a Bonnie Tyler song—really?"

"Sinatra and I have something in common: we try to stay relevant. But this is an opportunity to acknowledge the men and women in law enforcement. What better tribute than to have the songs performed by one of the best detectives I know and a lowly lieutenant from research and planning?" He paused. "My personal reason is, it's the best gift I can think to give my hurting wife. She'll be thrilled to have the role of women acknowledged—but to have you represent the women would be icing on the cake for her. You know she never got her dream of a ceremony when you all graduated from the academy or when she was promoted to sergeant. This is my way of making it up to her.

"Morton Solomon is a very different commissioner from Joe O'Neill. He and many others in the PD brass are forward-looking. It's the right thing for the right time. I can take the heat, but I don't think there will be any. And you are the right person at the right time. The chief himself told me he likes your sincerity, persistence, style, and results. That is high praise from someone who rarely compliments anyone. He requested that I make the Hero's Ball special, and I can't think of a better way."

"OK, OK, I'm in." Sam conceded. "I'll give it a go, but I predict you'll need to carry me."

"Not a chance," Ray said, chuckling. "Bobby O will arrange the music, and we have more than a month to practice. Bobby is also planning a special tribute to our female officers. Oh, one more thing. I'd like this to be a surprise—don't tell anyone."

"I am sworn to secrecy."

The truth is rarely pure and never simple.

—Oscar Wilde

THIRTY-FOUR

⎯⎯⎯⎯⎯⎯⎯⎯⎯⎯ •• ⎯⎯⎯⎯⎯⎯⎯⎯⎯⎯

LEIGHANN JORDAN WAS DRINKING A CUP OF COFFEE AND watching *Good Morning America* at her kitchen table when the phone rang.

"Hello, Leighann, this is Detective Kelly calling from Central Detective Division."

"Detective, I was going to call you. I saw in the paper about the officer found dead. You worked with her, didn't you?"

"Yes, I did. If you have a moment, I am calling to pick your brain about something."

"Sure, Detective. What do you want to know?"

"Do you recognize the name Terrance Owens?"

"Yes, they call him Bean."

"Who are 'they?'"

"Everyone at Green Valley. He's an aide there."

"Can you tell me anything about him?"

"He's a nice guy, seemed very pleasant. He was always kind to my father. Do you suspect him of something?"

"No, no, nothing like that. I think he might be able to give us some information."

"I'm pretty sure you've seen him before. He was there the day Brenda and I met with you outside the nursing home. He was talking to the other aide, Beth, and they were watching us."

Sam thought for a moment, searching her memory, and then asked, "Was he wearing blue scrubs and a knit cap the day we met?"

"Yes, that was him. He always wears that cap."

"Do you know anything else about him?"

"Nothing right now, but if I remember anything, I'll call you. I still have your card."

After hanging up, Sam immediately called Jonesy at home.

"Jonesy, Terrance Owens was and may still be an employee of Green Valley. Can you make some discreet inquiries and find out how we can connect with him?"

"Got it, Sam. I'll let you know what I find. In the meantime, your boyfriend seems to have guessed what we're up to. He told me to let him work on getting those reports—that I should lay low and let him take care of it. What do you think?"

"I think we need to operate in the shadows. Locke is right. Let him take care of accessing the reports, and I'll be sure to make it up to him. Can you make the inquiries to find Owens?"

"I'm on it. I'll do it next shift. It wouldn't hurt to see if he has a record. If I can ID him, I'll order a photo. Oh, by the way, Carmella and Len invited us to their house for their holiday shindig this Sunday. You should come and bring Locke."

"OK, I'll let him know, but even if he can't make it, I'll definitely be there."

Walt and Ray were watching the end to the Philadelphia Eagles game when Locke showed up. He searched for Sam as he politely greeted everyone. Sam was in the basement kitchen of the South Philadelphia row house, watching the pasta boil when she heard his voice upstairs. She joined everyone in the front room, made eye contact with Locke, and smiled. Carmella looked at them and said, "Sam, why don't you show Greg upstairs to put away his coat?"

Sam showed Greg up the steps and to a back bedroom, pointing to a bed piled with coats. Greg shrugged off his coat and tossed it on the bed, and then he pulled her to his chest and hugged her.

"Miss me much?" Sam said, chuckling. "I'm sorry."

"Sorry for what?"

"I want you to know I have always trusted your instincts. I just wanted this to end as quickly as possible because I didn't want you to go through any more pain."

"I realize," Sam started to say, and then said, "What's up, Locke?"

"AJ was left-handed. Wasn't she?"

"Yes."

"The entry wound was on the right side of her head."

"Oh," she said softly, "that's big."

"Yes, it is," Locke said, pronouncing each word slowly and distinctly.

"After dinner and Christmas carols, we should have a meeting with the rest of the team," said Sam.

"Team?"

"Yeah, I think we need to bring in Ray and Walt. They might become as open-minded and enlightened as you." Sam smirked.

Locke kissed Sam and held her for a long moment. "Nice to know I might have some redeeming social value."

From downstairs, they heard Carmella announce that dinner was being served. Carmella's holiday table included an antipasto plate, seven fishes, meatballs and gravy, pasta, a baked ham, and assorted Italian pastries. No one ever left hungry.

They trooped slowly into the living room, clutching their full stomachs. Always prepared, Kate handed everyone their own book of Christmas carols. Ray sat at the piano and played as they all sang and laughed through "The Twelve Days of Christmas" together. During a lull, while they considered the next carol, Len said, "Sam, why don't you sing 'Hallelujah'? You sang it so beautifully. I'd love to hear it again."

Sam's heart started to race. She thought of last year, when AJ sang the song like an angel. "I'm sorry, I can't—"

Carmella frowned and gave a tug of disapproval on Len's arm. Ray saw the panic on Sam's face and suggested, "Sam, how about a duet. 'The Little Drummer Boy'—the Bing Crosby and David Bowie version?"

Sam smiled in thanks at Ray. "Only if I can be David Bowie," she said.

When they finished the song, Carmella said, "That was beautiful. You two sound like you've practiced together."

Ray quickly changed the subject. "How about coffee and cannoli?"

After dessert, Sam couldn't keep Locke's news quiet anymore. She looked at Kate and Jonesy and said, "Locke was able to access the medical examiner's report."

Everyone stared at Locke. "Well," he said, clearing his throat. "The report indicates the entry wound was on the right side of AJ's head."

Silence gripped the room for a full minute as everyone contemplated what that could mean. Jonesy was the first to speak. "I guess it's good we continued to ask questions. We also found out that Terrance Owens worked at Green Valley."

"Who is Terrance Owens?" asked Locke, Walt, and Ray at the same time.

Ray looked around the table at the three women. "Have you been conducting an unauthorized investigation without the knowledge of the assigned detective? I don't need to tell you how this could impact *all* of your careers."

"Ray," said Kate, "the assigned investigator may be the doer." The room seemed to echo with her words as the men stared at her in shocked silence. "OK, time for us to come clean," said Kate as she looked at Jonesy and Sam, who nodded at her. "Ray and I went to AJ's apartment to pack some things for Mr. and Mrs. Harris. I found a notebook in her bedroom. Terrance Owens's name was written in it, as well as Wexler's. It looked like someone had ripped pages out, but they missed this one page. Sam, Jonesy, and I are trying to figure out if it means anything. We think the notes and her death might be connected to the Green Valley investigation and, potentially, to Wexler."

Ray's voice was quiet. "You didn't feel like you could tell me." He wasn't asking a question but making a statement.

"Our relationship felt too fragile to risk an argument."

"Kate, we argue all the time. Our relationship was never at risk before."

"We never let the gender problems at work come between us before. But when we argued about AJ's death, it felt different."

Ray looked at Locke. "Were you operating separately, or were you part of the plan?"

Sam answered for him. "He guessed what we were up to. He's either pretty tuned into me or just a good detective."

Greg locked eyes with Sam and said, "Would you consider both?"

Sam winked. "You bet, Inspector Poirot."

"Let me see if I'm tracking with all of you," said Walt, who was trying process what everyone was saying. "Michelle, Sam, and Kate have been conducting a secret investigation into AJ's death. Locke found out and joined the team. He remembered AJ was left-handed, so we know Wexler screwed the pooch on the investigation because of the entry wound. The ladies think it was on purpose because he murdered AJ?"

"We are not ready to type the affidavit of probable cause, Walt," said Jonesy. "We do, however, now believe it definitely was *not* a suicide."

Walt turned to Jonesy. "Once Locke was on the team, why didn't you ask me?" The hurt in his voice was clear.

"I didn't want Locke, or Ray, or you to be on the 'team.' You didn't believe in us from the beginning, and I thought that you would be an obstacle."

His voice laden with regret, Walt responded, "Why?"

Jonesy dug in and tried to fight past her brittle voice. "I knew you already drew your conclusions. Why would I ask you to get involved if it went against what you really think?"

"I believe in you. I wish you believed I'd want to help."

Carmella looked around the table at the sad, angry, and serious faces. "Everyone in this room has been suffering. You girls have lost a friend you loved dearly. You boys have also lost a friend, and you want to fix the hurt of the women you love, but you can't. Acknowledge what is causing your pain and just help each other."

Locke, who was standing behind Sam, wrapped his arms around her and pulled her back into his chest, kissing her hair. Sam turned her head to smile at him and said, "I couldn't have said it better, Carmella." The tension in the room began to dissipate. Soon, Kate was debriefing everyone on their investigation, from the missing drugs at Green Valley to the notes in AJ's house.

"Our best lead is Terrance Owens. Jonesy is going to track him down and find out what he knows. We thought it best she meets with him away from Green Valley."

"I have an update on Owens," said Jonesy. "He no longer works at Green Valley. I called there and asked for him, and I was told he no longer works there. I did find a Terrance Owens in a records search, and I have a couple of addresses to check out."

"I think you need to have someone with you when you interview Owens," Locke said. "It isn't safe. We can't rule him out as the doer. We could take an unmarked car and check out a few addresses together."

"Makes sense," said Jonesy. "Let's hope we can track him down quickly."

~

*Music is a moral law. It gives soul to the universe, wings
to the mind, flight to the imagination, and charm and
gaiety to life and everything.*

—Plato

THIRTY-FIVE

WHEN SHE WASN'T WORKING—EITHER ON HER ACTUAL CASES
or on her AJ investigation—Sam was practicing for the police benefit.
During the next month, Ray, Sam, and the band met at every opportunity, and the rest of the time Sam listened to Bonnie Tyler singing
"Holding Out for a Hero" and Jack Jones singing "The Impossible
Dream." Each practice, Sam felt better and better about performing
both songs with Ray.

The night of the benefit, Sam made plans to meet Locke, who
was working until 4:00 p.m., at his apartment. She donned her new
dress—a short black sequin number—and twirled in front of the
bathroom mirror. "AJ and Kate should be proud," she told her reflection in the mirror. "I've turned into a primper."

"And you look like a million bucks!" said Locke, walking in
the door.

"Hey, it's almost six o'clock, birthday boy. You need to shower
and get dressed."

Placing a kiss on her nose, he said, "I will, but how about I
make you a dirty martini first?"

"Take your shower. I'll make my drink and have a scotch waiting for you," Sam said, gently stroking his face.

While Locke was showering, Sam turned on the radio and stared out of the balcony door at the view of Philadelphia at night. The DJ on the radio played Willie Nelson's song, "Always on My Mind." As Sam listened to the words, she scolded herself for wanting to cry. Most of the time, she was able to keep the sadness edging her heart at bay. She knew she and her friends were doing the best they could to find out what had happened to AJ, but still, sometimes she missed her friend desperately.

"Pull yourself together, Sam. This is going to be a good night," she said, not realizing she said it aloud.

"Yes, it will, and I'll be with the prettiest girl at the ball," said Locke as he put his arms around her, pulled her into his chest, and kissed her neck.

"You sure you want to go out in public with me?"

"I'm very sure. I'm also very sure that you are scared to death to go out in public with me."

"I think I'm afraid you are going to change your mind about wanting to be with me. As Jonesy says, I'm a magnet for controversy."

"I've got big shoulders," he said, kissing her cheek. "I think I can bear it. Can you help me with this bow tie?"

"Yes, but first, I want to give you your birthday present." Sam opened her purse and handed him a wrapped box from J. E. Caldwell.

"I thought we decided not to give each other gifts. Hmmm, cufflinks with my initials, and in a Caldwell's box to boot. My girl has good taste. My mother would approve."

Sam fixed his bow tie while admiring how handsome he looked. "Perfect. You're irresistible in this tux. I think I'll need to keep my eye on you."

Locke smiled at her. "I have something for you, too. Wait here." He slipped into his bedroom and then reappeared with a box from Tiffany and Company.

Wide-eyed, Sam said, "Locke, it's not my birthday. This is too much."

"How would you know? You haven't even opened it yet."

Sam swallowed. "It says Tiffany. The box alone is too much."

Locke pulled Sam to him and kissed her forehead. "As you said, I'm the birthday boy. What I want for my birthday is to escort the most beautiful detective I know to the Hero's Ball wearing my jewelry."

Sam opened the box to a diamond pendant and matching diamond earrings. "Wow," she exclaimed. "I don't have the words to describe how beautiful…what this means…I don't know how… Thank you."

Sam's hands shook as she put on the earrings, so Locke took the necklace from her and draped it around her neck.

"Relax, Sam," he whispered in her ear, "you're trembling. Everything is going to be OK."

Sam smiled, but her eyes were glazed with unshed tears. He placed his hand over hers. "Are we good? I hate seeing tears in your eyes."

"I am feeling overwhelmed. This jewelry is so much. If you are trying to get me to fall for you, Greg Locke, mission accomplished. No further action required."

"Well then, let's just stay here for the night," Locke joked.

"I'd love to, but we are committed. Let's go before I change my mind."

Thirty minutes later, Sam and Locke arrived at Palumbo's to find Ray, Kate, Walt, and Jonesy were already sitting at a round table for six. Sam squeezed Locke's arm to keep herself from visibly shaking.

"I think you could use a martini," he said.

"I'd love one, thanks," replied Sam.

The ballroom was packed. The deputy commissioner gave the obligatory welcome speech, highlighting the importance of family helping family. He highlighted the importance of supporting the families of those who had fallen in the line of duty. The gala was an example of how first responders step up to honor the memory of the fallen by caring for the families left behind, he said.

After opening remarks, Ray took over as the master of ceremonies and opened with a Tony Bennett song, "If I Ruled the World."

Locke pulled Sam to the dance floor and said, "I think Ray does Tony Bennett better than he does Frank Sinatra. He's doing this song great." Sam nodded and said nothing. Ray turned the next set over to the DJ to up the pace of the music, and they all rejoined the table. Everyone made small talk, but no one seemed fully relaxed. Finally, Ray made eye contact with Sam, who excused herself to the ladies' room. Locke watched her for a second, noticing she didn't seem to be walking toward the ladies' room, but he was distracted by a question from Kate and didn't give it a second thought.

Where words fail, music speaks.

—Hans Christian Anderson

THIRTY-FIVE

RAY ROSSI, A SMOOTH-TALKER AND NATURAL ENTERTAINER, was completely at home on the stage as he reintroduced the band. He spoke of the shared quest of all law enforcement officers, past and present, active and retired, living and dead. Ray announced that the next two songs, intended to be tributes to heroes, would be sung as a duet. He waved to the side of the stage and Sam walked on to join him.

She looked flawless, sparkling in the black dress and the diamonds. As she took the mic, she outshone everyone else. Locke felt his breath catch in his throat.

Sam sang the opening verse to "The Impossible Dream," and Ray joined in the chorus for a duet. They ended with a standing ovation. After taking a bow, Ray spoke of the officers who had been killed or injured in the line of duty. He dedicated the next song to them and to his personal hero—Kate Rossi.

The band played several bars of the score to *Superman*, followed by the theme from James Bond. The room was absolutely silent. The piano player opened with a few bars, and the trumpet joined in, and Sam belted out the first verse to "Holding Out for a Hero." By the end of the song, the audience was standing and cheering. Sam was spent;

she hugged Ray and asked how he could possibly sing another song. Kate and Jonesy made their way to the stage to congratulate Ray and Sam on the performance. Locke sat in his chair, his eyes devouring Sam as she made her way from the stage, people shaking her hand, hugging her and patting her back and telling her to take the show on the road. When Sam arrived back at the table, Locke took her hand and pulled her to the dance floor.

Next, Bobby O took the mic. He began to sing James Brown's "It's a Man's Man's Man's World," dedicated to A. J. Harris. As Locke and Sam swayed to the song, he whispered, "I'm the luckiest guy here. My girl is a rock star."

"Did we do OK?" Sam asked, an uncertain smile on her face. "I was hoping Ray would carry me through the songs. Did he?"

"Yes and no," Locke said, pulling her closer when he felt Sam's shiver. "Yes, you did great, and no, no one had to carry you through the songs."

Locke escorted Sam back to the table and excused himself to the men's room. When he entered the room, he tried to walk past Wexler without an exchange, but Wexler decided differently. "I always thought you were sniffing around her skirts," he said with a sneer.

"Say another word, Wexler, and we can take it outside," warned Locke.

"Hard to believe you would threaten me over that cunt." Wexler snorted.

Locke grabbed Wexler by the collar and pushed him up against the wall. At that moment, Ray Rossi walked in and pulled Locke back, placing himself between the two men.

"Greg, you don't want to do this," said Ray.

Wexler laughed. "You tell him, Lieutenant. How many blow jobs did Kelly give you to get herself invited onto the stage?"

Rossi released Locke and said, "He's all yours."

Locke punched Wexler once in the face, knocking him to the floor. Blood spilled from his nose.

A toilet flushed, and the chief inspector walked out of an enclosed stall. "Is there a problem, gentlemen?"

Ray Rossi spoke. "No, sir. Detective Wexler slipped, and we were helping him up."

Wexler wiped the blood from his nose and nodded. "Wet floor."

Locke turned and left the men's room. Instead of returning to the table, though, he left the building and paced the sidewalk outside of Palumbo's.

This won't be good if Sam finds out, he thought. He'd expressly promised he would never try to defend her honor; he knew she was more than capable of defending herself. But he just couldn't abide Wexler's leer. Locke needed to get Sam out of there before she sniffed out what he'd done. Locke realized then that it had started to snow. He walked back into the ballroom, brushing the snow from his jacket. Ray was back on stage, singing "That's Life."

"Where you been, cowboy?" Sam asked.

"Checking the weather. Roads look bad, we should probably think about leaving."

"OK. One more dance?"

"Sure."

Sam felt him wince when she took his hand, and she loosened her grip. Kate had already told her about the men's room confrontation, and Sam wondered if Locke was going to 'fess up. She'd have to make it up to him for defending her honor and hurting his hand in the process. *Wow, Sam. You must be losing it; you made him promise never to defend you or your questionable honor.*

The snow was falling at a steady pace when Sam and Greg left Palumbo's. Sam smiled as she thought about how silly she was for pausing to look at snow-covered streets in South Philly, which reminded her of a beautiful winter wonderland. Was it the mood of the pleasant evening that was affecting her vision? Or was it a brief moment of appreciation that the fresh and untouched snowfall was able to cover the grime and filth of the well-traveled streets, if even for a short time?

Several minutes later, when Sam walked into Locke's apartment, she kicked off her shoes and walked barefoot to couch. "My feet are freezing. These," she said, pointing to the heels, "were not the best shoes for bad weather."

Locke began rub her feet to warm her up. "Would you like some hot chocolate or coffee? Would that keep you awake?" he said as he draped his mother's afghan over them both. Sam saw he was favoring his right hand. She took it into both of hers and smiled at him.

"You are very thoughtful, but I'm good. Do you think we should go for an X-ray to make sure it isn't broken?"

Locke flinched. "Sam, this doesn't change anything. I just couldn't just stand by—"

"Oh, but it does. It changes everything. You see, I thought I was crazy about you, but now…I know that I am completely, thoroughly, absolutely no-going-back in love with you. Let me be clear though: never risk a broken hand for me again." She smiled at him again, and she allowed all of the tenderness she felt to shine through. "Detective Locke, have I ever told you the legend of the kissing hand?"

Locke smiled. "No, you've never told me the legend of the kissing hand."

"Oh, well," Sam said. "First, let me kiss your boo-boo and make it better." Sam gently kissed the knuckles of his right hand, and then she turned his palm up. "And then, I hold your hand like this, and I kiss your palm like this, and then my love travels up your arm like this," she said as she gently walked her fingers up his right arm to his chest. "And when my kiss reaches your heart like this, your heart is filled with love and joy. I know this because your five-year-old nephew told you so."

"Then it must be true."

"Oh, it's true." Sam kissed his hand again and asked, "Do you have a plastic bag? It's my turn to take care of you." She walked to the kitchen, put ice in a plastic bag, and wrapped it up in a towel. When Sam returned to the living room, Locke had turned off the light and was standing at the glass door to the balcony, watching the snow.

"Give me your hand, cowboy." Sam wrapped his hand in the ice. Locke smiled at her the entire time.

"Thank you for everything that you do. I'm sorry if I don't say it enough."

She walked over to the glass door and looked out. "I love your view of the city. I could stand here all night." Locke pulled her into his chest and buried his face in her neck. "And this is my favorite position. Having your arms around me like this." Locke said nothing, still nuzzled in the crook of Sam's neck. "Did you hear me, Locke?"

"Uh huh," he said as he placed butterfly kisses on her neck.

"Isn't this where you say something reassuring? I was hoping to hear something like 'me too.'"

"Nope."

"No?"

"It's not my favorite position. I have a few other positions that I prefer more. How about I show you?" Locke swept her off her feet and carried her to the bedroom.

Heaven has no rage like love to hatred turned, nor hell a
fury like a woman scorned.

—William Congreve

THIRTY-SIX

"THANKS FOR MEETING ME OFF SHIFT, LOCKE," SAID JONESY AS she drove an unmarked police car north on Broad Street toward Olney Avenue. "I know you are working a case."

"Do you think we'll have more luck in the New Year, Locke? I'm getting tired of this ride."

Instead of responding to her question he said, "Pull over." Jonesy pulled over as Locke shuffled through a pile of police photos that were in the visor of the passenger side of the car. "Jonesy, do you have the photo? Is that Terrance Owens walking across the street?"

"One way to find out," Jonesy said. She rolled down the window and yelled, "Yo, Bean!"

When the subject of their interest turned around, both detectives jumped out of the car to confront him.

"Terrance, I am Detective Locke, and this is Detective Jones from Homicide. We need to speak with you."

Without denying his identity and exhibiting no surprise or alarm, Owens asked, "Is this about Officer Harris?"

Locke and Jones glanced at each other and nodded. "Yes, it is," said Jonesy. "Let's go to the car and take a ride? We'll buy you something to drink or eat."

"Can you take me out this neighborhood?"

"Yeah, how about the diner just off the boulevard at Levick Street? Is that far enough away?" Locke asked.

"Yeah. Let's go."

Twenty minutes later, in a booth in the back of the diner, Owens ordered a burger, fries, and a Coke.

"Thanks, I was hungry," he said. He looked at the two detectives sitting across from him. "I'm sorry about Officer Harris. Did they kill her, too? Is that why you want to talk to me? I'm surprised it took you so long."

Both Jonesy and Locke were startled but remained straight-faced. "Did who kill her?" asked Jonesy, trying to hide any evidence of her adrenaline rush.

Owens continued as if he hadn't heard the question. "I told Officer Harris it was dangerous for her to ask all those questions. I knew she was doing it unofficial-like. She wasn't in uniform when we met. We talked about those old people dying at Green Valley. I told her I didn't have proof, but something went down, and they're lying. That detective is helping them lie."

"Which detective?"

"Tall white guy with dark curly hair. He walks like he thinks he's Kojak."

Jones and Locke briefly exchanged a glance—Wexler—they acknowledged without words.

"What is he helping them do?" asked Locke.

"He's helping them with the cover-up," replied Owens.

"How would he do that?"

"Rumor was, Kojak wasn't gonna find anything wrong cause he was gonna get paid. That's what I told Officer Harris. I told Officer Harris about his extra benefits, too."

"What were his extra benefits?"

"One of the helpers was takin' care of him."

"Taking care of him?" asked Jonesy.

"You know, she was servicing him," he said, waving his burger before he bit into it.

"Who was servicing him?" asked Locke

"Employee number two. She's a helper, but she acted like she owns the place. She calls herself employee number two because she was the second employee hired. Gets away with bullying everyone."

"What's her name? Does she still work there?" asked Jonesy.

"I don't remember now, but I told it to Officer Harris, I think they called her Betty or something," Terrance said. "They let me go, but I was gonna leave anyway."

"Maybe we should start from the beginning," Locke said. "Let's start with the missing drugs."

An hour later, Jonesy and Locke drove back to the Homicide unit, still processing the information they gleaned from Owens.

"Well, this has gotten very interesting. I never liked her anyway, but clearly 'Employee number two' is Sam's sister, Beth," Jonesy said. , "I wonder how Sam is going to take it. Not only was her sister screwing Sam's ex-husband but also her public enemy number one," Jonesy said absentmindedly.

Locke was so surprised, he hit the brakes. "What are you talking about, Jonesy?"

"Ooops! I'm guessing that Sam didn't tell you much about Beth and Jeff?"

"No, we don't talk about the past. Sam never wants to talk about her family. I do know she divorced a scumbag named Jeff. I get the sense she's close to her sister Reagan, but if I ask her about the others, she always says, 'My mother taught me if you don't have something nice to say, don't say anything at all'. I also think she is haunted by the car accident that killed her parents and brother and thinks her family blames her for it. I only know about that because I was around when it happened."

"She isn't imagining her family. It's sad that her parents were such good people and their offspring are weak minded and wouldn't understand loyalty if they tripped over it. I think you need to know about her little sister, Beth. She's a real doozy. She is a master manipulator—always creating drama, and with few exceptions, the family buys into the tales and webs she spins. I'd like to think that Sam is the exception, but Beth plays the part of Betty Davis in *What Ever happened to Baby Jane*, and Sam is convinced that she is Joan Crawford and somehow responsible for the dark and creepy way that Beth covets all things Sam, including her ex-husband and now her arch enemy."

When she was done, Locke said, "I'm not sure who is more despicable—Beth, Jeff, or Wexler."

"They are all shameful sub-humans. So, what did you think of Owens?"

"I think he's credible."

"Do you think either Beth or Wexler are low enough to cover up murders? Or are they both so depraved, they thought they were putting Sam in her place by playing games with her—and with people's lives?"

"God, I hope I'm wrong, but Wexler has a lot to lose if any one of those accusations is true. I just don't see him looking the other way if he really thought the nursing home was hiding something."

"It's not a secret that he has a sick child and a lot of medical bills. I'm thinking he might be swayed by money."

"Lots of speculation, but not much evidence. We know the drugs that went missing could be deadly in an overdose, but we have no evidence because there were no autopsies. We also don't know how the drugs would have been administered. We need to track down the part-time nurse Owens mentioned—the one who left Green Valley. She might be the lead we need."

While Jonesy and Locke were driving around the Northwest Philadelphia, Sam arrived at the Central Detectives Division of the Philadelphia Police Department to work second shift; she came directly from City Hall court, where she had spent the day waiting to testify in a trial.

Finding a space to set up her typewriter, she pulled out a pile of Initial Report Forms from her file drawer, preparing to review and develop a plan to conduct follow-up interviews and prepare investigation reports. Sam was having a hard time distracting her thoughts from AJ and the lack of progress in the off-the-books investigation. *I need to get my head into an investigation and give my brain a rest from this,* she thought.

An hour later, she took a break from the paperwork and walked through the hallway from the squad room; she noticed a pregnant woman sitting quietly on the bench outside the door. An hour later, when Sam walked to the hallway restroom, she saw the same woman still sitting on the bench.

"Hey, Mike? Is there anything I can do help with the complainant on the bench?"

"No, she has some tall tale that includes a million-dollar jewelry heist, a Jamaican posse's drug deals gone bad, and murder most foul."

"She's been sitting for an hour, and she looks uncomfortable. I'll take the interview and get her out of here if you want."

"I'd appreciate the help. I need to focus on real complainants."

Sam walked back to the bench and introduced herself. The woman said her name was Darnella Jackson.

"Would you come with me so we can talk?" Sam asked, and Darnella nodded. Sam led her to a chair in the squad room.

"You comfortable, Darnella?"

"Yeah."

"Good. Before we talk, I want to be sure you understand how this goes. I am going to document that you are here of your own free will and ask you to sign it. After that, I'm going to type everything you tell me, and then I'll ask you to read it, make any changes you want, and sign it. Are you willing to do that?"

"Yeah," Darnella said in the same quiet voice.

Darnella signed the agreement that the interview was voluntary, and Sam rolled a clean sheet of paper through the typewriter. She looked at Darnella and said, "OK, what do you want to tell me?"

"I know where you can find stolen jewelry, drugs, stolen guns, a gun used in a murder, and the dude who did the Korean."

"How do you know where I can find all that?"

"I was staying at a house on Lehigh Avenue with the posse."

"Is this the same house that contains drugs, guns, and jewelry?"

"Yeah."

"OK, well, I will require more details, and I'll need to verify the information you provide. But before we do that, I need to understand why you would be living in that house and why you now want to tell me about it."

"I was living there with my baby's father. He stays there and works for the posse."

"And why are you snitching on your baby's father?"

"He isn't taking care of me. I have to think about my baby. I asked him for one ring after he got his share of the jewelry, and he didn't get it for me. I also have this, and I think it'll help me with my baby." Darnella handed Sam a flyer offering a $20,000 reward for information leading to the arrest of the individual who murdered a Korean businessman.

"OK, let's take it one crime at a time, beginning with the jewelry. I need dates, times, names, locations, and descriptions of the jewelry."

For the remainder of the shift, Sam documented every detail provided by Darnella, occasionally stopping to verify the crime wave that she described. Sam asked Darnella to draw and describe as many pieces of jewelry as possible. The jewelry heist was the most difficult to identify because it happened outside city limits, and Sam had to send a message to suburban jurisdictions to determine where the robbery actually occurred. Eventually, Sam received a response to her ping from a detective in Montgomery County. The detective confirmed an incident had occurred the day before near the Montgomery County Mall at a gas station.

Hogan helped by calling Homicide to verify the details of the murder, including the nine-millimeter handgun used in the killing. Hogan took the point on coordinating with Homicide, including telling them the name of the gunman. Homicide was going to show pictures of the suspect to witnesses for potential identification.

"Sam, I'm leaving for the night, can I do anything else?"

"Thanks for the help, Hogan. My luck, it would have been Wexler's case, and I'd find myself the subject of an IA investigation. Would you review my affidavit for a search warrant and let me know what I missed or should change?"

"I was reading over your shoulder. That search warrant has quite the wish list. Want to make any bets on how much you will find there?"

"You're going to bring me bad luck," Sam chastised him, with wide eyes and an arched brow.

"You think that I'm going to bet against you? OK, I withdraw my offer. I won't say another word—except to remind you that you do your best work when men underestimate you. However, I have never underestimated you. I've never seen anyone step in a pile of shit and come out smelling like roses like you do."

"We shall see," Sam said, smiling. "I need to drive to the PAB so the judge can sign the search warrant. Could you line up a stake-out unit to meet me at 6:00 a.m. at Broad and Lehigh?"

"Yes, ma'am. I'll also let Homicide know you're serving a warrant on the house at six. I can see you're going to have a long night. Good hunting, Sam."

By the rendezvous time, Sam's unmarked car was parked in a vacant lot at Broad and Lehigh Avenue, and she was reviewing her search warrant and waiting for a stakeout unit and wagon crew. Sam was beginning to drag from lack of sleep, so she stepped out of the car and began to pace. A few minutes later, another unmarked unit pulled up. Detectives Patrick Brennan and Greg Locke were in the car.

"Good morning," Sam said. "Are you two just passing by, or are you here for a reason?"

Brennan smiled. "We heard from Wexler that Detective Kelly was still trying to solve all our homicides. We decided if you can't beat her, join her. Thought maybe you could teach us a thing or two about developing informants."

"You are a regular riot, Brennan." Trying to act nonchalant, Sam turned to Greg and nodded.

" Hey, Locke, how are you."

"I'm splendid, and the day is getting better every minute," Locke said with a goofy grin.

After a wagon crew and the stakeout unit pulled into the lot, Sam debriefed the entire group passing around the details of the search warrant and summarizing by saying, "So, in addition to everything outlined in the search warrant, my informant says some of these guys might still be high and there will be guns in that house. One of them sleeps with a sawed-off shotgun under his pillow."

"I think we need another stakeout team," said one of the stake-out officers. "I'm going to give my sergeant a call. We don't want to be outgunned."

"I think we should also call for another wagon, Sam," Locke said as he passed around some photos. "Homicide has a warrant for this guy. His name is Marques McCoy. He was the shooter in a drug-related homicide. We are also looking for a nine-mil."

Just then, the second stakeout team pulled up. Sam recognized McDevitt and Gannon from her days on patrol in the Thirty-Fifth District, and she smiled at them as she felt a rush of warmth and nostalgia.

"Well, well, well. If it isn't jump-the-fuck-off-the-roof Kelly, in the flesh," said McDevitt. "Tracker of laundry tags and investigator extraordinaire. I can't wait to find out why you need two stakeout teams. What's up, Kelly?"

After Sam debriefed him, McDevitt took the point on coordinating a strategy for entering the house and conducting the search. The stakeout teams would enter the house first, followed by the detectives, and the wagon crews would take position in the front and rear of the property.

The stakeout team led the police caravan to the row house and gained entry. Kelly, Locke, and Brennan were close behind. Sam followed McDevitt to the second floor. When McDevitt called clear on the front bedroom, Sam looked around the room and focused on a floorboard in the corner. Darnella had told her she would find some of the jewelry and maybe some guns under the floorboard. Sam walked to the corner of the bedroom and considered how she would pull up the floorboards. Just then, a small, slender man jumped out from under a blanket on the bed and leaped onto Sam's back. McDevitt quickly hit him with the butt of an M 16 and pointed the gun in his face. As the suspect fell back, Locke saw the shiv in his hand and stepped on his forearm until he released it. McDevitt picked up the knife.

"Christ, did you really think you would get away with doing that?" McDevitt asked as he roughly cuffed him.

Sam stood up and saw the shiv. Locke remained stone-faced, with his eyes on Sam. She looked at her attacker and then at Locke. She didn't know what to say and finally blurted, "You're Marques McCoy."

McCoy didn't respond, but Locke did. "Yes, he is."

McDevitt shoved McCoy toward the patrolman who had just arrived at the bedroom. After the suspect was taken away, McDevitt turned to Sam and said, "I'm sorry, Kelly. I pulled off those blankets to make sure no one was in bed and threw them to the other side. I looked under the bed, too. He must've been under the bed and then rolled into the blankets when I threw them."

"Don't worry about it. I should have sensed him before I did." Changing the subject quickly, Sam said, "My snitch told me I'd find some jewelry and maybe guns under a floorboard in this room. Do any floorboards look loose?"

McDevitt used his heel to kick the floor, and then he knelt down. "Here you go, Kelly. Looks like there's a stash here. Guns, jewelry, and some drugs. Does that square it for us? Man, I blew it. You almost got hurt. Am I forgiven?"

Sam shrugged, trying to make light of the situation. "You saved my life, McDevitt. We're not square because I owe you."

An hour later, Marques McCoy was in custody for murder, and the search had recovered two kilos of cocaine, four handguns, two shotguns, and numerous pieces of jewelry, some with the price tags still on them.

Detective Brennan was walking to the unmarked squad car when he turned to Sam and said,

"I'm impressed, Detective Kelly. How much of what was listed in the search warrant did you find?"

Locke answered before Sam finished shrugging her shoulders. "She found it all, Brennan."

"Nice," Brennan responded.

"Yep. And all is a lot," Locke added as he winked at Sam. Sam rolled her eyes, smiled at him, and walked to her unmarked car. Locke followed her. "Sam, you're looking a little down and out. I don't get why. Aside from the twenty years you took off my life when I saw you wrestling with McCoy, this is an impressive bit of police work." When Sam didn't respond, Locke added, "You OK to drive?"

Sam nodded. "I'm good. I should be able to wrap this up in a couple hours. After a hot bath, a warm bed, and some well-earned sleep, I'll feel better."

*The most important things in the world have been
accomplished by people who had kept on trying when there
seemed to be no hope.*

—Dale Carnegie

THIRTY-SEVEN

JONESY INTRODUCED HERSELF TO SUSAN TRICKETT, THE NURSE
who'd found the twelve-year-old girl. She was assigned to the fourth
floor of St. Michael's Children's Hospital, where she was caring for a
girl being treated for an infection due to a weakened immune system. Trickett had checked the girl at 5:30 a.m., and her vitals were
fine. When she returned just twenty minutes later, at 5:50 a.m., the
girl was in distress. Trickett called the doctor, but they lost her. She
simply stopped breathing. Trickett sank down onto the bed, and that
was when she realized someone had tampered with the girl's IV line.
There was a used needle on the floor at the head of the bed; someone
had dropped it in their hurry.

Trickett rubbed her eyes. She saw plenty of sick and dying kids
at the children's hospital, but she'd never seen one murdered before.
"Her name is—was—Annamarie Wexler," she said, her voice raspy.

Jonesy sucked in a breath. "What are her parents' names? Have
they been notified?"

"We haven't been able to reach them," replied Trickett. "We left
a message on their answering machine and asked them to come to
the hospital. Their names are James and Denise Wexler."

Jonesy nodded, inwardly reeling but trying to appear cool. "Can I assume no visitors would be roaming the halls between 5:30 a.m. and 5:50 a.m.?"

"Generally, no, but if they were, the security guard would have signed them in on the log."

"Can you ask the on-duty security supervisor to meet me?" Jonesy asked. Trickett nodded. Jonesy reached out a tentative hand and placed it on the nurse's shoulder. "You did everything you could," she said.

The nurse looked at her for a long moment and then dropped her gaze. "It still wasn't enough," she whispered, and left.

Jonesy found a phone at the hospital and dialed Homicide. The deskman patched her through to Locke.

"It's Jonesy. I'm at St. Michaels on a case. Have you seen Wexler today? Does he have court?"

"I don't know, but I would guess he has. I've been on the street with Brennan. What's going on?"

"His daughter may have been murdered in her hospital room. I'm at the hospital, processing the scene with mobile crime."

"Oh, Christ, what a nightmare. Is…is he a suspect?"

"I don't think so. I think he's a parent getting ready to face his worst nightmare." She sighed. "The hospital left messages for him and his wife. Best guess is, it happened sometime between 5:30 a.m. and 5:50 a.m. I requested a copy of all security logs to see what visitors were on site as well as a list of all employees working this morning."

"Keep in mind if Wexler was there, he might have badged his way in instead of signing the log. You might want to ask security if a plainclothes cop fitting his description came through. In the meantime, I'll brief the lieutenant and he can start tracking down Wexler."

An hour later, Jonesy called Locke back. "Wexler and his wife are at the hospital. I was there when they told him. He was absolutely devastated. I'm giving them some time for the news to settle in before I talk to him. I have the visitor and employee logs from last night, and I found a name that jumped out: Beth Kelly. She works here. I confirmed she was here this morning, but I haven't been able to locate her. I just met with one of her coworkers, and apparently Beth knows that Wexler's daughter is dead and that I'm here. She told the employee, and I quote, 'That detective is a friend of my adopted sister. She and her friends have been trying to ruin my life.'" Jonesy took a deep breath. "Locke, I tried to call my house, and the phone just kept ringing. Sam would've picked it up even if she were in a deep sleep. I asked a Fifth District patrol car to check on the well-being of an officer and to proceed with caution. I'm on my way."

Locke ran to an unmarked police car, turned on the sirens, and drove down Route 76 toward Manayunk faster than he thought possible. Meanwhile, Officer Nancy Forelli responded to Jonesy's police radio, parking half a block away from 332 Baker Street. The front door was locked securely, but the back door had been forced open. Forelli stopped requested backup. With her revolver drawn, she stepped cautiously through the door.

Locke was exiting Route 76 when he heard the call for backup, and he advised police radio that a plainclothes detective would be responding in one minute. Locke crept through the back door, revolver in hand. Forelli nodded to him and pointed upstairs where they could hear two different voices arguing. The first woman was too quiet to make out, but the second was yelling every word. Forelli was quietly walking up the stairs with Locke right behind her when they heard the shot.

Several hours before, Sam had come home from a long shift and fallen into deep sleep. Suddenly, she felt someone shaking her.

She opened her eyes to see her sister Beth. Tired and groggy, Sam asked, "What are you doing here, Beth?"

Beth said nothing, but her face was filled with rage and her pupils were tiny pricks in her red-rimmed eyes. Beth slapped Sam twice in the face with such force that Sam fell off the bed, banging her head into the corner of the bedside table.

"You and your friends just can't leave me alone," Beth said. Her voice was like that of a wild animal, writhing and out of control.

Sam put her fingers to the spot where she'd hit her head. Blood. She was still stunned by the blow, but she knew she needed to stay calm in the face of Beth's fury. Sam quickly tried to remember where she left her gun—and then she saw the Smith & Wesson .38 detective special in Beth's shaking hand.

Sam's mind and pulse were racing, but she tried to speak in a steady voice. "Beth, put the gun down and tell me what is bothering you."

"We all hate you, you know. Gene and Kathryn's other children should be doing this. They just don't have the guts. They always get me to do the dirty work for them. None of us understood why Kathryn and Gene gave you the time of day."

"You don't have to worry about me anymore. Mom and Dad are dead. I know that I have always been an outsider with the family. I can disappear from your lives very easily. You can leave now. I'll never bother you again, and we can pretend this never happened."

"*THEY WERE NOT YOUR PARENTS!*" Beth screamed. "You should have never had a say in anything. You were *not* their daughter, and it's your fault they died." Confusion knitted Sam's brow. What was she talking about? But Beth raged on. "If you hadn't interfered with Denny, I wouldn't have needed to stop him like that. It's your fault that Denny is dead, that my parents are dead, that your girl-friend A. J. Harris is dead, and that you need to die, too."

Realization swept over Sam in a cold wave. "Beth, I under-stand why you killed Denny and AJ, but why did you kill those old people? They never hurt you."

"Finally! The big-shot detective is catching on," Beth spat out.

"But you have to know that if I figured it out, I'm not the only one who knows," Sam bluffed.

"Well, then, I guess it doesn't matter what I do anymore," Beth sneered, waving the gun at Sam. The hate in Beth's face transformed her into a monster.

"Help me understand, Beth. I get why you hated me and even AJ, but what did those people do you?"

"Do to me? I was *helping* them. Those people were old and miserable and so was everyone around them. Do you know how many times I listened to their relatives complain about feeling obli-gated to visit? Their lives had no point. I was helping them, and you interfered. Just like today. Your girlfriend Jonsey started asking ques-tions. Jim loves me, but he had to make a choice between a sick kid and me. The kid was going to die eventually anyway. I just helped it along for everyone's sake. As usual, you and your friends were out to screw me over."

Sam had no idea what to do, but she knew she was running out of time. "Beth, please drop the gun, and let's talk this through," she said in one last desperate bid. But then she locked eyes with Beth and knew that she was going to shoot. Sam dropped to the floor and rolled behind the bed as the gunshot rang out. Footsteps rushed into the bedroom. From the floor, Sam saw Philadelphia police uniform pants and then a pair of familiar men's dress shoes. Sam looked up from the floor at Locke while Officer Forelli tackled Beth to the ground. Locke secured the gun while Forelli cuffed Beth and escorted her down the steps. Locke offered Sam a hand and pulled her to a standing position.

"Are you OK, Samantha?" Locke asked as he placed his white handkerchief over the cut on her temple.

Sam nodded. "You are forever saving my butt. That's twice in one day. I really owe you."

"Yeah, and it took another twenty years off my life. I figure you owe me forty years now."

"Be careful what you wish for, cowboy."

"Come on, it's time to get dressed. I'm taking you to the hospital. You're going to need stitches for that cut. And then we'll need to visit Homicide for a statement."

During the ride, Sam told him that Beth admitted to the Green Valley murders and to killing AJ, Denny, and her parents. "I guess I have the answers I looking for, and some I wasn't. It was right in front of me the whole time, but I didn't see it. I didn't think of her as a suspect because I made her behavior all about me."

"Officer Forelli and I heard much of what she told you." Locke glanced over at Sam, and his gaze softened. "You have blood dripping down your face. Why don't you put your head back and hold the handkerchief to it? When we get to the hospital, I'll call Jonesy and let her know you're OK."

"Wait a minute, what made you come to Baker Street?"

"Jonesy is the assigned detective for a homicide investigation at St. Michael's Hospital. The victim's name was Annamarie Wexler."

"Oh no. No, no, no. And I thought this couldn't get any worse. Oh god, it was Beth." Sam choked. "Pull over. I'm going to throw up."

Locke kept his hand on her back as Sam dry-heaved over and over. "Sam, you might have a concussion. We should get to the hospital."

"I never liked Wexler, but I wouldn't wish this on anyone." Sam thought for a moment. "She must've been talking about Wexler when she said she loved him. Jim. Oh, this is so fucked up, Locke. It's like a bad dream you can't wake up from."

"Try to shift your focus for a little while," Locke said gently. "The next several hours will be grueling. Think about the parkway. Remember the night you told me that the parkway was the most beautifully constructed roadway in the world?"

While Sam received twelve stitches at the Hahnemann Hospital emergency room, Locke briefed Jonesy. "Beth is en route to the Roundhouse. She admitted to everything we suspected and more. You'll probably want to think about who should interview Beth and how, because she apparently hates you and Kate. Have you spoken to Wexler?"

Joe Falco is teed up to interview Wexler with staff inspectors. Staff inspectors aren't here yet. If I'm as good as I think at reading faces, I'm pretty convinced he had no idea what Beth was going to do."

When the doctor was done stitching up Sam's scalp, she and Locke drove to Homicide. Jonesy took one look at Sam and said, "To the ladies' room, girl." Once there, Jonesy wet some paper towels and began to clean up the blood still clinging to Sam's scalp and hair.

"How are you feeling?" she asked.

Sam glanced in the mirror and said, "Like I could haunt houses. Why didn't Locke tell me I looked this bad?" She turned her gaze back to Jonesy. "Has Beth said anything?"

"Locke didn't tell you how bad you look because a, he doesn't care and b, he knows better. In a situation like this, only a girlfriend would tell you that you look like shit. By the way, Beth keeps asking her interviewer, Pat Brennan, if she can talk to Wexler. Pat told her no, but it hasn't affected her desire to talk. She's been singing louder than Kate Smith. I'll get a copy of her statement for you to read once you're cleaned up. Your sister Reagan called twice. You should give her a call." Jonesy stepped back. "OK, you look presentable. Let's go back. Brennan will take your statement. If you're wondering, I don't think Wexler knew what Beth was doing."

As Jonesy and Sam walked back into Homicide, Wexler was being escorted to an interview room. He and Sam stopped and looked at each other.

"Wexler," she said sadly, "I am so sorry for your loss. My thoughts are with you and your family." Wexler didn't respond; he just walked away with a look of devastation on his face.

Before he began asking Sam about the break-in at Baker Street, Detective Brennan slid a copy of his interview with Beth Kelly across the table. Once they were done, Sam read Beth's confession. Sorrow and horror built within Sam as she read Beth's proud description of the eight lives she took at Green Valley over the course of a year. Beth said she was guided by God to identify nursing home residents who had become a burden to their family and had no quality of life. Beth felt it was her duty to send them to the next life. When she described killing AJ, Beth said AJ was a troublemaker, and God instructed her to eliminate any obstacles to her sacred duty. Beth admitted to the theft of benzodiazepine and fentanyl from the nursing home and to stealing the key she used to enter AJ's apartment from Sam's key ring. She acknowledged she shot A. J. Harris in the head with her service revolver and said that she intended to use Sam's service revolver to kill her. Beth also insisted she and Jim Wexler loved Annamarie and each other and she, Wexler, and God wanted her to end Annamarie's pain. Beth's one regret was the death of her brother and parents, which she continued to blame on Sam. She added that Sam was not her sister, that she was in fact the adopted daughter of Gene and Kathryn Kelly.

After reading Beth's confession, Sam called her sister Reagan. "Reagan, I'm calling from the Roundhouse. Beth is here, and she's being charged with multiple homicides, including Denny, Mom, and Dad, and a little girl at the hospital. She also tried to shoot me earlier today."

"Oh, God," Reagan said, her voice barely a whisper. "Are you OK, Sam?"

"I'm OK, but confused. In addition to confessing to most of it, Beth is saying that I'm not her sister—that I'm adopted. Do you know anything about that?" The line was silent. "Reagan?"

"I'm here. The truth is Mom and Dad were very loving people. You are adopted, and so is she. You were the daughter of Dad's best friend, a detective killed in the line of duty. His wife had died of cancer just after you were born, and when he died, you were orphaned. I remember the day they brought you home. Mom introduced you as my little sister. I asked where you came from, and she told me from God. I wasn't ever to tell because God wanted us to protect you. A couple years later," Reagan paused, "Mom showed up with another baby girl. It was Beth. Mom told me to never ask where she came from but I overheard a conversation. She was the daughter of Dad's brother, Charles. After Charles became a widower, he had a fling with a woman from Manayunk. She got pregnant, and she didn't want to marry Charles or have the baby. Dad and Mom took her in, too. I knew and Denny knew, but Mom made us promise we would never tell. A couple of years ago, though, Beth found your pictures and papers when she was going through Mom's things. She met with our sneaky siblings, and they all tried to pressure Mom and Dad to tell you. Mom and Dad said no and made all of them promise to stay silent and told Beth she was adopted to stop her from trying to alienate you from the family.

When Denny was still alive, he was able to put a lid on the argument. After he and Mom and Dad died, I found out Beth was meeting with the rest of the family and wanted everyone to cut you out of the estate. I told the family that she was also adopted and showed her the papers. She convinced the rest of them that because she was Dad's brother's child she was still family. She was furious, but I had no idea she was violent. I am so sorry, Sam."

"What she did was not your fault, Reagan. As for the family, they can pretend I never existed. I hope never to see any of them again."

"I hope that doesn't include me," Reagan said. "But I understand if it does."

"No, it doesn't include you. What Beth did had nothing to do with you. It was all in her own twisted mind. You're my sister no matter what, and the only one I care about anymore."

"There's one more thing I wanted to tell you, Sam. Dad's friend, your biological father, was a Philadelphia detective. His name was Cavanaugh. Mom and Dad were so proud of you, and they knew you were born for that job. They should have told you, but they were afraid you might feel differently about them and the family."

"I loved them," Sam said, drawing a ragged breath. "But I always felt like I was on the outside looking in when it came to most of the family. Telling me would have only helped."

Sam replaced the phone in its cradle and looked up to see Locke and Jonesy staring at her.

"Sam," Jonesy asked, pointing to an interview room, "do you have a minute?" Once Locke shut the door, Sam didn't wait for anyone to ask. "Well, I confirmed that Beth's statement about me was accurate. I am not her biological sister."

"How do you feel about that?" asked Locke.

Sam paused for a moment, and their eyes met. "Relieved. I'm not related to a serial killer. And now so much of my family life makes sense. I never respected the people I thought were my siblings, and I never understood the petty shit they did. I'll always love my parents, Denny, and Reagan, but if I never see any of the rest of them, I will rest in peace with a clear mind. Reagan did give me a gift, though. It turns out, my biological father was Dad's best friend. His wife died in childbirth, and he asked Dad to raise me as his own if anything happened to him. He was killed on the job—as a Philly detective."

Jonesy shook her head in amazement. "Whoever said 'what a difference a day makes' didn't know the half of it."

After several more hours of paperwork and debriefs, Sam looked at Locke and said, "I'm exhausted. Can I leave yet?"

"Yes, and you're coming to my apartment, and we're going to cuddle and watch old movies on my video player. We'll start with Errol Flynn and Olivia DeHavill and in *Robin Hood*."

"Sounds lovely, but don't forget Claude Rains. Let's make it a Claude Rains marathon. You have *Casablanca*, don't you?"

"Yes, ma'am—and corned beef sandwiches to add a bit of atmosphere. Jonesy said she and Walt will clean up Baker Street. Let's go, cutie, you're coming with me."

Sam narrowed her eyes at Locke and said sarcastically, "Corned beef sandwiches, wow—you've got the art of seduction down. By the way, did you call me cutie to make me feel better about how terrible I look?"

"Since I don't think I'm going to win any arguments today, I'll just apologize now," Locke said, throwing up his hands in amused surrender.

"Good move. Keep it up, Locke, and this could be the beginning of a beautiful relationship."

I'd like to end up unforgettable.

—Ringo Starr

THIRTY-EIGHT

It was Kate and Ray's first anniversary, and the three couples met Carmella and Len at the Four Seasons restaurant, where they'd had the black-tie reception. After they'd placed their dinner orders, Kate said, "We have an announcement to make."

All six heads snapped up, and Sam looked at her friend eagerly. "Ray is being promoted to captain!" Kate said.

"Oh," Sam said. "I thought...well, that's great, Ray! Congratulations."

"Oh yeah," Kate added, as if an afterthought, "and we're having a baby." The entire table whooped and cheered, clinking glasses. The other patrons looked over at them, and they just grinned. "If it's a boy, Ray will pick the name, as long as he doesn't choose Primo like he's threatening to do. If we have a girl, her name will be Angela, which is a two-for-one. Both AJ and my mother's sister were named Angela."

Carmella wiped tears from her eyes as she looked at her daughter. "Angela! What a beautiful name. You know we will adore this grandchild, boy or girl, and we've been over the moon since you told us we're going to be grandparents."

Not to be outdone, Jonesy announced, "We have some news as well. Walt and I are going to Europe for an extended tour of Scotland and England. On the way back, we are going to Paris."

"Your dream vacation, Jonesy. That's wonderful!" Sam exclaimed.

Jonesy reached into her purse and pulled out a wrapped gift. "Sam, we a have a group gift for you."

Sam pressed her lips together as she accepted the box from Jonesy. She unwrapped the paper and lifted the lid of the box. Instead, nestled in tissue paper, was a handsome leather-bound book.

"It's a scrapbook," Jonesy said.

"This is beautiful. Calling it a scrapbook doesn't do it justice," Sam running her finger over the smooth cover. She looked around the table as she grabbed Locke's hand to squeeze under the table. "Thank you all."

"As you open it, I'll give you the background. Soon-to-be-Captain Rossi helped us access the police archives. Walt and I spent several hours researching your biological father and found nothing. Locke joined the search and found the first reference to him. Walt discovered the biggest surprise. Turns out your biological father wasn't just any inspector. He was head of the detective bureau back in the day. We found pictures and copied documents he authored. Kate, Carmella, and I designed the book, and Len did the proofreading. Locke suggested the title, 'God, in his infinite wisdom…made Sam's father and then Sam.'" Everyone at the table laughed and then smiled at Sam. "By the way, once you start reading, you will quickly realize you're a chip off the old block. Your father was a superstar. And you share similar traits. He was persistent, stubborn, and apparently had a bit of a temper. Yes, he was your dad, all right."

Sam looked at the photos of her father, this man about whom she knew so little yet so much.

"I wonder what he would have been like if he were still alive. You know—what would he have said to Joe O'Neill for dissing his daughter and her friends when we graduated from the academy? Kate might have gotten that graduation ceremony she wanted after all."

"If the apple didn't fall far from the tree, I'm sure there would've been a graduation ceremony," Carmella said.

"I'd take that bet." agreed Walt.

Sam paged through the pictures and newspaper articles about Chief of Detectives Liam Cavanaugh. Seeing all of this made him real for the first time, and she worked hard to keep the tears at bay. Sam tried to calm herself by taking deep breaths, hoping that she was quiet enough to go unnoticed. Her friends sipped wine and water, pretending not to see.

"There is more, Sam," Jonesy eventually said. "I received a call from Kit Gibbons, that reporter from the *Bulletin*. After she did the series on the Green Valley homicides she received this letter." Jonesy handed a photocopy of a letter to Sam. Sam noticed that the letter was handwritten and printed. Jonesy continued, "In one of the articles, she mentioned your father, Chief Cavanaugh." Sam read the note.

Ms. Gibbons, I read your story about those old people who died. You mentioned that Liam Cavanaugh died in an accident. You have the story wrong. Chief Cavanaugh was murdered; he deserves his justice too. It happened a long time ago, but it has haunted me every day.

Sam looked up to meet Jonesy's eye, and the letter quickly circulated around the table.

After reading the note, Kate said "Wow, looks like we need a plan."

Walt straightened. "Wait a second, ladies. You can't be thinking of opening an investigation on a thirty-year-old accident."

All three women glared at Walt, saying nothing.

Ray put his hands up. "Careful, Walt. I'm getting a sense of déjà vu."

Walt looked toward Locke, who shook his head no. "You're on your own if you go there, brother. I've learned my lesson."

Carmella raised her wine glass and said, "I'd like to propose a toast. We have a lot to celebrate. Let's focus on today and good friends."

Everyone raised a glass to the toast. Carmella continued, "Ray, don't you want to sing a song or something?"

Ray stood up and said, "I thought you would never ask." He walked over to the center of the room to the piano player, who didn't seem to be surprised. He handed Ray a microphone. Ray said, "This song is dedicated to Sam and Greg."

Sam winked at Ray, took Locke's hand, and said, "I think they're playing our song."

Ray sang the Nat King Cole classic "Unforgettable." Once on the dance floor, Locke spun Sam and pulled her toward him. Looking down at Sam, he smiled and said, "Good choice. Our time together has been anything but forgettable."

Sam pulled him a little closer and whispered, "I just hope you don't get bored with me."

"Oh, Sam, you and your friends are never boring. Everything you do is definitely, well, unforgettable. I'll never get bored, and I'm looking forward to the ride."